When Laura and
chiatric Institute
area just off th
thing here. How
identification ca
small with dra
guarded by a cold orderly.

"I'm going to bring Mr. Cromwell in now," the orderly said curtly. She returned with Cromwell to the room. "You've got ten minutes."

Press extended his hand. "My name is Preston Lennox, and this is Dr. Laura Baker."

Abruptly, Cromwell's fingers came together, hard, like a man who'd suddenly decided it was time to launch a desperate prayer. "I know why you're here . . . I'm a molecular biologist," Cromwell hesitated.

Laura shot a glance at Press. Cromwell continued, "At the present time, Mars is a little over four and a half billion years old. It had water, an atmosphere, and a hospitable climate. I believe the aliens that landed on that planet made it the hunk of useless rock we see today. They spread like a plague across its surface, the life-form depleted its supply of water and raw materials."

When no one said anything, Cromwell again folded his hands and continued. "When I heard the United States was sending a landing mission to Mars, I strongly urged the government to reconsider."

"Why?" asked Laura.

Cromwell's cheeks flushed. At its best, it would have always been a harsh planet on which only an extremely strong, hardy life-form could exist. A life-form that would no doubt be incredibly dangerous and harmful to humans! A species that could very possibly go dormant and leave its own DNA on the surface—like spores—so that any attempt by another form of life would result in biological contamination!"

Both Laura and Press jumped as Cromwell's hand shot out and snatched a fly from midair, "We will be to these aliens what this fly is to us." He opened his palm and held it out, showing them the insect's crushed carcass.

SPECIES II™

A NOVEL BY YVONNE NAVARRO

BASED ON A SCREENPLAY BY CHRIS BRANCATO

BASED ON CHARACTERS CREATED BY DENNIS FELDMAN

TOR®

A TOM DOHERTY ASSOCIATES BOOK
NEW YORK

SPECIES II

A Tor Book
Published by Tom Doherty Associates, Inc.
175 Fifth Avenue
New York, NY 10010

Tor Books on the World Wide Web:
http://www.tor.com

Tor® is a registered trademark of Tom Doherty Associates, Inc.

ISBN: 0-812-57075-8

First edition: July 1998

Printed in the United States of America

0 9 8 7 6 5 4 3 2 1

This one is for Dennis Feldman,
with gratitude for dreaming up such
a wonderfully wicked creature
in the first place.

ACKNOWLEDGMENTS

Thank-you to Dennis Feldman and Howard Morhaim, who worked so hard and fast to make this project come alive. As usual, thanks to Don VanderSluis for tech/engineering and weapons help, and to Dr. Johnny Ellison for his medical expertise. And I certainly won't forget all the people who patiently answered my pesky questions: Robyn Fielder, Matthew Woodring Stover, Sean Jordan of ZEntertainment (who prowled the Internet for me in search of photographs), and yet again, Don VanderSluis. Special appreciation goes to my Dad and Elaine, who kept me fed and brought me turkey leftovers on Thanksgiving so I could keep working. (What—me cook??!)

Thanks, too, to everyone who wrote or e-mailed to say how much they liked the first book, and to all of you who shelled out hard-earned money to buy and read the second.

And as always, *Darke Palace* is open:

http://www.para-net.com/~ynavarro
Come visit.

PROLOGUE

"Even now, Mars, the god of war, is still sending men to their graves . . ."

Approaching Mars—Two Hours from Orbit

"Have you ever seen anything so beautiful?"

Captain Patrick Ross reluctantly pulled his gaze away from the viewport and turned toward the speaker. It was hard not to smile at the sight of Dr. Anne Sampas as she leaned forward over her control console, her green eyes filled with childlike wonder below the heavy waves of her deep auburn hair. "No," he said honestly. "I don't think I have."

When she didn't say anything else, he spun his chair until he again faced the heavy glass, felt himself once again get lost in the scene in front of him:

Mars.

The planet looked like a huge red marble suspended against a backdrop of sparkling black velvet. Slashed by canyons and painted with shadows that ran from orange to dark red to utterly black, in his mind Ross knew the Martian surface was cold and lifeless, but right now it looked anything but. It looked . . . *hot,* and very much alive, as though any moment might bring an eruption from one of the dormant volcanoes that spotted its surface: Ascreus Mons or Pavonis Mons perhaps, silent, murky spots on the Martian surface to the west through the viewing portal.

"Control, this is *Excursion.* We have OMS cut off, over." The deep voice made Ross jump then look to his left, where the flight navigator, Dennis Gamble, was already deftly flipping switches on his control panel.

There was a static-filled blast of noise from the capsule's communicator, then the whine of an unidentifiable voice. *"Excursion, this is Control. Please advise when ET umbilical doors are open, over."*

"Roger that." Dennis's dark gaze caught and held Patrick. "Time to start suiting up." There was a pause, then Gamble added, "You've got two hours, Patrick."

Ross nodded and squelched the urge to swallow, afraid Dennis or Anne would see the movement and know he was nervous. Not afraid, just a little . . . jittery. No big deal, he'd done this half a dozen times. Walking in space or on the moon was commonplace; walking on Mars . . . now *this* was something. The first time, and he was going to get to do it. God, sometimes he felt like the luckiest man alive.

Ross made his way carefully toward the back of the ship, his thoughts divided between his mental checklist for the upcoming mission and wondering what his dad was doing back home on Earth. Watching the mission at NASA, of course, but what was he *doing*? Standing proud and tall in the Mission Control Room next to Melissa, Patrick's girlfriend, with his six-foot-five frame towering over everyone else? Or sitting on someone's chair so it wouldn't be obvious that he might have had a belt or two of Old Grand-Dad?

Shaking away the thought, Ross slipped out of his

in-flight suit, then meticulously began setting out the components of his Extravehicular Activity space suit—his life depended on nothing being overlooked, but he was too familiar with the routine to be concerned about forgetting something. Besides the oft-repeated space walks he'd performed, the practice sessions at NASA were too numerous to count. He could, simply put, don the EVA in his sleep. Plus, Anne Sampas, the flight's M.I.T. mission scientist, would do everything but look at his suit-up job under a microscope before she'd let him strap down in the landing module. A final vision check and then, pulse heightening, Ross took a deep breath and stepped into the absorbent underwear to begin the final steps of suiting up.

"Mission Control," Dennis Gamble said clearly into the microphone. "We have module at gimme five seven gimme." After a few seconds, a confirmation message came back and Dennis flipped more switches on the console, his fingers a blur of efficiency. "Disengaged," he barked into the transmitter. A few breathless seconds, then he grinned at Anne. "Hope he's holding onto his hair. He's gonna feel a little bump—"

To punctuate his words, there was a faraway clanking sound and a slight vibration ran through the floor.

"—and grind."

Eyes wide, they both leaned forward to peer out at the void of space through the viewport.

The landing module shuddered and gave a short, metallic groan as the hold-downs to the *Excursion* were released, then it tilted slightly. A fleeting sensation of giddiness sank into Ross's stomach as the craft spun gently, bringing the main vessel into view. For a moment, all he could do was gawk at the *Ex-*

cursion's size, let himself feel like a fly buzzing around the hide of a huge horse. Then the realization that now it was just him suddenly hit home. I've been orphaned, Ross thought, and somehow the idea that this was Mars—*Mars*, for God's sake—just made it all the worse. The moon versus Mars . . . the difference was like being separated from home by the width of a town or the stretch of a continent.

He felt weightless and lost, temporarily out of control, as Dennis steered the landing module back around, giving him a full shot of the parent spacecraft in all her glory. It was hard not to feel small and abandoned as he watched the gleaming alloy ship slide past; it seemed to go on and on, moving silently from burnished silver to a grand, panoramic view of the patriotic red, white, and blue painted on the hull. Ending, of course, with the requisite colorful logos of the corporate sponsors that had so generously pumped money into the National Space Exploratory Group and made the mission possible.

Abruptly the loneliness was gone, and Ross wondered if his two partners were smirking as their video playback gave them the same scene. Or was he the only one who found it amusing to see the traditional red-and-white logo of Classic Coca-Cola, the famous Golden Arches of McDonald's, and the simple black-and-white Nike swoosh emblazoned across the side of the massive spaceship?

The module lurched and picked up speed, the cockpit rattling around him with enough noise bleed-through to make him feel like a piece of popcorn in a microwave. He ground his teeth and found the radio switch. "Dennis, ease up on those thrusters, would you? Bring turbo alignment to negative seven, over."

"Roger that." Dennis's voice sounded grainy and already far away. "ETA twenty-eight minutes, seventeen seconds." A beat of silence, then Dennis spoke again. "Make that fifteen . . . no, wait. Fourteen."

Patrick grinned and ignored him, feeling the module's movement smooth out under the navigator's capable hand. Never a doubt, obviously—he knew no one else in the world who could do a better job of this than Dennis Gamble. The black man was the best and could steer a missile ship into a landing bay with the door half-closed, his good eye taped shut and only one finger free. And Ross's opinion had nothing to do with the fact that Dennis Gamble was his best friend.

He'd thought the next half hour would pass slowly, each torturous minute trudging along while he fidgeted beneath the straps—he hated these tiny cockpits with a vengeance—and Dennis did all the work back on the mother ship. Anne, too, was likely buried in last-minute calculations and notes, that overly intelligent mind of hers no doubt cranking out another two dozen experiments to conduct on the soil samples he would bring back. Patrick had pictured himself sitting bored and impatient in the module while he performed his routine checks, just another matter-of-fact landing well on its way to completion.

Yeah, right.

The half hour was gone—*zip*—seemingly before Patrick could blink, the slice of time utterly erased by the sight of the sprawling Martian landscape that filled the screen of his console. His training still carried him through the flight routines but had he not been tied into his chair, he would've jumped in surprise at the voice crackling over the communications line from Mission Control. "Copy that," he said instantly, his gaze tracking the numbers on the instrument panels. "Descent target zero one niner. Synchronous orbit phase cycle is a go. We are on the mark."

"Turbo alignment is two seven Cavalier. Descend, defend, watch your rear end."

Patrick chuckled but before he could respond, Anne's voice came over the transmitter. "And don't forget to watch out for little green men."

This time he laughed. "If there were any little men here, I'm fairly certain they'd be the color of rust. Don't worry, Annie. I'll be fine."

"Of course you will," Dennis shot back. "You're Patrick Ross, all-American hero, remember?"

"Aren't I supposed to have a cape?"

"Forget it. It gets tangled with the EVA suit."

Patrick laughed again, then grew serious and frowned at his instruments. "Hey, shouldn't I be—?"

"You *are*," Dennis said smoothly as the module lurched to one side, then the other . . .

. . . and settled itself on the bleak red rubble of Martian soil.

Inside the *Excursion*, Dennis Gamble and Dr. Anne Sampas slammed their palms together in a high-five that neither would admit was painful. "Yee-ha!" Anne whooped. "We made it, Dennis!"

Her partner gave her a wide grin, then turned back to the console. "Mission Control," he announced loudly. "We have surface interface. I repeat, we have surface interface. IMU alignment is complete. We show two eight degrees, three six minutes. Over." He paused, then spoke again. "Patrick, do you copy?"

"Loud and clear."

Damn, Dennis thought as his smile widened, along with Anne's. If I get any happier, my face is going to split in two. "Congratulations, brother," he said into the microphone. "You just became the first man on Mars. Set your digital readout. You've got one hour till party time. Make yourself useful until then and bring back some souvenirs for our scientist friend here."

"I can handle that."

Anne pushed her hair behind her ears and leaned over the console. "Is everything functional down there?" Her voice had gone from jovial to strictly professional. "No problems to report?"

"Not a one," Patrick came back immediately. "You see me on the video screen?"

"Got it," Dennis said. "Clear as Monday-Night Football."

They heard Patrick snicker, then saw him reach for an LED display and start the counter. Every now and then, a white line of solar interference would cut across the display, but that was to be expected, and they still saw the bright numbers start counting up from 0:00 as the astronaut in the module adjusted an array of telemetry switches. "Annie," Patrick said, "I think things are just about ready for you on my end. If your connection is clear, we can go on and fire up your toys."

Anne Sampas nodded, her eyes glittering emerald green with excitement in the glow of the instrument panels. "I'm going to switch on an external camera," she said. "Right . . . now." She gave a flick of her forefinger and there it was in full color—red and orange and rusted brown—so completely spectacular that it nearly took her breath away.

"Man," Dennis said from his seat. "Is that unbelievable or what?"

"God, yes. And Patrick—he's down there, right *on* the surface. He's going to *walk* on it in just an hour." She shook her head, but her gaze never left the display. "Can you imagine how completely, utterly *tiny* he must feel?"

"I heard that, Annie. You forgot to toggle off the transmitter."

She blinked and looked at Dennis guiltily, but he only gave her an it's-too-late-now shrug. "Sorry, Patrick, It was just a foolish thought—"

But the first video display showed their comrade down on the surface as he waved a hand in dismissal. "Aw, I'm just kidding. And anyway, you're right. It's a pretty damned lonely feeling—but I know I've got you guys looking out for me." On the vaguely grainy display, Dennis and Anne could see one corner of his mouth lift.

"You bet," Dennis cut in. "Annie, let's get those Land Rovers going. We need to bring 'em out and at least start collecting our samples before Patrick hits the ground. Can't have him doing all the work."

She nodded and settled herself at the console. "I'm set. Patrick, are you ready to synchronize?"

"Ready when you are."

"Great. One, two, three, *mark.*" On the dual cue, a small hatch in one side of Patrick's landing module flipped down with a precise movement of hydraulics. "I've got the camera carrier," Anne said, her voice shaking with exhilaration. "You're in charge of the drill."

"I knew it," Dennis quipped. "The man comes all this way and gets stuck digging in the dirt."

"Always did like making mud pies." Patrick's voice was enthusiastic, his face set with concentration despite his easy words, his fingers light on the remote controls in the landing module as he worked his Rover around the rock obstacles on the surface.

"I'm afraid for those you'll need water," the doctor said absently. She was piloting her camera-armed Rover close to where Patrick's mechanism had stopped on the near side of a dark-colored, three-foot-long rock and was slowly working a drill into the barren soil. "Not enough of that on Mars."

"There's considerable evidence of subsurface ice," Dennis commented.

"True," Anne agreed. "But liquid water can't exist on the planet's surface at the present time. I'm afraid Patrick's mud pies would have had to be made in the first third of the planet's life—the last of the Noachian Period, or perhaps the first part of the Hesperian Period."

"More?" Patrick asked, breaking into the discussion. They saw him point toward the Rovers and the small pile of red material it had gouged free of the Martian landscape.

"Yes, please. There are three canisters in the storage hatch. Ultimately you'll need enough samples to fill all of them, and from different depths and areas, too. You might as well get started before you go out, so you have more time to explore the terrain. Besides, the less time you're in proximity to the drilling mechanism, the happier we'll be."

Patrick nodded and bent back to his task, then looked up and smiled. "Go on, Anne. Take your Rover out for a ride. Mine is positioned so that I can see well enough with the module's external camera, and we'll want as much film as we can get. Staring at the same spot on the ground is no fun."

The doctor's face lit up. "Wonderful!" She bent closer to the screen, nose nearly touching its surface as she focused on piloting her miniature Land Rover in a tight arc around the base of the landing module. "God, look at this. Wouldn't it be great if we had one of those ships they're always flying in those science-fiction shows? Then we could just zoom around wherever we wanted, see what's really in the deeper regions of the Valles Marineris canyon system, the Hebes Chasma." Her words were starting to come so fast they were running together. "Or the Olympic Mons—can you imagine going down into the crater of a volcano that rises over fifty *thousand* feet high?"

"I wouldn't go," Dennis said, more to slow her down than anything else. Not just an observer, he was continually monitoring and adjusting the position of the *Excursion* relative to the landing module down on the Martian surface. "What if the volcano erupted?"

"Oh, there's no indication of current volcanic activity," Anne responded. "Face it, this place is empty."

Dennis glanced at her. "I distinctly remember a media blitz a few years back about microbes having been discovered in a Martian meteorite—"

Anne raised an eyebrow at him. "Dead microbes are a long way from the kind of life needed to make mud pies, Mr. Gamble. There's nothing out there now but wind and oxidized dust."

Patrick's voice interrupted them. "Afraid I'm going to have to side with Annie on this one, buddy." A pause, then, "What do you say? Are we ready for me to go out and start the in-person collection process?"

Dennis chewed his lower lip nervously and checked the digital readout—1:00:37. Jesus, where had the time gone? Finally, he nodded. "Ready when you are."

For a few moments, the radio remained silent. At last Patrick's determined voice spilled from the multiple speakers in the control panel at the same time they saw his image on the screen reach for the spacesuit helmet. When it was in place and locked down, Patrick said one more thing over the solo feed to the mother ship to make sure the audio connection was working:

"All right, Mars. Say hello to the human race."

Patrick Ross stepped off the landing module's ladder and onto Martian soil at about ten minutes after eleven on what was a perfect Saturday morning back on his home planet. If he could have seen the celebrations across the United States, he would have been embarrassed at all the fuss; he wasn't quite sure how he'd become an all-American hero, and the truth was, all this attention just made him flustered. He couldn't show that, of course—he'd been raised to speak clearly and proudly in public and to do right by the image of his father, Senator Judson Ross. There was the memory of his mother to consider, too—if he didn't always agree with his father, he was determined to do right by her. She had been sweet, patient, and taken from the family way too soon. Without getting too Freudian, Patrick saw some of the same character qualities in his lovely girlfriend, Melissa. She didn't know it yet, but someday she'd be the wife of an American astronaut and the mother of his children.

He felt the life-support system on his EVA suit register the swift drop in external temperature and adjust the body temperature-control unit to accommodate it. Numbers flashed across the small optical display just above eye level on the inside of his helmet, and one of those numbers told him it was slightly under one hundred and eighty degrees Kelvin on the Martian surface—a staggering one hundred thirty-five degrees below zero Fahrenheit. After all these years and all the moon and space walks he'd done, it *still* amazed Patrick that he, or any man or woman, could actually be walking around in an environment that brutal.

He stopped and just stood there for a few moments, drinking in the sight of the Martian landscape in a close-up way that no one else in history had ever experienced: the terrain filled with dark, porous rocks; the rusty-red, sandy-textured soil; a sky painted the color of salmon from atmospheric dust. The view stretched across his vision and beyond for as far as he could see with a stark, unrelenting beauty that was almost mesmerizing.

Patrick broke the spell himself, knowing that if he didn't move forward soon, the radio would cut into the silence around him and ruin the moment. With graceless movement, he turned and punched in the code to unlock the exterior storage compartment; when the hatch dropped open, he lifted out a small folded package and the rack containing Anne's trio of bright orange canisters. Five halting steps took him far enough away from the landing module to give the mother ship a view on the video screen that was unmarred by any man-made object but the one he painstakingly unfolded. He snapped open the metal rod at one end, then pushed it deep into the dry, blood-colored soil. Patrick knew that when he spoke, the transmission would fill his voice with static from atmospheric interference, so he said his words slowly and as clearly as he could, while the cold Martian wind straightened the folds of the American flag:

"Not for one nation, one people, or one creed, but for all humankind."

Mankind had finally conquered Mars.

Back Home on Earth

Millions of people across the nation raised their voices in celebration, hoisting everything from beer bottles to coffee cups to cans of soda. Fixed before their television sets at home, in bars, in health clubs, and during reluctant Saturday work sessions at the office, they all listened, exhilarated by the success of the Mars mission and captivated by the voice of Peter Jennings.

> *In a world beset by violence, hunger and strife, there are still occasions when mankind surpasses the petty struggles of daily existence.*

Nowhere, however, was the elation more intense than at Mission Control in Houston, Texas.

Of the three huge screens that dominated the room, two of them showed a live feed from the landing. The massive room was alive with applause and yelling, the workers and technicians at a hundred and ninety-seven work stations slapping each other on the back with glee and spinning foolishly in chairs before their consoles to celebrate the culmination of years of work. In a glass-paneled viewing room behind the main control area, a smaller but no less elated group laughed and raised glasses of champagne to toast each other and the space-suited figure on the screen as newscaster Peter Jennings supplied them with the media viewpoint via a small television set off to the side:

> *The* Excursion *voyage to Mars is one of these occasions. Today, America is proud!*

Impeccably dressed in a deep blue suit, every silver hair in perfect place, Senator Judson Ross put his arm around Melissa Evans and gave her a gigantic, fatherly hug. "He did it, Missy!" He let go of her and began shaking hands with the NSEG officials milling happily around the room, his mouth stretched in a beaming smile. Excitement made his words slip into the slight southern drawl that he'd worked to shed, but right now that was okay. This was his grand moment, the day that brought the United States success in the Mars Space Program that he himself had pioneered, the red planet conquered by none other than his own son Patrick. "Look at him up there," he exclaimed. "He's on *Mars*!"

"Your son's a hero, Senator Ross," an NSEG official whose name he couldn't recall told him. "A true-blue hero—congratulations!"

Senator Ross nodded, delighted at the response, relieved that Patrick was up there and seemed to be doing okay, safe as you please; he never would have told anyone how scared he'd been at the prospect of his boy traveling over thirty-five million miles—a distance nearly inconceivable to him—and stepping out of his spacecraft. But it was okay, he was there and safe, and everything was fine. Thank God.

The smile plastered to his face, he made his way around the room again, downing a glass of Dom Pérignon on the way.

The Garberville Psychiatric Institute in Maryland was lovely, a top-of-the-line facility reserved for special people thrust into "special" situations. From the outside, the Institute looked like a New England mansion: quaint red brick; shutters painted bright white framing lightly tinted windows; petunia-filled flower boxes even adorned the windowsills above neatly shaped hedges. A long, curving drive flanked by marigolds led to a locked—discreetly, of course—double front door next to which was a small brass doorbell and an inconspicuous sign that read "Visitors By Appointment Only." The grounds were quiet and peaceful, intentionally inviting.

Inside, the environment did an about-face.

Beyond the scrupulously decorated and maintained entry foyer, reception area and receiving offices, the walls were pitted and cracked, both from age and the force of blows thrown by residents for one reason or another. Well hidden behind the exterior's solar tint on the windows was a layer of steel mesh embedded on the inside of the glass. Furniture was sparse and strictly functional: hard-cushions on the couches and chairs that couldn't be used to smother a fellow inmate, steel legs and arms on the tables that couldn't be broken off and used as a club. The Institute was old enough so that the bare tiles on the floors were asbestos-based, but the directors and big-armed orderlies didn't care. They had enough to worry about just trying to keep the residents' behavior at a level vaguely approximating acceptable control.

In the game room—checkers and cards only, no sharp objects allowed—the television was mounted high at the juncture of the wall and the eight-foot ceiling and turned on. Only a few of the ten or twelve men and women in the room were paying any attention to the running report of the Mars space landing; many were tranquilized to keep them quiet and to ensure the safety of their fellow residents. The television was, quite simply, something with movement and noise on which they could focus beyond the misery surrounding them. One of the orderlies—Joey—had tried unsuccessfully to find a sports game, but the Mars landing was on all the main channels, and the Institute wasn't about to spend good money on cable television.

One of the residents, a patient named Herman Cromwell, had pulled a chair to a position directly in front of the television, he could focus completely on the screen without having his view obstructed by any of the others in the room. Joey watched him suspiciously, but he seemed okay, doing nothing other than listening intently to that Peter Jennings guy on the tube—

> *Patrick Ross. Son of a senator, football star at Yale, and now the first man on Mars. Intelligent, dependable, caring—a perfect hero for these imperfect times.*

Cromwell leaned forward on his seat, his face straining toward the screen. It was chilly in the game room—it was chilly everywhere at the Institute—but perspiration gleamed on his shaved head. His eyes, a disturbingly intense cobalt blue, were wide and anything but vacant. When he spoke, it was with such conviction that everyone in the room, drugged-out or not, turned to stare at him.

"I told them not to go!"

Aw, Christ, Joey thought as he saw Cromwell's fingers dig into the armrests of the chair.

Here we go again.

On the Surface of Mars

"How's it going out there?" Anne Sampas asked. Beneath the radio headset, her gaze was fixed on the video feed, watching the diamond-tipped mechanism on the Land Rover plow into the sandy red surface of Mars. The picture had deteriorated, then straightened out again, fading back and forth as it fought against unseen pulses of solar interference. Right now it looked pretty good, and she could see Patrick using a small scoop to fill the second of the three sample canisters. At the navigator's console a few feet away, Dennis was keeping his usual close eye on the *Excursion*'s orbit position relative to the location of the landing module on the planet's surface.

"Not bad," Patrick answered. "The soil is loose but the drill is still showing signs of wear and tear."

"One more area," she noted. "Sector one twelve. It looks like it might've been a canal bed."

Dennis looked over from the control chair and smiled. "Signs of water?"

"That's what we hope to find out."

Patrick's voice came over the radio again, fuzzy at the edges but understandable. "Eight years of training and I'm a Martian ditch-digger."

Dennis pressed the audio button on his own headset so he could join the conversation. "Quit complaining. I thought you said you liked making mud pies."

"Like Anne said," Patrick came back, "there's no water."

Anne smiled. "Sorry, pal. Mining is part of the job description."

Dennis glanced over at the LED display that was synchronized with the one in Patrick's landing module: 4:27:38 and counting. "You've got about an hour and a half of surface time left, Patrick."

"Roger that."

"Don't push it, Patrick. You need to be off-surface well before Martian nightfall. If you think it's cold now, try dropping to a hundred and thirty degrees Kelvin," Anne said.

"For the temperature challenged like you," Dennis interrupted with a smirk, "that's two hundred and twenty-five below zero."

"Gee," Patrick responded. "Thanks so much for your help. I couldn't function without you."

"Look at him down there," Dennis said an hour later. He and Anne studied the wide-angle video feed from the landing module, which showed Patrick taking halting steps across the rock-strewn surface, moving carefully around the jagged edges of large, dark stones. "He's just like a speck of . . . I don't know . . . dust." He followed his friend's movement, his forefinger tracing the screen. "See? A little dot moving across the horizon."

Anne leaned toward the display. "Wait—what's he doing? Why did he stop?"

Dennis thumbed his voice feed. "Patrick?"

The barely recognizable form on the screen paused for a long moment. Finally, Patrick spoke. "Did you know that Mars got its name from the Roman god of war?" he asked. "But I can't figure out why—I've never felt such peace. It's like I'm here with God."

Anne smiled. "Perhaps you feel that way because

the Roman god Mars was not always so destructive. He was originally the god of spring vegetation, Mars Sylvanus. Among other things, Mars was also known to be the lover of Venus."

"Patrick," Dennis broke in, "I'm afraid it's time for you to leave your gods behind. Shake your legs and head on back to the module. ET until module liftoff is thirty-five minutes and counting."

On the display, Patrick gave them a choppy-looking salute. "Copy that, Dennis. I'm on my way."

An hour and ten minutes, no more—

And Dennis Gamble and Anne Sampas turned to stare as the airlock door to the docking bay slid open. Patrick Ross grinned at his cohorts but didn't say anything, and for a long moment, neither did they.

Then they all started whooping and hugging at once.

"You are the *man*!" Dennis shouted. He whirled a laughing Patrick around the small control area, then gave him a push that sent him toward Anne.

She caught him in an amiable hug, then ruffled his dark hair like a schoolboy's. "Great job, Patrick. You've done us proud, young man!"

"Aw, knock it off, you two," Patrick said. "It was no big deal, not really." He took a step back to the docking-bay door and retrieved the rack of sample canisters, then snapped it into its holder on the rear wall.

"No big deal, huh?" Dennis rolled his eyes. "If that's so, then why is the President of the United States waiting to talk to you?"

"Oh, boy—why the heck didn't you say so!" Patrick hurried over to the command chair and fumbled on the headset, pushing the switches to bring up the audio and video feeds. "Commander Patrick

Ross here, Mr. President," he said respectfully. "I apologize for keeping you waiting."

A few beats, then the President's smooth, practiced voice rolled into the *Excursion*'s cockpit, and the three astronauts could tell by his words that the rest of the world was hearing him at the same time. "Captain Ross, this is a tremendous achievement that once again proves to the world that if we rise above partisan politics, America can climb to the heavens."

Patrick smiled at the clearly rehearsed speech, pleased nonetheless. "Thank you, Mr. President. But the credit should go to my crew. I couldn't be up here without them."

"The three of you definitely make an excellent team. Please accept my invitation to be my guests at the White House."

"We'd be honored, sir," Patrick replied. He glanced at his two partners, an impish grin tugging at his mouth. "But I'm afraid you won't change my mind. I'm still a Democrat."

Rich laughter filtered over their headsets. "Come home safe, Commander Ross. Our prayers are with you."

"Thank you, sir."

Dennis hit the cut-off switch and turned to his companions. "Ready to head home?"

For a moment, neither spoke. Then Anne exhaled. "Wow, I can't believe it's over. All those years to prepare, and now—already it's just a memory."

Dennis chuckled. "Then let the memories begin. We've got a lot of those to go through when we hit home, not to mention the flight time back to Earth."

"Yeah, but the actual Mars walk—" Patrick began.

"Oh, quit your griping," Dennis said lightly. "We'll walk with the Martians again sometime. You'll see."

Anne smiled. "Little green men?"

"I thought you said they'd be red."

"Whatever."

Patrick snickered and bent to his work. "Knock it off, you two. Let's get down to business."

Unnoticed against the aft wall, bright beads of condensation had begun a slow drip down the outside of the last of the sample canisters.

Thirty minutes later, the three astronauts had finished their final checks and were strapped into the harnesses of the cockpit chairs. Dennis's expression had slipped into his standard mask of concentration, a sure sign that what was uppermost in his mind was getting the *Excursion* free of the Mars orbit and on her way home. His gaze tracked the readouts on the system monitors, his fingers ran confidently over the switch panels. "Control, this is *Excursion*," he said briskly. "All systems are go. Request update on the ETD."

The response was nearly instantaneous. *"Excursion, this is Control. You are a go for de-orbit burn. Activate main thruster panel, over."*

"Thank you, Control. De-orbit burn sequence completed . . . now." Dennis snapped the final toggle switch to the GO position. "We are homeward bound."

"Roger that, Excursion. Starting propulsion engine countdown. Twenty, nineteen, eighteen . . ."

Dennis looked over at Patrick and Anne. "We're in the money, folks."

"Seventeen . . ."

He grinned and stretched a hand toward Patrick, who slapped it, then grabbed it in a homeboy shake.

"Sixteen, fifteen, fourteen . . ."

Beneath them, *around* them, the engines began to pulse with power. Anne gave the other two a thumbs-up, knowing that the low, throaty hum would effectively wipe out all conversation until the *Excursion* had pulled them out of orbit and set herself into a steady cruising speed. As the ship began to vibrate, Anne turned her attention to the mainframe computer, intent on entering the final log notations for the trip. Only a few feet behind her chair and despite the perfectly monitored, low-humidity air of the small control center, water was now dripping freely off the third orange canister and forming a small puddle on the metal floor.

"Thirteen, twelve, eleven . . ."

Hunched over their tasks and momentarily deafened by the increasing roar of the thruster engines, none of the crew heard or saw the metal band cinching the edges of the sweating sample canister release with a snap, nor did they notice the still tightly sealed lid as it began to bulge.

"Ten, nine, eight, seven . . ."

Eyes locked on the LED countdown display, forehead creased, Dennis deliberately began flicking the first of a long sequence of switches on the control console.

"Six, five, four . . ."

Suspended on the rear wall, a fracture grew between the canister's lid and body, a break in the regulation quarantine seal. A thin line of slime the same rusty-red color as Martian soil squeezed out, then slid down the side of the orange metal, dripping and melding with the water already beneath it.

"Three . . ."

As the astronaut team counted down its final seconds in the Martian orbit, the spot of sludge on the floor began to bubble and expand—

"Two . . ."

—doubling, then tripling its size.

"One."

As Dennis Gamble opened his mouth to tell Mission Control that the *Excursion*'s thruster engines had fired, the mass of cellular muck twisted and reshaped itself into three separate segments—

—which leaped toward the crew of the *Excursion* with a ghastly chittering wail.

Back Home on Earth

With the successful firing of the thruster engines, the *Excursion* was on her way home and the back-patting and celebrating at Mission Control in Houston began anew. When the two direct-feed video screens went blank but the status screen kept relaying data, for a moment, one—

—long

—moment,

—no one breathed. Then the communications specialist slammed his hand on a button on his keyboard and his speaker-driven voice cut through the merriment and ground it all to a halt.

"Sir, I have LOS radio blackout. We have lost contact."

Pandemonium.

The grim announcement sent technicians and specialists vaulting back to their stations. Thomas Duncan, Flight Director for the Excursion Mars Space Landing Mission, strode across the room and stopped before the terrified-looking communications technician. Normally confident, Duncan's lean face was ghost-white beneath the pale blond of his crewcut, his eyes as wide as those of the young man awaiting his orders. A muscle ticked in one side of his jaw as he scanned the tech's screen but found nothing there to answer the thousands of questions suddenly jumbling in his mind.

"Activate the emergency satellite network," Duncan said between clenched teeth.

"Yes, sir." Young, capable, impeccably trained, the specialist's fingers were a blur on the keyboard. A final jab at the ENTER key hard enough to make the keyboard jump, and he said, "You have an open line, sir."

Duncan glanced over his shoulder and saw the people in the viewing room—Senator Ross and all the other family members, not to mention a significant number of NSEG officials—crowded against the glass, their frightened faces grim testimony to the seriousness of the situation.

Duncan snatched at the headset the technician offered him and slipped it on. "*Excursion*, this is Mission Control," he barked. "We are on emergency satellite frequency. Do you read?" A pause, longer and longer. *"Do you read,* Excursion*?"*

No response.

With a growl Duncan yanked off the headset and flung it at the technician, who barely noticed it as he frantically began typing emergency-check commands into the keyboard, desperately trying to troubleshoot the communications problem.

Around him, dozens of people did the same, rapid-firing orders into headsets and over telephones as their flight director paced the aisles between the consoles like a panicked lion. "Open O-2 pumps," he snapped at one technician. "Mobile auto-pilot thrusters," he ordered another. "Bounce the communications beam off the retro satellite. Do it *now*!" Beneath a red-bordered sign bearing a cigarette beneath the standard circle and slash, Duncan fumbled a cigarette from a pack of Pall Malls in his shirt pocket, then lit it. "Holy Christ," he muttered. His gaze cut to the viewing room and he sucked in a lungful of smoke in dismay.

Senator Ross had already thrown open the door and was on his way down the stairs. The babble of voices in the control room did nothing to drown out his strong voice. "What's going on?" he bellowed. "That's my boy up there!"

Close behind him came the girl—what was her

name? Melissa something-or-other, Patrick Ross's girlfriend. She had her hand to her throat in a classic display of southern feminine dismay, and her greenish-brown eyes had gone huge. Even from where he stood across the control-room floor, Duncan thought he saw her mouth form a single word . . .

Patrick.

In a pleasantly disguised psychiatric ward across the country, Herman Cromwell listened to the words of Peter Jennings—

> *For the past three minutes, every attempt to communicate with the* Excursion *has failed. Let us say a prayer for the safety of the astronauts and for the safe return to Earth of this spaceship and its fine, brave crew.*

—and went ballistic.

He had an orderly on either side of him, both big men with brawny arms and short tempers.

They couldn't hold him.

"I told them!" he screamed. *"I told them not to go to Mars!"* He lunged forward, then back, and forward again, a bucking motion that suddenly set him free. Before the closest orderly could grab him, Cromwell hefted the metal-framed chair in which he'd been sitting only moments before and hurled it at the television set. The screen imploded and hundreds of shards of dark glass sailed over the heads of the residents and orderlies amid the crackle of an electrical short and the hot smell of ozone and sizzling electrical components. One of the other residents began screaming, a high-pitched sound like the yowling of a cat on fire.

The orderly named Joey tackled Cromwell before he could find anything else to throw. "Tranq him, damn it!" he hollered as he and Cromwell hit the floor, followed quickly by his coworker. Two more orderlies barreled into the room and flung themselves at the still-struggling Cromwell; in the midst of all the flailing arms and legs, there was a flash of a hypodermic needle sinking into flesh.

Five seconds later, Herman Cromwell sagged, not quite unconscious, to the floor.

Defeated, the communications specialist looked up at Thomas Duncan. "Still no contact, sir. It's been seven minutes—she's drifting off course and we can't explain why the remote pilot functions have been disabled. Without something from the crew, we can't bring her in."

Duncan ground his third cigarette butt out against the technician's console, then turned and snapped at a black-suited woman hovering nearby. "Get me General Metzger."

She started to acknowledge the order, then blanched at something she saw over her shoulder and backstepped instead. Duncan scowled and turned, then gasped as the lapels of his jacket were crushed in the fists of a red-faced Senator Judson Ross.

"You are *not* giving up on my boy," the senator hissed into Duncan's face. Ross towered over the flight director, his strength fueled by fury and fear for his son's life. There was no escaping his grip as he shook Duncan to emphasize his words. "Do you hear me? You are *not giving up*!"

"Senator, please!" Melissa Evans tried to put her hand on Senator Ross's arm, but he ignored her and shook Duncan again. Trapped, the flight director's teeth rattled together with the assault.

"You get my boy back, damn you!"

"Sir, I have LOS blackout lift!" the communications specialist a few feet away suddenly shouted.

"Repeat—I have LOS blackout *lift*!" The last word was nearly a shriek of excitement.

Duncan didn't even notice when Ross released him, just found himself crowding around the technician with everyone else, leaning forward over the man as the tech rapid-fired commands into his keyboard and reinstated Mission Control's connection to the *Excursion.* The huge room was silent as the moments ticked past; finally, first one, then the other, of the viewing screens flickered and stabilized, at last showing the serene face of Commander Patrick Ross.

"Mission Control, this is the Excursion. *We have experienced a system malfunction, total blackout of telemetry, communications, and life-support operations."*

Still paralyzed with fear, Senator Ross and Melissa stared at the screen, unsure if Patrick and his crew were all right or not.

"I was able to repair the communications connection and reboot the life-support systems. Sorry for the scare."

As a cheer went up in the Mission Control Center, and indeed, around the world, Senator Judson Ross and Melissa Evans bowed their heads in thankful prayer . . .

. . . While, straitjacketed in a cold and solitary padded cell at the Garberville Psychiatric Institute, a heavily sedated Herman Cromwell still heard the final transmission on the television from the day-nurses' station around the corner—

"Excursion *crew is fine. Headed on de-orbit burn for Big Blue. It's gonna be good to get home. Over and out."* —and felt a single, lonely tear slip down his cheek. His whispered words were slurred by the drugs but still came from his heart:

"May God have pity on us all . . ."

CHAPTER 1

Five Months Later

"This is Mission Control. Link-up proceeding on Earth-orbit telemetry, shuttle to make Canaveral landing at 00:17 hundred. Over and out."

For a mission that had been nearly a decade in the making and had taken almost a year of travel time to complete, the end of it came amazingly fast.

The shuttle's touchdown on the Shuttle Landing Facility was a flight director's dream. The ground station microwave scan-beam landing system functioned perfectly on final approach, and everything on the surface was timed precisely to the second; the personnel-retrieval vehicle locked itself onto the shuttle without a problem, and the *Excursion* crew, smiling and healthy, climbed into their seats and were quickly carried away to the Kennedy Space Center's medical facilities. As part of standard operating procedure, the press was excluded from the initial reintegration; reporters had to be content with waiting in permanently leased facilities at the Space Center or in hotel rooms around the area as they waited their turn at the press conference scheduled for the following day.

And with the press, the whole world waited.

"On preliminary examination, all three of you are in remarkable health, although I'll continue with more specific blood testing, of course." Dr. Ralph Orinsky pushed his bifocals lower on his nose so he could peer over the top of them at the three crew members. "In fact, you're not even exhibiting the usual symptoms of long-term space travel. At the very least, we would have expected each of you to gain a minimum of an inch in height because the spine tends to stretch out during long-term exposure to a weightless environment." He tapped his pen against the sheaf of papers on the clipboard he was holding. "There's no evidence of that, however. All three of you are exactly the same height as you were eleven months and fourteen days ago. That's most unusual."

"So we're done here?" Dennis Gamble asked hopefully. It was the first time any of the three had spoken since disembarking from the transport vehicle except to answer questions from the medical team. "We can go?" He shot a glance at the glass partition that separated him, Patrick, and Anne—each stripped down to regulation NASA undergarments—from the rest of the medical facility. A half-dozen nurses and female technicians had found excuses or errands that had allowed them to congregate outside the window and stare in at the returned space team. "Oh, man," Dennis said now. "Look at that. Surely enough nurses out there to cure what ails *me*."

Dr. Orinsky cleared his throat pointedly. "I will remind you, Mr. Gamble, *again*, that you are under intimate-contact quarantine until we have a chance to conclude our scheduled tests. There are a few people here who require that we perform further in-depth examinations, and the National Space Exploratory Group regulations are going to insist on the standard quarantine period." His sharp gaze paused on each of them. "This means all of you, of course."

"Actually, I'm sure that the regulation was meant just for him," Patrick Ross said with a straight face. "I think it was instituted to save the women of the world."

"Kiss my butt, Ross," Dennis grumbled. "It'd better apply to all of us, or I start hollering discrimination."

"What's the matter, Dennis?" Anne asked sweetly. "Don't you feel special?"

Dennis opened his mouth to retort and ended up just shaking his head in defeat amid their laughter.

The next day started bright for the crew from the *Excursion*, with their first full Earth sunrise in over three quarters of a year. All three of them rose early enough to watch it, thankful for the clear Florida morning; then they met for a breakfast of NASA cafeteria coffee and powdered donuts before heading to the press site in the Launch Complex 39 area for the nine-o'clock news conference that had been arranged by NASA's public relations people.

"Christ," Patrick said under his breath as he sat between Anne and Dennis at a table placed on a platform at the front of the auditorium. "How many people are out there? It's like being tossed to the wolves."

"Nah," Dennis said, eyeballing the microphone suspiciously and checking to be sure it wasn't turned on before continuing. "Wolves are friendlier." He scanned the expectant faces. "And you're right—not so damned numerous, either. How many—"

"The auditorium seats ninety, and you can see it's standing room only," Patrick said, answering his friend's unfinished question. "Be grateful. It's clear now but there's a storm predicted. If it weren't for that, we'd be outside in the grandstand and facing three hundred and fifty."

"You two just behave," Anne said. The most reticent of the trio, she had plastered a strained smile on her face and was struggling valiantly to keep it there. "This is going to be hard enough."

"Oh, I'll keep your mind off of it," Dennis promised.

"That's what I'm afraid of."

"Get ready, guys," Patrick warned. "They're starting the footage, so the rest can't be far behind." As he spoke, two television screens above their heads flickered to life; after a flash of blue screen, a carefully edited official NASA version of the journey began to roll simultaneously.

"Ladies and gentlemen," said NASA's public relations director, "NASA, as well as the National Space Exploratory Group, welcomes you to this first press conference with the extraordinary crew of the *Excursion* Mars Space Landing Mission. Please note that our crew members—Commander Patrick Ross, Flight Navigator Dennis Gamble, and Mission Scientist Dr. Anne Sampas, are still recovering from this incredible, seventy-*million*-mile journey. We ask that questions be limited to one per newsperson, and that you keep your inquiries short and to the point." The director, a polished woman bearing a strong resemblance to an actress who starred in a popular television series about aliens and secret government files, gave the crowd of reporters a somewhat condescending smile. "We and the crew of the *Excursion* appreciate your cooperation. Also note that NASA has prepared detailed press kits for all of you, including video clips of the *Excursion*'s journey, which you may pick up on your way out."

She stepped back, and despite her request a double dozen of the reporters started firing questions at the same time, creating a completely unintelligible babble. The crew sat there for a few moments, then Patrick Ross finally held up his hand. As the noise died away, Patrick leaned forward and spoke carefully into the microphone. "I think we'll make this a simple question-and-answer session. I'll just call on people, one at a time, and we'll try our best to get to everyone." He paused. "How about you there, down in front."

A random choice, and the woman Patrick pointed to was delighted. "Thank you, Commander Ross," she said as she stood. "I'd like to know if the NSEG has come up with any explanation for the communication breakdown and the failure of the other systems onboard the *Excursion.*"

From the corner of his eye, Patrick saw the public relations director and her companion NSEG officials frown, but the question was out now and on-camera, and it would have to be addressed. No matter; he was great at diplomacy.

"All sorts of things can go wrong when you're thirty-five million miles from home," he began. "We—"

"I can explain the breakdown," Dennis interrupted.

Patrick raised an eyebrow at his friend and tilted his head to indicate that Dennis had the floor. The reporters in the audience leaned forward in anticipation, and one or two of the suits standing next to NASA's PR directors looked ready to wince.

"I'm sure you all realize that communication is an extremely expensive industry," Dennis said with deadly seriousness. "NSEG didn't pay the phone bill. Government cutbacks, you know."

The people in the audience laughed and looked at each other. When most of the chuckling had died down, the same woman fired another question before Patrick could single out a different reporter.

"Can you describe how you felt during those moments of tension?"

For a long, painful moment, none of the three spoke. Finally, Anne reluctantly pulled the microphone toward her mouth. "It was . . . a blur," she said.

"I don't recall," Dennis added.

Not good answers, and Patrick could tell by the expressions on the faces before him that this had the potential to be on the front page of the next batch of tabloids—hell, it probably would be, anyway—if he didn't jump in and fill in some blanks for these people. He cleared his throat to pull the audience's attention off his floundering crew members and sent the reporters the most engaging smile he could manage. "Remember that we spent five years training for this mission," he explained. "Much of that training was devoted to troubleshooting the what-ifs in a situation, so that if something were to go awry—as it did here—your training and your preparation and your *instincts* kick in. You go into a sort of autopilot function, as we did, and the next thing we knew, we were headed home."

That seemed to satisfy the woman, and Patrick passed the lead to Dennis as she sat down. Dennis scanned the faces in front of him, then arbitrarily picked a woman four rows from the back. "You have a question?"

"How do you feel about the corporate sponsorship that made the mission possible? Isn't that a sell-out?"

Dennis tried to arrange his face in a glare but he couldn't hide the smile that came out with his answer. "You're damned right it is. And do you know what I'm doing right after the longest space voyage in history?" He sat up on his chair, straightened his tie, and sent a glitzy grin at the cameras trained on them. "I'm going to Disneyland!"

Another round of laughter, at the end of which Patrick looked over at Anne. The smallest shake of her head told him she had no desire to go one-on-one with anyone in this room, so Patrick chose again, finding a harmless-looking fellow a couple of rows back. But the reporter, a balding man in his late forties, asked a question that startled Patrick enough to bring a little color to his cheeks.

"Patrick, are you surprised at your status as a sex symbol for the nineties?"

"I'm afraid that's something you guys in the press cooked up to sell newspapers," he replied. "I'm a one-woman kind of man." He looked to the far left and saw Melissa standing straight and beautiful next to his father, sent her a tiny wink. Let the reporters notice her—in fact, he hoped they would. Maybe that would put a stop to all this nonsense. But still . . . he should keep it light. "My girlfriend would kill me if I didn't say that."

"Any thoughts about NSEG's sexual-quarantine policy?"

"It's standard mission procedure," Patrick replied. "No different this time than any other."

"After eleven months in space," Anne put in unexpectedly, "ten more days doesn't seem too long."

"Correction," Dennis said. He looked intently at his watch. "Nine days, twenty-two hours, five minutes, eleven seconds."

Anne grinned, her face going red. "Talk about a one-track mind."

"I believe that what the world wants to know, Commander Ross," spoke up another man without being asked, "is whether there's alien life on Mars."

"Perhaps on a microscopic level there once was," Patrick answered without missing a beat, "although it almost certainly died out billions of years ago. As someone who's been there, I can tell you that as far as I could see, there were definitely no little green men walking around up there." He glanced at Anne. "Or red ones either."

Patrick Ross turned his piercing blue gaze back to the audience and sent the folks down there a perfect smile. His next words earned him and his crew a well-deserved round of applause.

"When it comes to evolution, I think we're the ones to beat."

CHAPTER 2

Monroe Air Force Base is heavily guarded, one of the most secretive facilities in the United States. It is a series of long, low-slung buildings made of dull gray-and-white cinderblock interspersed with steel-sheeted, whitewashed hangars, all surrounded by walled towers and firepower-laden sentries. For the most part, it is drab and nearly camouflaged. Harsh and sparse, from the outside it looks like the most unwelcoming, most unfriendly place in the world.

For some, the inside can be just as inhospitable.

"What you are about to see here in the BioHazard Laboratory is 'For Eyes Only' and may not be shared with anyone other than your superiors, who already know of its existence and by whose direction you have been brought here," Dr. Laura Baker said from her position in the main control crane a good forty feet above the floor. "Only the people who work at this facility, plus a very few others, know about this project. I'm sure you're all aware of the ramifications of disclosing top-secret information." This was an unnecessary warning perhaps, but one the molecular biologist felt compelled to make one that she wanted on record—the audio was always on and recording everything in this room. Laura's own security clearance was unquestioned—the badges plastered all over her lab coat attested to that. After all, what they were about to see was her own specially altered recreation of something that once could have destroyed mankind.

Standing silently behind the glass of a viewing booth ten feet above her and next to Colonel Carter Burgess, Jr. were the men she'd come to think of as the "Pentagon Three." That trio probably comprised a hundred and fifty years of uninterrupted military experience, and as for Colonel Burgess . . . he was what Laura privately termed a professional hard-ass, and she despised him. She had an ex-lover who fell into that category, and she was realistic enough to recognize that Press—the infamous former significant other—was probably the reason for her opinion. At least the two didn't look alike: where Press had been dark and rugged, more fit than was apparent at first glance, Colonel Burgess was just . . . big. Slightly taller than average and on the burly side, the tautness of his muscles was finally loosening with age; Laura thought that now he most likely hired others to do his dirty work for him. No doubt the loss of one of his eyes—the glass replacement gave his face a strangely skewed look—had taken him out of the physical foray.

The other three men weren't much different—craggy faces, stiff manners—except perhaps that their identities had been kept secret even from her. They were probably all retired four-star generals, but the fact that they still worked for the government wouldn't be found on public records anywhere.

No one in the booth said anything in response to her warning, so Laura inhaled and began her demonstration. "We have re-created the alien being known as "Sil" from a frozen lab embryo. If you look to the center of the work area, you will see the results of our efforts."

Laura entered a series of commands on her control keyboard and there was a ratcheting sound as unseen switches were released, followed by the hiss of hydraulics. In the middle of the floor, a petal-shaped circle spun open and a glass cylinder rose smoothly into sight. Standing inside, her beautiful face deceptively innocent, was—

Sil.

No—not quite.

"This, gentlemen, is . . . *Eve.*"

Laura heard a murmur from above and resisted the urge to sneer. Had they thought she was exaggerating? Well, she hadn't been. The same DNA, a combination of human with the alien formula transmitted in a coded message to Arecibo in 1992 and decoded in 1993 . . . the same mixture that had nearly caused a global disaster when the resulting creature had escaped.

The same kind of creature that stood before them.

Tall and stunning, Eve stood naked in the glass tube, the portrait of a perfectly formed woman. Slender but shapely, with small, perfect breasts, a flat stomach and lean hips, she looked like anything *but* the uncontrollable life-form she had the potential to become. Staring around her at the lab and the workers beyond the unbreakable quartz-glass panels—no stupid mistakes this time—Eve gave the impression of nothing more than a terrified, captive victim.

But Laura Baker knew better. God, how she knew.

"The test capsule is mirrored on the inside, and she cannot see the technicians in the lab while inside it, nor can she see you. As you've all probably noticed, Eve's enclosure is in the upper part of a larger living arrangement, a sort of human 'habitrail.' The environment has been specifically designed so that all areas of it, including a small garden on the upper level, are in full view. The creature can hide nothing from us." She raised her hand so that her small audience could see it, then gestured toward the floor below. "We have a fully staffed testing laboratory, complete with technicians, biologists, and heavily armed guards—all, of course, female."

When there was no comment from the men secluded above her, Laura continued. "Our goal is to discover a means to defend ourselves against this species should it, in its natural and purest form, ever find its way to Earth. What you see here is of necessity a genetically modified version of what we speculate that form would be, half alien and half human. She appears to be human in every respect, but I assure you that she can still be quite deadly." Laura glanced upward, but none of the men in the viewing booth were looking at her; their gazes were riveted on the woman in the cylinder, and Laura was far too intelligent to think it was for sexual reasons.

"One of the things we've developed here in the lab is a hydrochlorine-based toxin. In a moment, you will witness the effects of this chemical agent on the alien." More commands into the keyboard, a firm stroke of the enter key, and suddenly a blue-tinted mist spewed from nozzles set at regular intervals around the inside of the glass cage. Within the tube, Eve gasped and her chest began to hitch in human-like sobs as she twisted and turned in a vain attempt to avoid the haze.

"As you can see," Laura said grimly, "Eve is not only repulsed by the hydrochlorine toxin, but it results in distinct physical injuries. If you'll turn your attention to the monitors across the room, you'll be able to view close-up images from two perspectives. One is a magnetic-resonance pattern of Eve's body, the other is a real-time video feed that shows the damage being done as we speak." One of the screens flicked to a close-up and showed Eve writhing in agony, her formerly smooth skin covered with ugly, raised welts. Laura gave her audience a few moments to register what they were seeing as she checked the biological information scrolling beneath the film views, then she leaned forward.

"Unfortunately, it's far too early in our experiments to celebrate. Watch very closely, gentlemen. What you are about to witness will shatter any notion that you might have that the young woman below you is a member of humankind." Laura almost *felt* their interest elevate as she thumbed the switch that brought her voice down to the technician in charge on the main floor. "Clear the tube."

Somewhere out of sight, a reverse fan whirred to life and the air in the glass capsule began to reverse, the noxious blue mist spiraling down to thin ribbons as it was sucked out via the same nozzles it had entered. In a few seconds, the glass was once again unobstructed, this time giving them a view of a different Eve—swollen, red, and crying like a child.

Laura didn't say anything more—she didn't have time to—before Eve's healing began.

It was like watching a layer of sand shift and bubble across the woman-form's skin—a *vibration* of cells rearranging, *regenerating*, right in front of their eyes. Two seconds, then three . . . and every indication of physical harm was just . . .

Gone.

Eve stood there, rosy-skinned and perfect, blinking but seemingly unsurprised at her own metamorphosis, completely at home in her own skin despite the blatant display of her nudity. She was healed; she was whole.

She was *Eve.*

When Laura glanced up at the viewing booth, she saw all four men staring down, their expressions frozen with disbelief. She cocked an eyebrow and broke the spell. "Now you understand what we're up against here. Every toxic chemical agent that we've come up with has had the same result: as an offense, whatever we employ against her works only once, and only *very* briefly. The alien's biology immediately adapts and renders the weapon useless."

For the first time, the speaker on her console came to life and she heard Colonel Burgess address the others in the booth with him: "Simply put, this is it. Nothing we've found so far works, and we still haven't figured out an efficient way to deep-six these alien bastards."

Wow, Laura thought with a roll of her eyes that thankfully couldn't be seen from above. A man of eloquence. Still, she felt compelled to add her own measure of important information. "There's another extremely important thing. The species displays a very measurable sixth sense—a form of telepathy. We believe it's essentially a Darwinian survival mechanism that enables it to communicate with others of its kind in what it perceives to be hostile environments."

For a long moment there was no response, and Laura could imagine the Pentagon Three considering this new bit of information, turning their strategy-oriented thinking toward the concept of a savage being capable of communicating without their knowing it. When the response finally came, it was short and to the point.

"Continue the testing, Dr. Baker."

Was there ever any doubt?

Laura gave the three figures in the viewing room a brisk nod, snapped on the control that would drop Eve's glass capsule back to the lower level for unloading, then climbed out of the control pod and went back to work.

It took only a few minutes to store the notes from the experiment and make backup copies for the data banks, but in that short time Eve had already been released into her habitat by the safety crew on the main floor. Laura found her getting dressed in one of the simple-patterned jumpers that made up her wardrobe, anger sparking from her clear blue eyes as she yanked the cotton fabric down and over her head, then jammed her feet into a pair of white canvas flats. Eve stood when she saw Laura, then backed up a step and folded her arms defiantly, like a schoolgirl standing up to a teacher. "Why did you do that to me?" she demanded.

For a moment, Laura couldn't answer. Guilt suffused her, robbing her of the scientific reasons that she knew would justify her actions; all she could see was this blond-haired, fresh-faced young woman standing in front of her, all she could hear was Eve's righteous indignation. This was the image that stayed with her at the end of the day and the reason she sometimes had to forcibly remind herself that the being in front of her was an alien creature, *not* the exploited woman she appeared to be now.

"I-I'm sorry, Eve," she managed to say. "We lowered the dosage as far as possible, but the purpose of the test was to show the toxin's effect. It could have been so much more painful . . ." Her voice faltered as she belatedly realized that her words sounded like nothing less than a threat. "I've explained why we have to do this," she said at last, her voice low and as reassuring as she could make it. Eve said nothing, just continued to stare at her. "What happened with Sil—"

"—and why you have to be prepared," Eve cut in bitterly. "Survival of the fittest and all that. Right."

Her voice softened and she looked away from Laura, gazing longingly at the color television, now dark, built into one wall of her living area. "I suppose that one must be cruel in order to survive."

Stung, Laura opened her mouth, then closed it. What could she say to that? In nature cruelty was a given, brutality accepted and even admired. But in the human race, were they not expected to be civilized? Or even kind?

"You know," Eve said when Laura remained quiet, "I watch all these programs on television and see the places I can't go, the people I can't meet—I bet you didn't know that I'd give anything to visit the Pyramids, did you?" She gave a short, harsh laugh. "No, of course not. How could you?"

"Eve—"

"A lab rat," Eve said suddenly, her eyes narrowing. "To be tested and poked and prodded. *Tortured.* Is that all I am to you? I wonder what your animal-rights people would say to *this.*"

"Stop it," Laura said, more sharply than she'd intended. Her face was heating up with exasperation and she hated that—if she didn't put a stop to this now, the constant videotape would make her look like she'd painted rouge on her cheeks. "I'm doing the best I can under the circumstances." With effort, she brought her tone back to the carefully measured level she always used when talking with Eve. "Part of the reason I took this job was to make sure these experiments were done with regard for the subject—"

"Subject," Eve said with a sneer. "Yeah. That would be me." Gazes locked, for a long moment neither woman said anything. Then, feeling chastised, Laura broke the gaze and turned to go.

"Tell me," Eve said from behind her, "what was the rest of your reason? Curiosity, perhaps?"

Laura stopped and turned back. "Aren't we all curious?"

Eve cocked her head. "Yes, I suppose that's true." Her expression relaxed a little and she looked thoughtful; then hesitantly she reached out and touched Laura on the arm. "I know you've been good to me, Laura. But remember one thing . . .

"I'm human, too."

Laura gave her a small smile and briefly squeezed Eve's hand before stepping out of the habitat and into the exit corridor.

God help her, a big part of Laura wanted to believe that.

CHAPTER 3

"Look at it," Melissa said dreamily. "Have you ever seen anything like this?" She glanced at Patrick and he smiled and followed her gaze to where she was staring, out the best window at The Willows Steakhouse. The view from this prime corner booth was indeed spectacular: on the other side of the glass was a rare, clear night sky showing a faint sweep of crystalline stars overhead, their sparkle diminished only by the butter-yellow glow of the White House in the distance. Not many places in Washington, D.C. could boast a panoramic scene like this, and not many people rated the one table in the restaurant that offered it.

"It's very pretty," Patrick agreed, and he meant it.

"Oh, silly," Melissa said. "I know you're only indulging me—it's probably nothing compared to what you saw while you were on the *Excursion*."

The smile he sent her was genuine, and the warmth in his dark eyes made Melissa's breath quicken. "What it can't compare with is how beautiful you look tonight. The dress suits you perfectly."

"A-hem," Senator Ross said with mock seriousness.

"No kidding," Dennis Gamble put in. "The two of you could light the candle here without touching it."

Melissa blushed and made herself ignore the other two men, instinctively smoothing away a fold in the red-velvet fabric along the line of one hip, knowing that Patrick's gaze would follow the movement appreciatively. She didn't want to be rude, but she wished Senator Ross and Dennis would just go on home and let the two of them have the rest of the evening together. The dress was right, the mood was right—even if the quarantine wasn't lifted yet, she could at least make sure Patrick was thinking only of her. God knew, the competition for his attention got harsher every day, especially now that his dark-haired, handsome features were plastered across the front of every news magazine in the world. She was about to hint to Patrick that they should leave when a stranger's voice cut into the conversation.

"Uh, excuse me, Commander Ross?"

The four of them looked up to see a young man, hardly out of his teens, standing nervously about four feet away, clearly too afraid to come any closer. "I, uh, hate to bother you, but . . ." He aimed a glance over his shoulder at a table somewhere in the room, swallowed, and tried again. "I was wondering if I could, uh, get your autograph?"

Melissa beamed with pride as Patrick gave the admirer a friendly nod. "Sure," he joked as he pushed aside the remains of his dessert to make room on the table. "What am I signing—a napkin or a menu?"

"Actually," the stranger said shyly, "it's just a piece of paper my girlfriend had in her purse."

"That'll work just fine," Patrick said as he scrawled out his name with the pen the guy offered. "There you go."

"Wow, thanks—now I've got yours *and* Michael Jordan's!" His face split in a huge grin, the young man hurried back to his table, his prize autograph clutched firmly in one hand.

"Well, you made his day," Dennis said with a chuckle.

Patrick looked at Melissa. "Hey, you think Michael Jordan gets hand cramps?"

Before she could answer, Senator Ross leaned forward. "Popularity, boy. That's the name of the game." Melissa's pretty features slipped a notch as she heard the slur in the senator's words. Darn; he wasn't going to get loud right here, was he? Jesus, not tonight. This time, however, he surprised her by lowering his voice instead of raising it. "I got the head of the Republic National Committee telling me you're a shoo-in for a Senate seat, Patrick."

Like Melissa's, Patrick's expression sobered a bit. "No thanks."

The senator leaned back again, studying his son, and Melissa could've sworn the look in his eye was more calculating than anything else. "Come on, son. There's no harm in at least exploring the possibilities. You could be one of the youngest ever—"

Patrick cleared his throat. "I'll leave the politics to you, Dad. It's just not my line of work."

"I spent four years in flight school with your son, Senator." Dennis smiled amiably. "He doesn't lie well enough to be a politician."

Bless Dennis for making them all laugh and turning the conversation away from government employment and exactly the kind of future Melissa, if not Patrick, wanted to avoid. She supposed it was probably inevitable—didn't all astronauts grow up to be politicians of one sort or another? What a strange predicament to find herself in, madly in love with the son of a powerful United States senator and who, let's face it, was destined to someday sit in an office in the nation's capital.

"So, Dennis," Senator Ross said when the gaiety had diminished, "Patrick only talks about the good stuff for dear old dad. Tell me what it was *really* like up there for eleven months."

For just a beat too long Dennis didn't answer, and Melissa frowned. Before Patrick's father could pick up on the hesitation, however, Dennis looked over at Patrick and gave him a sappy smile. "Not much that I can tell you about the details, sir. But I will say this: Patrick and I are getting married."

"Hey, just a minute," Melissa exclaimed around the hoots of the three men. "He's mine!"

"But you could draw a lot of liberal votes like that," put in Senator Ross.

More laughter as the talk turned again to Senator Ross's favorite subject and Melissa's least preferred, and it was only a few minutes when she noticed that Patrick had sort of faded from the conversation. Now it was mostly Dennis and Patrick's father, bantering back and forth like old college buddies while the older man put away his usual few too many. "Patrick," she said in a low voice, touching his arm. "Are you feeling all right?"

He shook his head and Melissa saw him squeeze his eyes shut, then open them, his gaze darting around the restaurant in a way that struck her alarmingly like the gaze of a trapped animal. "Hey, you guys excuse me, okay?" he said abruptly. "I need some air." Without making further excuses, he rose and headed away from the table, and Melissa noted with amusement that most of the women in The Willows seemed to be tracking his every move.

Dennis and Patrick, of course, had cleaned their plates and then some—understandable after eleven months of vacuum-packaged food on board the *Excursion.* Across from her, however, the senator's slice of tiramisu had hardly been touched in favor of his once-again-empty drink glass. "What's the matter with him?" he asked, bewildered.

Melissa folded her napkin and stood. "I'll take care of him." As she headed after Patrick, she had to smile at Dennis's candid quip:

"Actually, I think there were two too many people at this table."

In good weather, patrons of The Willows often waited outside, in a tiny, tree-lined plaza to the side of the restaurant. Melissa found Patrick there, sitting on one of the wrought-iron benches with his hands folded between his knees, staring down at the quaint pattern of cobblestones on the ground. Around them a soft, warm breeze ruffled the leaves and drove away the last of the humidity that had been so stifling earlier in the day. She joined him on the bench and sat quietly for a moment without touching him, sensing that he needed undisturbed time to collect himself. It seemed like a peaceful oasis here—private and dark, lit only by the glow of the four old-fashioned gas lamps at each corner of the paved square.

Finally Patrick lifted his head, his expression a little more relaxed. "My head was ringing like crazy," he explained. "For a minute I felt like I could hear people whispering about us from thirty yards across the room." He laughed ruefully. "Meet Commander Patrick Ross, the Amazing Hearing Aid."

Melissa touched his knee. "Patrick, I think you should talk to the doctor. These spells you've been having—"

"Sweetheart, I had a full physical from the NASA physician after the landing, you know that. He and his team said I was fine."

"Maybe you need a second opinion."

He shook his head. "Forget it. I've been poked and prodded enough for now. They can wait until the next mission." He lapsed into silence and studied her, and she watched his eyes tracing her features. "You're so beautiful, you know that?" His fingers reached out and lifted a strand of her hair and held it up to the soft light. "These lamps make your hair almost look like sand spread with stardust." He let the hair fall, then rubbed his face with both hands. "You know what I think it is?" he said. "The damned pressure. People think this is fun, but it's not—it's just a drag, like having a boulder tied around your neck. 'You gonna fly another mission, Patrick?' 'You gonna run for office, Patrick?' " His voice lightened a bit. " 'You gonna marry Melissa, Patrick?' " He gave her a sideways glance, a sparkle in his eye that hadn't been there a moment before. "I tell them 'maybe,' 'no,' and 'yes.' "

Melissa blinked. "What—"

"You'll marry me, won't you, Missy?"

"You're proposing to me?" she asked. "Right here? Now?"

"I sure am." He raised his hand and opened his fingers. Melissa didn't know how long he'd been hiding it, but nestled on his palm was an exquisite filigreed gold band with a pear-shaped diamond mounted on it. Patrick took her hand in his and slipped the ring onto her ring finger, then brushed her knuckles with his lips. "Don't you know that I've loved you since the day we met? You're everything to me—my love, my world, my *life.* I want you until death do us part."

Tears filled her hazel eyes. "Oh, Patrick—I don't know what to say."

He grinned. " 'Yes' would be a good answer."

She threw her arms around him and hugged him fiercely. "Then yes! Yes, yes, yes!"

He laughed happily and stood, pulling her upright with him. There in the small, shadowed plaza, his mouth came down on hers in a sweet, slow kiss that warmed her like nothing else in the world could or ever would. Melissa responded without thinking, pressing her body against Patrick's, her well-toned form molding to his in a way familiar but long denied. The pressure of his lips increased as he pulled her closer, hands slipping down and along her waist as her lips parted to admit his tongue. Heat coursed through her, riding on the hunger for him that she had controlled for nearly a year. His mouth broke free and found its way to her jaw, then down her neck.

"If we keep going," she said breathlessly, "I'm going to say to hell with the quarantine—"

"Hey, Patrick!"

Startled, she and Patrick broke apart, turning their faces in the direction of the voice. The flash of a camera sent a spike of light into the plaza, then another; suddenly flashbulbs were popping all around the main entrance, nearly blinding them and utterly destroying any notion of privacy. A dozen reporters crowded through the wrought-iron archway and rushed toward them.

"Look this way, Patrick!"

"Smile for us, Melissa!"

"Right here, Patrick!"

Patrick grabbed her arm and pushed through the knot of paparazzi, guiding her back to the restaurant, where he knew the maitre d' would cut off the photographers at the door. "Come on, sweetheart."

Smiling despite the pesky cameras, Melissa hurried to keep up with Patrick's longer stride. "Let's go back inside and tell your father the news."

But Patrick stopped just outside the door, ignoring the still-flashing cameras. "You go on."

"By myself?"

"Go on—get Dad and have him take you home. I'm getting out of here."

"Patrick, what's wrong?" Melissa demanded. "Are you not feeling—"

"I'm fine," he insisted. His hand on her elbow turned her toward the maitre d', who was hurrying to meet them, an apologetic look on his face. "I just need to clear my head."

Hurt, Melissa started to step away, but Patrick turned back and pulled her close. "I'll call you later," he whispered. "I promise." He gave her a quick, sweet kiss, ignoring the camera flashes that increased to a frenzy when their faces came together.

"Hey, lovebirds," Dennis said from behind them. "I have to fly—my date awaits."

"For heaven's sake, Dennis," Melissa said. "Why didn't you include her tonight?"

But Dennis shook his head. "Nah—this is too much like family. Takes a little more time to get to this level."

"Later," Patrick promised her again. "Come on, Dennis. You go one way and I'll go the other. They can't follow us both."

"I hate to tell you how many famous people have thought that," Dennis retorted. Nevertheless, he dashed in one direction while Patrick headed in the other.

And left Melissa standing there with the maitre d', staring after him, feeling strangely frightened.

CHAPTER 4

No doubt there were people somewhere within the bright cluster of government buildings that made up the Goddard Flight Center in one quadrant of the NSEG grounds, but they were certainly few in number at this time of the night. On the most complicated matters, however, Dr. Ralph Orinsky worked best alone, and on those things he also worked best during the darkest of the night hours.

Or at least he'd once thought so.

Now the white-haired man walked back and forth in front of the specimen table in his laboratory, a cordless telephone held so tightly in one hand that his fingers hurt. "If I can't speak to him, then I need to leave a message for Mr. Herman Cromwell," he said urgently into the receiver. He jammed his bifocals up to his forehead and they immediately slid down again. His voice was rising in desperation and he tried to control it—if the operator on the other end decided he was a loony, she'd pretend to take a message and Herman would never know he'd called. "He's a patient there," he said. "I believe he's in Ward B. I realize it's rather late, but if he could call me at his earliest opportunity, it would be most helpful." He bit his lip at the woman's reply but managed to hold his tongue—getting angry would only destroy any chance he had of getting through to Herman. "Yes, of course," he said. "I realize it's late. Tell him that Dr. Orinsky called. I'm a former colleague."

When the Garberville operator broke the connection, Dr. Orinsky allowed himself a full scowl as he clicked off the telephone and slammed it on the table. Foolish woman—could she not tell from the tone of his voice how important it was that he speak to Herman Cromwell? If it hadn't been so far and so late, and if he didn't have these samples on which he needed to run further tests, he'd drive there tonight, demand to see the administrator and generally raise hell until he made them let him meet with his old partner.

The samples . . .

Orinsky whirled and stared at the lab table, but of course everything was as it should be: sample bottles, beakers and burners, several clipboards of crumpled paper upon which he'd scribbled copious notes, and obviously, the rack holding the tubes of blood that had prompted his post-midnight call to the Garberville Psychiatric Institute in a vain attempt to connect with Herman. They'd all come from the half pint that made up beaker number three, and Orinsky picked up the wide-mouthed glass container and peered at it as if his naked eye could somehow explain what he'd seen only a few minutes earlier beneath the lens of the electron microscope. The thought almost made him smile, and he set the beaker back on the table and returned to his stool in front of the microscope. How he wished Herman would call, if only to hear an apology from Orinsky for scoffing . . . no, for *condemning* the findings that Herman had tried so hard to share. Foolish people, it seemed, came in all walks of life.

Unable to resist, Dr. Orinsky bent his head to the microscope and peered into the eyepiece. He wanted to view these cellular changes again—

Something rattled and Orinsky looked up in time to see the container he'd set down had inexplicably fallen on its side and rolled to the edge of the table. The contents had sloshed over the side and were now sending a slow, scarlet stream onto the floor. For a second, he just stared, trying to reconcile in his mind how this could have happened. "Damn it," he finally muttered. "I knew I should have capped that."

Sliding off the stool, he grabbed a towel and yanked a pair of disposable rubber gloves from the box next to his microscope. But before he could pull on the gloves, the blood on the floor . . .

Moved.

Dr. Orinsky froze for a moment, then gave a hard, mind-clearing shake of his head. Too many damned late nights, too many hours, too much *work*—now he was seeing things that couldn't be, hallucinating alone in his laboratory in the middle of the night. I'm getting too old for this, he thought as he shifted the towel and gloves to one hand and rubbed at his eyes with the other.

But when he opened his eyes again, he watched with open-mouthed amazement as the crimson puddle of blood moved again, more rapidly this time, pushing itself across the room with a snakelike rippling motion until it reached the junction of the wall and the door to the medical-supply storage room.

"Mother of Mercy," Dr. Orinsky breathed.

What was causing this? Some kind of unseen electromagnetic charge? He should stay away, call for an assistant—a witness, for God's sake—but it was too fantastic to let out of his sight. And if it didn't happen again, who would believe him anyway?

Moving cautiously, Orinsky followed the blood trail left by the now-placid puddle over by the doorway. A thin track, really not much more than a smear . . . nothing notable. If he hadn't seen it with his own eyes, if he wasn't looking at this puddle right now that was ten feet away from where it had dripped off the side of the lab table, he wouldn't have believed it. Heart pounding with a mixture of excitement and fear, Orinsky stood over the stain and peered down, then bent lower when nothing appeared to be out of the ordinary. What on earth—

There was a tremendous *CRACK!* then something fast, large and dark went with blurring speed by and buried itself into his stomach. All the air went out of his lungs, and everything below his rib cage went strangely cold and numb, as though someone had sprayed him with liquid nitrogen. Dr. Orinsky looked down and saw with a vague sense of surprise that something ugly—like a shiny, brown hand but with barbs across its oversized back—was pulling . . . *out* of his stomach, and taking away with it a good portion of the internal organs that he needed to stay alive.

"Oh—not good," he croaked. "Not . . . *good.*" He forgot about the traveling blood as his hands slammed over the hole in his abdomen in a belated attempt to hold in the parts of his body that he now realized were being pulled away through an opening smashed through the door that separated his lab from the medical supply room. He tried to straighten up and step toward it but staggered backward instead, unable to do anything but watch in stupefied horror at the bloody gray lengths of intestine that were trailing over the ragged edges of the opening at knee-height—

Mine!

—and the mottled, talon-tipped fingers that were clenched around them.

The breath he tried to take for a scream choked off as blood welled in his throat from injuries he hadn't known about. He gasped and collapsed, still thankfully numb and growing moreso by the moment. Perhaps the lack of pain was a blessing, but he knew he was surely bleeding to death. He didn't have long.

Strength fading and on a fast track to death, Orinsky rolled on his stomach and dragged himself toward the far wall.

Behind him, unnoticed in his final moments, the surface of the ruby-colored blotch shifted, then shifted again. And finally crept up the door and disappeared through the fracture made by the alien hand.

CHAPTER 5

Morning sunlight streamed over the eastern roof-line of the Pentagon, spreading across the roof and chasing away the night's humid haze. No one, however, in this particular unlabeled conference room saw the bright, cheerful light, because there were no windows. Underground, secure in every respect, only those with the highest levels of clearance even knew of its existence.

Contrary to the images displayed in all the popular movies, the room was decorated in light colors. The Tempest-shielded walls were covered in polished ash paneling behind which was wired a sophisticated sound and video system, as well as the expected set-ups necessary to insure the room was free from unwanted monitoring. Telephone, video, fax and data lines were unquestionably safe, and all transmissions in and out were newly upgraded DES encrypted; as part of the nerve center of America's defense, no one in the world who shouldn't hear what went on in this room would ever have a chance to do so. The conference room table dated back to World War II and was original to this room. The table's wood was the same light ash as the walls, and although it was a little worn around the edges—a lot of decisions had been made here over the decades—the piece was still sturdy and serviceable. The chairs had been reupholstered a few times, but they, too, were still functional.

Much like the four men seated in the room.

Colonel Carter Burgess turned toward the multi-sided speakerphone in the center of the table, flipping through the sheaf of papers in his hands as the other three men—Laura Baker had been overheard referring to them as the "Pentagon Three," which had made even him smile—waited, their faces solemn and silent. Today Burgess wasn't smiling, though—no one was.

Least of all Dr. Ralph Orinsky.

Spread across the table in all their lurid detail was a stack of eight-by-ten color photographs of the crime scene, and now Burgess tapped the one closest to him, as though the person on the other end of the secure telephone line could see his movement. "The FBI lab came up with significant irregularities in their test results," he said, more for the benefit of his three comrades. "Thus we sent Dr. Baker samples from the Orinsky crime scene and asked her to study the DNA. Dr. Baker, if you would, please tell us what you discovered."

One of the things he found most appealing about Laura Baker was the way she came straight to the point. No frills, no fancy words. She just went for the short and sharp, and sometimes killer, statement.

"The substance found in Dr. Orinsky's wounds was a combination of alien and human DNA."

"What do you mean, 'substance'?" asked one of the men at the table. "Are you talking about blood?"

"No, I'm not. We have more investigation to do with Dr. Orinsky's notes and the tests he was apparently running on blood samples which were found in his lab, but I've been advised to leave that to the FBI team and work with them if they need my assistance. Rather, I'm talking about a conspicuous amount of an unidentifiable mucouslike substance. The DNA in this substance is structurally similar to Eve's, but it is not a perfect match. And obviously, Eve has not left the compound."

All four men were now staring at the speaker phone as if the woman on the other end could see and interpret their expressions. "What are you saying, Dr. Baker?" demanded Colonel Burgess. "Are you suggesting that—"

"Yes, gentlemen," came her reply. "*This means that there's another one out there.*"

There was no hesitation. "How can this be?" demanded the first of the three men seated around the table. By far the heaviest, now his pudgy face had gone an unpleasant shade of pink. "Who could've generated one of these creatures? The Japanese? The Russians? Or maybe the Chinese—"

"Christ," said the man next to him in disgust. His fingers ran nervously through his dull, steel-gray hair and his eyes were small and flinty.

"I don't know who else has the technological expertise to carry out this sort of experimentation," Laura interjected. "It is quite possible another government picked up and recoded the message originally sent to Arecibo containing the DNA code. But we're not talking about a simple medical experiment that can be performed in even a well-equipped medical facility. These are specialized procedures that require unique equipment and machinery, much of which is available only here in my lab at Monroe. As you are all aware, the expense of this project is tremendous."

"None of our Intelligence sources suggests that any foreign power is involved," Colonel Burgess said with finality. "We can't rule it out, of course, but the probability is extremely unlikely."

The third man in the Pentagon Three team, the one who was usually the quietest and whom Burgess knew wielded the most power in this room, finally spoke. "Why do you think Dr. Orinsky was targeted?"

There was a beat of silence as Dr. Baker considered this. "I haven't a clue," she answered at last. "But my staff and I hope to find some answers among the research notes found in his lab. We're still working our way through them."

The first of the trio spoke again. "Dr. Baker, given your background with these creatures, how would we start looking for this thing?"

This time there was no delay in her answer. "Blood testing is the only way to identify the presence of alien/human DNA. Based on what happened previously, and also because we have created another form of the alien species, my team at Monroe has developed a very specific precautionary procedure to follow. The plan includes a suggestion for investigative procedures and ways to identify possible initial suspects." As she paused, silence filled the room, broken only by the faint hum of the unseen signal-scrambling equipment. When her voice came over the speakers again, it was so quiet, the four men had to lean forward to hear her words. "I don't expect you to be pleased at the initial list. You have my recommendations, of course."

They all nodded as if she could see them, glancing automatically at the "Top Secret" folders they'd been given just half an hour earlier.

"Thank you, Dr. Baker," said the second man. He took a deep breath and held it for a moment before continuing. "You will, of course, help us track down this creature."

It wasn't a question and they all knew it. Colonel Burgess raised an eyebrow at her wry response—

"Oh, I'll wait with bated breath."

—but none of the other men seemed surprised. Without bothering to say good-bye, Burgess reached across the table and hit the DISCONNECT button on the speaker. He waited until they heard the sound of a dial tone, then hung up the line altogether.

For a moment, no one said anything, then Burgess watched as his three superiors held a whispered conference to which he wasn't privy. Annoying, true, but in his military career, he'd become accustomed to following orders, and the fact that he sometimes didn't have input into them was something about which he could do nothing. At this particular point in his life, Burgess had only so much power, though there might be a point in the future when if he could help capture the alien bastard running around out there by using whatever means were necessary, he might be able to change that.

After a few seconds, one of the four-star generals at the table looked up and caught Burgess's gaze; his expression left no room for argument.

"Get Preston Lennox," was all he said.

CHAPTER 6

They hit the Hungarian Embassy in broad daylight.

Not a single shot was fired. The men were heavily armed but even suppressed firearms made far too much noise for the leader's liking, and they knew to use them only if there was no alternative. For this job, the commander needed stealth and speed, but he would risk only as many men as were absolutely necessary—his boss would not take lightly to the loss of a team member's life. And if a life was lost and they couldn't bring the body back, then they might as well not come back themselves. He sent a ground team of twenty in and, once they were established, brought another four men in via a swift-flying Huey helicopter painted a dull black. By the time the air team was dropping down the ropes to the garden below, the terrorists guarding the entrances to the embassy's mansion had been utterly disabled and his team was inside; another thirty seconds and the hostages were freed and being hustled to the roof, where the helicopter was waiting to lift them to safety. Two of the air team would return with the helicopter to defend the pilot should one of the hostages turn out to be a plant; the other two would melt into the surrounding estate with the ground team, leaving the terrorists tied and gagged on the grounds for the locals to deal with as they would.

Had it been a real assault and rescue, he and his team would have killed the terrorists.

"There you go, gentlemen," Press Lennox said amid a round of enthusiastic applause. He smiled graciously at the collection of Eastern European diplomats gathered a hundred yards away from the front of the mansion, where his crack team members were helping the would-be terrorists to their feet. The "terrorists" had been supplied by the group, which had asked him to demonstrate his company's skills, and what a sad defensive they'd shown—so-called experts who had hardly been worth the effort and were certainly not deserving of the expense of taking the helicopter up. Supposedly comprised of trained men, yet all Press saw now were bloody noses and bruised egos. Ah, well.

Press gestured at his team, the men already lined up and waiting for his next command. He knew he looked good: a fresh haircut and a manicure would do that, and let's not forget the two-thousand-dollar Armani suit and Oliver Peeples shades that gave him the "operative agent" look these European guys admired so much. If this were real, he'd be wearing jeans and a sport shirt, plus a good pair of Asics running shoes, no one would be able to pick him out of a crowd. As far as he was concerned, however, the guys on his assault team were the important ones, and they looked better than he did, better than *better*, as a matter of fact. All were dressed alike in well-fitting black-cotton BDU outfits, and all had striped their faces with black greasepaint that made them indistinguishable from each other. Only their eyes were different—beyond those, they could've been moving shadows even, in the daylight. Damn, but he was proud of them.

He smiled wider, adjusted his tie, then gave them all a look of pride. "In addition to the clockwork demonstration of special services you just witnessed, Press Lennox Diplomatic Security provides the best in embassy guards and protection against kidnapping and assassinations. We have numerous contacts around the world and—" Press broke off his sales pitch as he saw his assistant, a reedy, mild-looking young man nicknamed Hawk who could kill a person in under three seconds, hurrying around the far side of the knot of observers. Damn it, now what?

"You've got a visitor," Hawk said into Press's ear. "I told him to fuck off but he says it's a matter of national security. And he claims it won't wait until the end of the demo session."

"All right," Press said as his jaw tightened. He turned back to the curious stares of the crowd waiting for him and plastered another charming smile across his face. "If you'll excuse me, there's something that requires my attention. My assistant can answer all your questions."

Knowing glances were exchanged, and he thought that was immensely funny—what did these people think they knew about Press Lennox's life that could do them any good? Press resisted the urge to shake his head as he strolled nonchalantly away toward the shaded area where he'd parked his baby, a brand-new soft-top Porsche Boxster. There it was, all those coats of custom black lacquer, and some asshole in a colonel's uniform was leaning all over it. He was five steps away from throttling the bastard when the older man turned and saw him.

Press stopped and grimaced. "Well, well. Carter Burgess."

Burgess made a game attempt at a pleasant smile. "Hello, Press." He glanced at the Boxster. "Nice car."

"The answer is no."

The colonel held up his hand. "Wait—hear me out. We've got another one of those fucking aliens on the loose—"

"My sympathies," Press said flatly. "But I'm in the private sector now. Get someone else."

"Come on, buddy. We're talking about national security. Your country is calling."

Press didn't budge. "You can skip the buddy-calling and flag-waving, Burgess. How clear do I have to make it? I'm not interested, and in case you missed the fun here, I've got a business to run." A line of dull red crept across Burgess's forehead just below the line of his blond-gray crewcut. For a moment Press thought the man was going to take a swing at him, and he almost smiled outright. Go for it, old man, he thought. We'll give my future customers a live one-on-one.

But Burgess only reached up and pointed to his glass eye, his voice cold and stiff with anger. "Listen to me, Lennox. You know how I got this damned piece of glass in my eye?" he ground out. "It's a sacrifice I made for my country, and I'd make it again in a heartbeat. Maybe you need to learn the meaning of the word *sacrifice.*"

"No, *you* listen, pal." Press was practically snarling now, right up in the colonel's face. "I almost got killed chasing the last alien she-bitch you guys spliced together. If the government was stupid enough to make another one—and I don't doubt that for a moment—let *it* clean up the mess!"

Surprisingly, Burgess stayed cool. "We didn't make this one."

"Yeah?" Press turned and started to walk back toward his demonstration area. "Well, too bad. Count me out of the search party anyway."

"One million dollars."

Press stopped—he couldn't help it. "What?"

"Cash," Burgess said softly. "Non-traceable, nontaxable. For two weeks of work." He waited a beat, then asked, "Are you sure you won't reconsider?"

Press swiveled on one heel and turned to scowl at the smug-looking Carter Burgess.

God, he really hated this bastard.

"I can't tell you how much I despise getting up this early," Press said as he stared morosely out the side window of the government-issue Chevrolet sedan. Dawn over the city of Washington, no matter how beautiful the day promised to be, did nothing to cheer him up.

From the seat next to him, Colonel Burgess ignored Press's comment and opened the leather briefcase on his lap. A quick check to make sure the soundproof glass between them and the driver was closed, and he began flipping through a packet of papers inside. "After the Sil fiasco," he said matter-of-factly, "the President authorized the Pentagon to form a committee to study the situation and how it was resolved. Absolutely classified, of course."

"Of course," Press mimicked. He turned his level gaze on the colonel. "Why worry the public? Besides, the American taxpayers definitely need more committees."

Burgess was looking at him, but Press could've sworn the man hadn't heard a bit of his sarcastic comment. "The committee is composed of four-star generals," he continued. "These sons of bitches have seen this country through every military crisis since World War Two. They make the kind of decisions that grunts like you and I can only dream about—"

"Speak for yourself," Press cut in. "I'm fairly certain we have different career goals." He paused. "Besides, that alien—Sil—wasn't a military crisis. She was a government fuck-up, pure and simple."

Burgess opened his mouth to reply, then held back as the car rolled to a stop at the double-gated outer checkpoint of Monroe Air Force Base. There would be no mistakes here; the armed guard checked everyone's papers, including the colonel's, before allowing the sedan to pass through the gate with instructions to the driver to turn right at the directional sign marked BIOHAZARD 4 and stop for another identification check. He finished his instructions with a crisp salute that disappeared behind the tinted glass as Burgess's driver hit the button to raise the windows in the car.

"The Sil experiment was a mistake," Burgess admitted. He pulled a small bottle of Visine from his pocket and dribbled a bit into his good eye before turning to look at Press. "But we're ready for them now that you're back in the game."

A game, Press thought wearily, although this time he kept his mouth shut. The fool was actually calling this a *game*. These types never learned. "Why are you involved?" he asked aloud. "You were always strictly search-and-destroy."

Burgess shrugged carelessly as he indicated his glass eye, but Press wasn't fooled. This man still cared very much about that loss. "What happened in Costa Rica put an end to my field-mission days." He grinned, but it, too, wasn't a genuine expression. "So Uncle Sam found me a new niche."

Press grinned nastily. "Hire the handicapped."

"You're a funny guy," Burgess told him with a sour look. He glanced out the window and appeared to study the buildings that went from camouflage-patterned to cinderblock to white paint as they rolled past. "Used to be a man could make an entire career out of knocking off communists. Times are a lot thinner since the Iron Curtain came down."

A corner of Press's mouth twisted. "No offense, Burgess, but maybe you ought to catch up with the nineties. From a military viewpoint, aliens are the growth industry now."

Burgess's chin lifted and his eyes hardened, his entire appearance just a little too much self-satisfied to make Press entirely comfortable. "Oh, I'm on the cutting edge, Lennox. You just wait and see."

Before Press could respond, the sedan swung into a parking slot outside a bunker-style building with a discreet sign and logo matching the one they'd seen a few moments before. The BioHazard 4 building looked like any of the others on the base, a small square block attached on one side to a whitewashed, oversized version of an airplane hangar.

"Welcome to Monroe Air Force Base," Burgess said as the driver released the security locks on the sedan's doors and the three men climbed out. Press started to say something cutting; then choked it back and laughed instead.

The idiot driver had pulled into the handicapped slot.

"Okay, I'm intrigued," Press said as he followed Carter Burgess down the most recent of a series of long corridors. He paused before a door marked EMERGENCY ARMORY and watched as two uniformed military guards hefted several boxes onto a table, then proceeded to unload a cache of M-16s and Mossberg 590 shotguns. He couldn't see any farther into the room. "Since when does a bio-facility need an armory?"

"We're like the Boy Scouts, Press." Burgess's voice was a little glib and Press looked at him sharply. The older man only shrugged and gave him an enigmatic smile. "You do remember the Boy Scout motto, don't you? Always be prepared."

"I was never the Boy Scout type," Press countered.

Before he could say more, an airlock door slid open with a muted *whoosh.* Burgess stepped through and Press followed automatically, not particularly surprised at the high-tech equipment and the med-staff and biologists—all female—scattered around the bio-environment. "This is BioHazard Four," Burgess announced.

Press nodded, then saw that even the small contingent of SWAT guards were all women, and all armed to the eyeballs with 9mm H&K MP5A3s. "What—" he began, then his voice choked off.

"Jesus Christ!"

These days, Press's own weapon of choice was a small, concealable Glock 26 9mm. He yanked the gun from beneath his arm without conscious thought, raised it and aimed—

Sil.

It was only the shock of seeing her, of knowing somewhere deep in his subconscious that the creature in front of his eyes was safely restrained, that let Burgess snatch the weapon from Press's hand without getting himself killed in the process. "Put that thing away, Lennox," the colonel snapped. "You won't need it here."

Inside the confines of a glass-walled set of rooms that reminded Press of a human-sized hamster cage, the new Sil-creature sat cross-legged on a comfortably upholstered hassock in front of a built-in television set. To Press's shocked eyes, she seemed to be utterly fascinated by a commercial on the screen—some stupid thing with an animated leprechaun dancing around the rim of bowl full of cereal and twittering *"Frosted Lucky Charms—they're magically delicious!"* Still paralyzed, Press saw the alien woman cock her head to one side like a dog trying diligently to understand its master's commands.

"Magically delicious," she repeated, her voice echoing softly over a speaker system in the laboratory. Suddenly she blinked as if something had interrupted her chain of thought, then turned her head and saw Press and the colonel. The television forgotten, she stood gracefully and moved to the glass of her enclosure, her head lifting as she reached outstretched hands and pressed them against the glass. A chill ran across the nape of Press's neck as he realized that she was actually *smelling* them through the walls of the habitat.

Sense returned abruptly and Press wheeled on Burgess. Furious, he grabbed the military man by the front of his coat and shook him as hard as he could. "You glass-eyed son of a bitch," he growled, his face nearly pushed against Burgess's. *"You grew another one!"*

"Lennox, calm down—"

"Why?" Press demanded. It was all he could do to keep his fist from drawing back. "Tell me why!"

"What the hell are you two doing in here?"

That voice . . .

Press released Burgess with a shove and spun, stopping short at the sight of the so familiar face. A hundred, no a *thousand,* memories crashed together in his head—love and laughter and fighting, then bitter pain at the end of a relationship gone bad. And the worst of them all, involving a relative of the she-creature watching everything with keen interest from behind a glass barrier a few feet away. "Laura?" he asked stupidly.

Laura Baker ignored him and directed her icy words to the man at his side. "You know the rules, Colonel Burgess. *No men in the lab.*"

Burgess stood stiffly, unaccustomed to being chastised. "We have an emergency here, Dr. Baker. We can take it outside if you like—"

Laura's laugh was cold and disgusted, her expression rigid. "It's a little late for that, don't you think? You've already contaminated the atmosphere. But please—let me say thank-you for wasting two *years* of work inside of thirty seconds. Your forethought and ability to obey biohazardous instructions are truly amazing." She glanced over her shoulder at the habitat, where the young woman inside still stood at the glass, studying the men with shrewd interest. "Great," Press heard her mutter. "So much for a controlled environment."

Press finally found his voice. "I can't believe you're involved in this bullshit," he said incredulously. "Of all the people who should know better—"

"Dr. Baker is in control of this facility," Burgess told him as Laura folded her arms and scowled at both of them. "It was under her direction that the alien was re-created."

He shoved the Glock back into its holster, but Press could feel his face grow hot. "That bitch killed friends of ours, for God's sake," he hissed. "How could you breed another one. *How?*"

For a second Laura looked at though she might shout at him; then her face softened. "It's different this time, Press. Half of her alien genes are dormant—"

"Oh, great," he said angrily. "Sil *Lite.* I feel *much* better!"

"Her name is Eve," Laura snapped, "not Sil. And this is *not* the same creature. We've dampened her mating instincts, strictly avoiding the presence of testosterone in this laboratory." Her mouth twisted and she sent another look of resentment toward Colonel Burgess. "At least until you two brainwaves barged in."

"This has got to be the most insane thing I've ever heard you come up with." Press turned and would've pounded his fist on something, but he couldn't find anything that looked like it wouldn't break. "What if she gets *out*?" he yelled instead.

Laura's response was amazingly calm, considering how completely freaked out Press felt right now. "She won't. But if she does, we have that." She turned and gestured across the laboratory to a gleaming gold control console affixed to the wall. Next to it stood another of the female guards with an unconventional American Arms twelve-gauge slung over one shoulder and a standard-issue Beretta 9mm in a holster at her waist; one hand rested on the console and the hard-faced woman's attention was exclusively focused on the habitat and its occupant. Spray-painted in the usual black military stencil across the side of the control box were the words TETHER MECHANISM. "It's an electronic tethering device," Laura explained. "One step off the premises and a toxic capsule will explode in her brain. She'll die instantly."

Press gaped at her, then looked over at the creature still gazing fixedly at them from the habitat. He didn't like the look of . . . *seductiveness* painted across the Eve-thing's features, but there was still the fact that she—*it*—seemed disturbingly human. "So what happened?" he asked finally. "I knew you were ambitious, but at least you used to have a little soul."

Beneath the shining strawberry blond hair, Laura's face and her china-blue eyes blazed. "You thick-headed jerk—who the hell do you think you are, coming into my lab and questioning my motives? You—who have all the conscience of a rattlesnake!"

Press opened his mouth, but Burgess stepped between them. "Both of you, knock it off," he barked. "You know we have a national emergency on our hands, and you *will* work together—that's a direct order from the Pentagon." He stared at them, and both Press and Laura finally dropped their gazes. "You killed one of these aliens before," Burgess continued. His voice was flat, devoid of emotion or concern for the female life-form still watching them avidly from across the laboratory and who could no doubt hear their every word. "Do it again."

The three of them automatically turned toward the glass enclosure. Press felt himself clenching his jaw and forced himself to relax, despite the awkward silence that followed Colonel Burgess's brutally direct order. He pulled his gaze away from the habitat and made himself look at Laura again, who finally met his eyes. He gave her a sarcastic smile and allowed himself one final bit of derision.

"You heard him, Laura. Piece of cake."

CHAPTER 7

Whistling along with the radio, Dennis Gamble pulled his Explorer into the private driveway of Patrick's Georgetown townhouse. Bright red, loaded with enough extras to jack the price up to where no normal Joe Schmoe could afford it, the four-wheeler had less than two hundred miles on it and was a comp, courtesy of Ford Motor Company. No fools there; they'd jumped on a tie-in between space exploration and the name of their best-selling product immediately. Wait till Patrick sees this baby, he thought gleefully. Me and Air Mikey—this'll teach Mr. Conservative what endorsements can do for a guy. After all, a fellow had to plan for his future.

Dennis shut off the engine and climbed out, careful to set the car alarm even in this area—if this vehicle was a babe magnet, it would also draw attention from other not so desirables. It never hurt to take precautions.

A quick glance at his watch and he knew he was

right on schedule. When they weren't flying around the universe together, he and Patrick always met at Patrick's townhouse on Tuesday mornings, when they'd buzz off to their favorite health club for a game of racquetball. After working up a good sweat, they'd have a long, hot session in the sauna, complete with about half a dozen other regulars and at least an hour's worth of guy talk, covering topics that ranged from cars—today Dennis planned on monopolizing that subject to which woman had been the hottest one on the exercise floor that particular day.

That was always a heated discussion, and the memories brought a grin to Dennis's face. He and Patrick made a great-looking pair on that racquetball court, which was on the lower level of the club and surrounded by an overhead glassed-in walkway. They were both in tip-top shape and competitive as hell; the walls shook with the energy of their games and their shouts of enthusiasm and verbal sparring were guaranteed to draw an audience—mostly female—to the windows. While Patrick had eyes only for Melissa, Dennis had no reservations about taking advantage of the hero worship that had surrounded both of them since their return from the Mars landing mission.

Taking the stairs three at a time, Dennis rang the bell and waited impatiently. He was itching for a workout today, feeling the strain of too many hours in too many meetings. He hated being stuck indoors—how the heck did people survive in those grueling nine-to-five office jobs? He'd go nuts in that kind of rut, and maybe a similar feeling made Patrick instinctively shy away from the prospect of a permanent political career. What faster way was there to get pinned behind a desk and the accompanying mounds of paperwork than as an elected official? The idea made Dennis shudder.

He rang the bell again and rechecked his watch. Damn, where was Patrick? They had reservations on the court, and while Dennis didn't doubt for a moment that the club wouldn't hold the slot for them—after all, this was Patrick Ross and Dennis Gamble—he hated being late.

Backing up to the edge of the small concrete porch, Dennis tilted his head back and inspected the front of the building. Everything was shut tight despite the cooler-than-average, beautiful weather—Patrick probably had the air conditioning on automatic and didn't want to fool with raising and lowering the windows. There was, however, an air of desertion hanging over the place, and the longer Dennis stood there, the more convinced he became that Patrick simply wasn't home. He rang the doorbell a third time just for giggles, but he didn't believe anything would come of it. Something must have come up and Patrick hadn't been able to reach him—belatedly, Dennis remembered that he hadn't turned on his cell phone all morning.

He stood there for a moment more, then shrugged and headed back to the Explorer. He'd give him a call later on; no sense dialing up Patrick now unless he wanted to talk to the answering machine.

He heard the chime of the doorbell all three times that it rang, understood what it was and what the sound meant in some part of his brain that had remained detached from whatever was misfiring right now in his mind and his body. Sick, so very, very *ill—he couldn't stand or walk, probably couldn't even crawl. And talking? Answering the persistent call of that doorbell? Not a chance. All he was good for right now was sitting in the corner of the master bedroom upstairs with one hand on the window sash while Dennis walked away, sweating and shaking while some kind of unidentifiable fever raged inside him. If only he could've reached out to his friend, asked for help, somehow let his longtime partner know that something was horribly wrong . . .*

But he couldn't.

He'd tried, fighting so hard to speak against something he couldn't comprehend, a physical feeling of restraint that wrapped around his muscles and kept him pinned to that spot on the carpet and prevented him from so much as knocking against the windowpane to let Dennis know that he was inside. There was a strange, selective binding around his throat, one that kept his vocal cords paralyzed and soundless but still allowed air to wheeze in and out of his windpipe. His vision was skewed, fragmented. Gone was the rich red-and-blue Southwestern design of his home—everything in the bedroom, from the yellow-pine furniture and his football trophies to the framed photographs of his family and Melissa—had taken on a twisted, unnaturally brownish-gold tinge that made it look dark and wet. And so much pain, *pulses of it spiraling through his insides and head, jabbing along his nerve endings like unseen lightning. It made him want to do nothing more than pull off the clothes that seemed to be cutting into his skin, stretch out his arms and legs and fingers, reach on and on and on until he got beyond even the boundaries of his own flesh.*

But he didn't.

He wouldn't.

Now that Dennis had gone, the belt around his throat loosened and disappeared. He'd wakened this morning covered in blood, and the pain had already started, blotting out the reason that should have sent him to the police; he'd climbed into the shower instead and washed it away, searching vainly for the wound that must've been the source. Cleansed, he found nothing, and logical thought afterward had been blotted out by his suffering. Now he groaned and sucked in a lungful of air, feeling his voice gather strength, fueled by the agony, ready to just let go—

But . . . no.

He wouldn't.

Patrick Ross didn't know what was wrong with him, but he wasn't about to give in. He was a fighter, damn it, a United States astronaut and a hero. Whatever this was, he knew he could beat it. He had to.

He bent his head and bit savagely into his knuckles to keep silent the screams within.

CHAPTER 8

"If this wasn't so frightening, I'd be laughing right now," Laura said.

Settled on the driver's side, his eyes fixed on the road, Press said nothing as he drove a government-issue sedan past the familiar checkpoints within the boundaries of the National Space Exploratory Group's facilities.

"I feel like I'm reliving an old nightmare."

"Oh, come on," Press quipped. "Our relationship wasn't that bad."

"Bad is a relative term," Laura replied gloomily as he pulled to the curb outside the Goddard Flight Center's main building. She unbuckled her seat belt and started to climb out, but Press's hand on her arm made her stop.

"You seeing anyone?" he asked softly.

"That's none of your business."

But she'd waited just a measure too long and she damned herself as one of his eyebrows raised. "Oh, let me guess," he said. All the gentleness had gone out of his voice. "He's got family money and he's tall, blond—after me, you're probably ready for a change—and handsome. He's got a Ph.D. in B.S. from M.I.T., a weekend house in Connecticut, he jogs a whopping two miles every morning, and I'll bet he even he drives a BMW. Oh, yeah—and sleeping with him is about as exciting as watching mold grow in a petri dish."

Laura felt her cheeks flush in spite of her determination not to let Press get to her. Still, she managed to keep her voice steady as she pulled free of his hold and got out of the car. "You never fail to surprise me, and this time is no exception. The return of the male chauvinist pig—I thought your species became extinct in the late eighties."

Always the jokester, he gave her a conciliatory grin and she knew he was hoping she'd smile in return. Instead, Laura just looked at him and when she did respond, she couldn't hide the sadness in her voice. "You might not believe this, Press, but I've learned a lot working with Eve. You look at her and see nothing but a monster, but in technical terms, she's half human and half alien. Built into her are two distinct strands of DNA, and that ancestry fights a constant battle within her body."

She waited but he didn't say anything. "Genetically speaking," she continued, "she's part of a never-ending struggle for dominance that can't continue indefinitely—one will eventually win out. Alone and separate, those two halves of Eve would be fine; each would know and understand what it is and how it should act and survive. Side by side, they just can't coexist." She stopped and they stared at each other; then she shook her head and walked toward the building, letting him consider her final words:

"Sort of like us."

* * *

When the trio of military guards standing before the entrance to Dr. Orinsky's laboratory moved aside the barricades and lifted the yellow tape so that Laura and Press could enter, they walked into a bloodbath.

"The last time I saw something like this was in Hollywood Hills," Press said. "Remember Robbie Llywelyn? Sil killed him at his house when he tried to force her to have sex with him."

The glance he sent Laura had all the markings of a class "I-told-you-so," but she ignored it. "Sil's dead," she said shortly. "And Eve has never been out of her habitat. This isn't her handiwork."

"Sure looks familiar though." Press followed her as she stepped over a long, smeared trail that bisected the room, then moved to inspect a door marked MEDICAL SUPPLIES on the other side. He hooked a finger around it and pulled it open, then bent and peered through the hole that had been smashed through it at knee height.

"I think there are substantial differences in the outcome," Laura said dryly.

"You got that right," Press replied. She could see one of his eyes through the ragged opening. "What possible motive could an alien have to rip this old guy apart?"

"I have no idea." Laura moved through the dead doctor's work area, carefully stepping over the splatters of blood that seemed to be everywhere. "Press, this is very sophisticated blood-testing equipment and the computer records indicate which samples he was working on, although he didn't record the results. The strange thing is that I can't find any of them—all these tubes are empty. Where the hell did they go?" She scanned the floor as if the scarlet puddles could tell her the truth. "The FBI coroner says they've sampled all segments of the blood on the floor and it's all Orinsky's."

Press stood, then stepped around to the front of the damaged door. "I don't get it. According to the homicide report, Orinsky's abdomen was punctured over here and he was relieved of a good portion of his lower internal organs." He frowned at the floor, then went over to where she was standing. "But his body was found by a colleague all the way over here. That's a good seven feet away from where he was assaulted."

"So he was alive—and moving—for a short time before he finally expired."

"Exactly." Press shoved his hands in his jacket pockets. "So why did the soon-to-be-dead man cross the room?"

Laura's mouth tightened. "Not funny, Press."

"Sorry. But you didn't answer my question."

She shrugged. "Who knows? It might have been some kind of involuntary reaction." She stopped, considering her own words. "Don't you think it's far more likely that he was trying to get away from whatever had attacked him?"

Instead of answering, Press squatted and looked at the area where Orinsky's body had come to its final rest. "The crime-scene team said Orinsky had blood on the tip of his forefinger."

Laura lifted one eyebrow. "So? Orinsky had blood all over him. The man was gutted like a fish."

"So maybe he was trying to leave us a message."

Laura gestured in disgust at the circular smears of blood across the floor, then folded her arms. "Forensics says that Orinsky's colleague tried to wipe up the blood and destroyed the integrity of the crime scene." She shook her head in disbelief. "These people are doctors—you'd think they'd know better."

"Still," Press said, "all may not be lost." One hand dipped inside his jacket and came out with a small leather case. He pressed the latch on one side and showed her the small aerosol can nestled inside. "This is leuco malachite."

"And?"

"It'll give a green shading to blood-particulate matter," he explained as he began to painstakingly spray the wall and the floor around where the front of Orinsky's body had been found.

"But—"

"If Orinsky wrote something and it had any chance at all to dry before his partner came along and mucked everything up, this'll show us."

"Wait," Laura said as something began to form where the wall and floor met. "Look right there—what's that?"

They leaned forward and studied the area as it slowly began to show a vague green outline—a smudgy, slightly lopsided circle. A few more seconds and a spike appeared at the one-o'clock position, then was topped off by a pointed mark.

"You're right," Laura said excitedly. "He did try to leave a message!"

"Yeah, but I don't get it." Press pointed. "This line here is probably an arrow, extending upward. Isn't this whole thing the symbol for male? Was he saying that a man killed him?"

Laura nodded. "It sure looks that way." She chewed at her bottom lip thoughtfully, then moved a little closer to the faint greenish mark on the floor. "Press . . ."

Something in the tone of her voice must have given away her uneasiness, because he looked up sharply. "What is it?"

"It's also the astronomical symbol for Mars."

CHAPTER 9

The flashbulbs were nearly blinding, blotting out the stars overhead, the lights on the street and around the sumptuous hotel. Even the faces of the people held back by the barriers of velvet-covered rope, manned by discreetly dressed government guards, couldn't be seen. Hundreds of people pushed at the barriers, constantly testing the patience of the guards, who fought to keep pleasant smiles pasted on their faces while listening to their ongoing orders through tiny speakers tucked into their ears. Whatever transmissions were coming through, however, were lost in the cheers of the onlookers and a thunderous round of applause as the two limousines the multitude had been waiting for finally arrived.

Seven o'clock at night and the cameras—reporters, paparazzi, television crews—made it seem like high noon as the two sleek white vehicles rolled smoothly to the curb at the front entrance of the

Watergate Hotel. The first to climb out was Dr. Anne Sampas; with her auburn hair done in an impeccable French twist she looked lovely in a sparkling black Nina Ricci dress. One hand rested on the arm of her dark-haired husband, the handsome Dr. Harold Friedman, a noted professor of history at the University of Maryland. They made quite the picturesque couple, a perfect example of opposites attracting, as they smiled and waved on the way into the hotel.

Right afterward a pair of exquisitely long, coffee-colored legs slid into view. Jemila Asante, Dennis Gamble's date for the evening, exited the limo with the grace of a dark young gazelle, all legs and arms wrapped in silver lamé and matching high heels, her glossy black hair swept up and around a jeweled comb. Following her out of the car was Dennis himself, replete in a black tuxedo with a silver cumberbund that matched Jemila's dress perfectly. Cheers from the waiting onlookers escalated when the black couple laughed and waved as they headed up the front walkway.

But it was the second limo that drew the most attention. When the door was opened by a black-tied doorman and Senator Judson Ross stepped out of the limo with his son Patrick and Patrick's fiancée Melissa, the crowd went practically insane. The barrier ropes were virtually useless as the government bodyguards, conveniently decked out to match the hotel's doormen, tried vainly to keep them in place. As had their friends in the first limousine, the three of them smiled and waved, and Patrick, in keeping with the all-American hero image he'd unwittingly cultivated, fed the excitement by pausing to shake hands here and there and to autograph whatever the people thrust toward him, be it handkerchief or matchbook. When one young woman with long brown hair leaned forward over the ropes and momentarily grabbed onto Patrick's lapels, hung on, then began shrieking joyfully—

"I touched him! I touched him!"

—Melissa only smiled indulgently and pulled Patrick out of the woman's grasp and back to her side.

"Jack Kennedy and I started out in Congress at about the same time," Senator Ross told a delighted crowd during his speech after the banquet. He smiled expansively and gripped the podium. "We both championed the exploration of space," he continued. "I'd like to think that Jack's spirit is alive and well. You can find it carried on in my son, Patrick."

There was a thunderous round of applause from the two hundred-plus dignitaries assembled around the banquet hall. Senator Ross waited a few moments, then continued with his speech.

"Look at him," said Harry. "See how he's using the podium to pull himself upright? It makes him look taller. Even for a man his size, politics means always trying to look bigger than you are, especially to your constituents."

Anne and the others laughed. "Stop that," she admonished. "To you, the world is nothing but an ongoing history lesson."

"And to the senator, this room is a big bowl of potential votes," he returned with a smile. "For him *and* his son."

Anne glanced around, puzzled. "Speaking of Patrick, what happened to him?"

When their gazes turned to her, Melissa just looked down at the table. "He hasn't been feeling well lately," she said. "I asked him to go back to the doctor, but he keeps insisting that he's fine."

For a minute no one said anything as they considered this, then Anne picked up her napkin and twisted it nervously. The brightness of her green eyes clouded over. "To tell you the truth," she admitted,

"I haven't been feeling that great either."

Her husband glanced at her in surprise. "Why didn't you mention this earlier?"

Before she could answer, Dennis gave Jemila a long, hangdog look. "I think what we all need is a little tender loving care."

"Two more days until the quarantine is over," Anne reminded him. "We've waited this long. You can hold on."

"Shit," Dennis said crudely, then looked embarrassed. "I've been holding on too long already."

"Anne, this thing about you not feeling well—I think we should talk more about that," Harold Friedman said with a frown. "You haven't—"

A new round of applause drowned out the rest of his statement and the group at the table looked toward the podium, where Senator Ross was finishing his speech and gesturing somewhere offstage. "But enough hot air from this old windbag," he said graciously. "As a man gets older, he gets wise enough to know that people would much rather hear from the younger populace, and there's no greater thing that can do a man proud than to introduce his son to a roomful of people. So how about a word now from Patrick himself?"

Senator Ross waited as the seconds stretched on, turning into five, then ten. At the fifteen mark, the confident expression on his face started to slip, then he motioned to an assistant at the end of the stage—

"Go find him!"

—and grinned at the crowd. "Guess I'll have to send someone to the lounge to retrieve him. This is what happens when you have to try to please the American people—every time you turn around, you're expected to be in two places at once. Give us a moment, and my assistant will remind Patrick that his public awaits.

"In the meantime, you poor folks are going to be

subjected to my joke-telling skills. Once there were these three tomatoes walking down the road—''

''God,'' said Dennis, watching from the table. ''I hope they find Patrick soon. That's the tomato joke from *Pulp Fiction.* As much as the old man's had to drink tonight, I don't even want to *think* about what he'll move on to after that!''

''Has anyone seen Patrick Ross?''

That voice—Patrick didn't know whose it was, but it pierced the fog layered over his brain like an arm sweeping aside a pile of feathers.

Where was he?

Offstage, of course. He'd excused himself from the table and headed to the men's room. That done, he'd washed up and gone to the area blocked off by the curtains hung there to separate the platform on which the speeches were given and the back of the room. Behind him were piles of wires that fed the lights and the sound system and boxes of extra supplies. Napkins and whatever other things a huge hotel like the Watergate had to store.

Before Patrick could figure out more, someone kissed him.

Not just a kiss, but a *kiss*—passionate, intimate, more demanding than anyone in the world except his fiancée had the right to be. He started to say her name—

''Meli—''

—but the sound was cut off by a mouth closing over his, a tongue that pushed past his lips and explored his mouth hungrily. There was a heat in places on him where there shouldn't be—

The quarantine!

—and the kiss itself wasn't familiar, or even good. In fact, it wasn't—

''Stop,'' Patrick said into the mouth that covered his. He grabbed the side of the woman's head with both hands and pushed her away, trying not to think about where her hands had been rubbing until he'd broken the embrace. She was tall and busty and very beautiful, with streaked blond hair and chocolate-brown, doelike eyes that promised an innocence she clearly didn't possess. The ball gown she wore fit every curve of her upper body and Patrick had hiked up its long, layered-satin skirt to hip level and planted himself firmly between her legs. Thank God his pants were still on, because he had no idea who this woman was.

"I have to go," he said inanely and tried to back-step.

The woman glanced around, then gave him a short, sulky nod. Before he could stop her, she leaned forward and squeezed the erection straining against the fabric of his slacks. Patrick gasped and had to literally fight not to grab her again. She was a stranger, some oversexed Washington debutante out to put an astronaut on her scorecard, but he didn't even remember meeting her, didn't know her name—what the hell was going on here?

"The Lincoln Suite," she said in a low voice. She yanked her skirts down and with a few expert pats of her hand looked as if nothing in the world had happened. Her eyes were commanding when they caught his. "Upstairs. Later." She licked the tip of her finger languidly, then trailed it along the line of his jaw. Then she was gone.

He stood there for a moment, trying to get his bearings and thankful that both the unidentified socialite and whoever had been looking for him had gone. Christ, he was so hot, and so . . . *aroused.* How was he going to get enough control of his body to walk across the platform to the podium without the entire audience seeing that? And Melissa—good God. He'd never been interested in anyone but her. What on earth had he been thinking?

Another few breaths, more precious seconds passing while some dim part of his brain told him that his father must have introduced him a while ago, that he was supposed to be *out* there by now, and damn it, he'd better get his ass in gear. A final deep breath and he thought he had it—amazingly, his erection was gone, his heartbeat had slowed to a fast walk from the roaring it had been, the surface of his skin no longer felt like a lit burner on a stove. Incredible and unexplainable, but he'd worry about that later.

Right now, John Q. Public awaited.

A sea of people stared at him, expecting to be impressed by the man who had walked on the surface of the red planet more than thirty-five million miles away. They had made him into a demigod, placed him on the pedestal of American heroism, and now they waited, breathless, to hear what he had to say.

No problem.

"When I looked through the viewing portal, at first all I could see was blackness. It goes on for an eternity—certainly for anything we'll ever live to see—broken only by the sparkle of a million stars we'll never reach, a million more planets that man, with his limited lifespan, will never visit. Then the ship swung homeward and the Earth filled my sight—a beautiful blue globe covered in white swirls."

Patrick gazed at the audience, knowing they were mesmerized by his voice, by this retelling of an experience they would never know. He waited a beat, then held out his hand in a gesture that was a perfect balance of drama and entreaty. "Seeing it from up there," he continued, "makes it look so small. So . . . *fragile.* I couldn't help but think about how painfully easy it would be to destroy this most beautiful of God's creations. In the whole of the universe, we are nothing but a *speck* in the eye of God, and we could be wiped away so effortlessly. As we look into the future, perhaps we will see that our greatest mission should be to nurture what we have right here at home."

An excellent finish and one that garnered him a standing ovation. As he stepped from the podium, Patrick felt strangely as though his eyesight had increased tenfold. He could see his father's eyes—red-rimmed and clearly well-liquored—all the way from here, as well as Dennis and his date, Anne and Harry, and, of course, the lovely Melissa. He smiled and waved as they stood with the rest of the crowd and applauded enthusiastically, caught up in the moment with everyone else. Pride shone from his fiancé's hazel eyes and her radiant smile was only for him; still, Patrick felt vaguely disconnected from her and whatever tenuous hold she might have on him, from *all* of it, as he waved a final time and stepped off the platform and beyond the curtain an usher held aside for him.

All those people out there. When they looked at him, they saw a budding politician whether he wanted to be one or not, a man who was fair and kind and whom they believed could take their world into the stars and beyond while keeping a firm eye and a stable grasp on what was happening on the homeworld. They recognized his intelligence, his charm, his wit, his righteousness. They *believed* in him.

And how very easily they were . . .

Deceived.

The fifth-floor corridor of the Watergate was deserted when Patrick stepped out of the elevator. It hadn't been difficult to elude the crowds and his family—Melissa had proven the biggest challenge, but even she had believed him when he'd pleaded a headache because of the stress and the crowd. Another little speech about how people didn't understand the pressure he was under, all the expectations, et cetera, and her bewilderment had changed to concern. She'd wanted to ride home with him and stay with him, all night if necessary, but Patrick wasn't ready for that just yet.

He had other things to attend to tonight.

He strode down the hallway, checked once again to make sure none of those annoying reporters had followed him, then knocked on the door of the Lincoln Room.

"It's open."

Patrick twisted the doorknob and stepped inside, then took the "Do Not Disturb" tag and hung it on the outside knob. When he closed the door behind, he made sure to flip the double bolt.

"We've been waiting for you."

We? Three steps took him past the door to the bathroom and into the main area of the suite. Sprawled atop the king-sized bed were two women, each stunningly beautiful and clad only in nearly matching silk lingerie. The sexy young woman he'd almost taken behind the stage in the ballroom inclined her head toward the dark-haired newcomer lying next to her, then reached over and ran her hand slowly up the woman's thigh. Her fingers slid beneath the line of fabric at the hip joint, and her companion shuddered. "I'd like you to meet my sister," the brown-eyed woman purred. "We share *everything.*"

America's Number-One Astronaut smiled and began unbuttoning his shirt.

"Pulse rate is twenty percent below human and her temperature is stable." The young biologist—the name BREA was embroidered across the pocket of her lab coat—made a face at her coworker. "This certainly isn't the most exciting part of my career."

"What do you expect?" retorted Vikki, the second biologist on shift. "She's watching the Yankees and the Orioles." She made a few notations on her clipboard, then peered at the monitoring console again. "With that in mind, she ought to be asleep. Don't you think she looks a little restless?"

"She's an idiot," returned Brea. "She's got the remote—if she's that bored, she ought to change the channel instead of just sitting there and staring at it. Not exactly the exciting Movie of the Week. That game is about as much fun as watching grass grow—or us watching her watch the game."

Vikki sighed and snapped the clipboard shut as Brea settled at a terminal and began keyboarding the latest round of data into the computer. She leaned her chin on her fist and stared down at the alien woman in the habitat, who in turn gazed at the television screen and seemed completely engrossed in the utterly boring drone of the baseball announcer. None of the electrodes taped to the life-form's body were registering anything interesting, so there was absolutely nothing for Vikki to do right now. She'd gone through a lot of bullshit and background investigations to get the clearance needed to work on this project with Dr. Baker, but somehow she'd thought that research on an alien would be a lot more scintillating. A few toxin experiments took place now and then, but most of what everyone did here in the laboratory seemed to be just . . . look.

"I should've gone into oceanography," Vikki said glumly.

But right now, there was nothing to be done but sit and wait for her time to be over.

Sated for the moment, Patrick rolled off the first woman—he vaguely remembered her telling him her name down on the main floor, but that piece of information was gone now, as was any notion that he might have once been faithful to Melissa. Faithful—what was that, anyway? The concept no longer made any sense to him. Something in his body had changed and now demanded not only that he mate, but that he do so as often as possible and with as many *different* partners as he could find. Once he spilled himself into a woman, some dark, newborn instinct told him he could never do so again.

"Oh, my *God,*" breathed the woman. She quivered next to him, as if she could still feel the power of his lovemaking inside her. "You really *are* a hero."

Her dark-haired sister came over and curled herself next to Patrick, her hands roaming at will across his muscled chest and stomach, then farther down. "Hey," she said coyly. "I think it's *my* turn now."

Patrick grinned, his first conquest already dismissed. He turned on the bedspread and pinned the young woman down, feeling the firm globes of her breasts against his chest, the curve of her belly, the heat between her thighs as they parted. Already he was hard again, completely ready. God, he felt *great.*

"Yeah, baby," he said with a satisfied smile. "It's your turn, all right."

She licked his ear in response and pressed herself tighter against him. "You've got a dangerously gorgeous body, Mr. Astronaut."

Patrick's smile widened. "And it's got something really, really good for *you.*"

Lindsey closed the door to the bathroom behind her while she cleaned up. She could hear Patrick Ross rocking on the bed with Claudia, who wasn't really her sister at all but her best friend. She and Claudia went all the way back to college, when they'd done this same type of thing a time or two, usually on a dare with each other and involving the most unreachable of the hierarchy on the faculty. And just like the almighty Patrick Ross, every damned man the girls had set eyes on had fallen victim to their charms, been used and ultimately—just like Patrick Ross would be—used up.

She checked her face in the mirror—flushed, of course. My goodness, but that man could move! She pursed her lips, then broke into a smile when she heard Claudia practically screeching. That silly girl, the whole dorm had always known when she made orgasm. What the hell, Lindsey thought and turned to open the bathroom door. No one ever said I couldn't join in—

A nasty wave of nausea spiraled through her belly and up her throat. Lindsey grabbed for the sink, fighting not to retch as sweat popped out on her forehead and across her upper lip. What the hell was this—some kind of food poisoning? It had to be that; what else could make her want to throw up so badly, spin the room on her, and send a knife-twist of pain through her gut like this?

She groaned and leaned over the sink, closing her eyes in anticipation. But nothing would come up; her ears were ringing with the sounds of Claudia's cries, the noise all mixed up and distorted in her head until it sounded like Claudia was screaming and Patrick was roaring at her. God, couldn't they just shut up? Didn't they know she was sick in here, damn it?

Something cold touched the skin of her naked belly and Lindsey forced her eyes open and looked down, trying to see, trying to function around the urge to vomit that was pulsing through her. The sight that met her eyes would have made her scream had she been able to draw enough air into her lungs.

The "something" that had touched her was the sink, and actually it was her *belly* that had touched it, not the other way around. Her stomach was huge and distended, belly button thrust out by the pressure of whatever was inside her and making her gut bloat further by the second. Lindsey sucked in air, then gagged and stumbled backward against the wall as a tremendous pain knifed through her abdomen, circling around and under her rib cage to finally twist deep within the center of her pelvis, all the way to her groin. The floor came up hard to meet her as she slid down the wall, the knobs of her spine grinding along the tile edges, leaving tiny spots of blood from scrapes she never felt.

Lindsey's eyes bulged and all she could manage was a low groan as her stomach rippled, then ballooned out even farther. The scream she'd wanted so badly found its voice at last when the flesh along the grotesque mound that was once her stomach, stretched and *split*. The agony was unspeakable but she voiced it anyway, for as long and as loud as her shock-washed system would allow, never realizing that the sound was indistinguishable from the howls of her friend in the room beyond and the wailing of the hellish infant to which she'd just given birth.

She lived exactly five more seconds.

Long enough to see the blood-covered brown creature, half human and half something she'd never imagined, reach up and pull itself free of the ruins of her body.

"What's the matter, baby?" Patrick demanded. His movement never faltered, despite the struggles of the woman beneath him. Something about him had suddenly freaked her out, a . . . *movement* of something along his back, the release of some new part of himself that he hadn't known wanted to be freed. Now that it was, his partner had hold of it and was wailing like a terrified cat, while he worked his way toward his second climax of the evening. "I thought you said you *liked* my body!"

Instead of answering, the delusional woman thought she could choke him, wrapping her puny hands around the corded muscles in his neck and trying to squeeze. "Let me up!" she screeched. "Get off of me, you fucking monster—Lindsey! Lindsey, *help me!*"

Patrick just laughed and kept hammering at the woman's body. "One...more...second," he panted. "Just . . . one . . ."

All that noise, and the woman jerked when she finally realized that her sister was doing her own screaming in the bathroom. She bucked savagely beneath him, clawing at his face, her body's gyrations unwittingly bringing Patrick so very, very close—

"Enough," he snarled. He gripped her shoulders and pinned her arms in place, holding her down as a few more deep thrusts finally gave him his release. Patrick sighed deeply and rolled to the side, letting his rigid body relax as fully as he could, while the screams from the bathroom ceased abruptly and all that was left to hear was the quiet mewling of his already maturing son.

"What's that? Lindsey? Are you all right?" Her face twisted with hate, the woman with whom he'd just mated started to climb off the bed, then she froze. Her eyes widened in horror as she saw her unwanted lover's new, freer form.

When she would have screamed, Patrick clamped a hand over her mouth and held her thrashing body down on the bed.

All he had to do was wait a few minutes.

"What the hell's going on?" Brea demanded. "Haven't you been watching her?"

"Of course I've been watching her!" Vikki snapped. "Why do you think I called you over here?"

"Maybe it's an equipment malfunction. How did it start?"

"Beats me," Vikki said. Her hands were a blur as

she worked her way across the medical console, running spot checks and comparing figures. "The last I checked she was still watching that stupid ball game and playing with the baseball—maybe Ripken hit a home run or something. The next thing I know her pulse rate's gone through the ceiling, her temperature's up ten degrees—"

"That would kill a human!"

"Which she's not," Vikki reminded her coworker.

"Look at her," Brea said in awe. "She's sweating like an ice cube in the sun, and—*shit*!"

Something cracked loudly inside the habitat, and both biologists froze, expecting the worst. Across the facility's floor, the half-dozen guards had their H&Ks instantly pointed toward Eve's enclosure.

Vikki's gaze settled on something inside Eve's glass walls, and she thumbed on the intercom to the main floor. "It's all right," she yelled into it. "It was just the baseball—it popped, that's all."

"She *broke* it?" Brea asked incredulously as the nervous SWAT women below reshouldered their weapons. "Do you have any idea of how strong you have to be to do that?"

"I don't want to think about it," Vikki said grimly. Her short bangs were plastered to her forehead and she was perspiring just as much as Eve. "All I want to do is get through the next few minutes without that thing breaking out—look at her electrocardiogram stats. She's writhing around down there like she's got a bad case of the hives. And she's moaning."

"Maybe she's sick," Brea said. "I think we should call Dr. Baker." Her voice had risen a notch, the situation already headed out of the realm of their expertise. "She's got a pager on at all times. The number's right here—"

"Hold on a minute." Vikki leaned forward and studied the screens across the control console, then stared hard down at Eve's glass home. "She's stopped."

"Stopped *what*?"

"Whatever she was doing. Look for yourself."

Down below, Eve sat tranquilly before the closing credits of the baseball broadcast—

"Strike three! Batter out!"

—while the remains of the baseball rolled away from her in a lopsided path.

"Hi, honey. We're headed home," Patrick said with wicked glee as he sat behind the wheel of his black Mercedes SL. Such a dark and beautiful night it had turned out to be—moonless, with the stars blotted out by just the right amount of cloud cover. Perfect for cruising back to the old home state, as the state sign whipped past the window—

Virginia is for Lovers!

—just to prove it. It seemed like only a few minutes more and Patrick was turning into the immense circular driveway that led to his mother's Georgia-style summer mansion. Just a few lights shone through the windows; this late at night, it would be only in the servants' quarters that the minimal staff members would still be awake. His father might be here, of course, packing away another few belts of Old Grand-Dad bourbon, or if his tastes were running a little more expensive tonight, some brand of hundred-year-old Scotch—as if he hadn't gotten enough at the banquet earlier. If he was here at all, the elder Ross's indulgences would be taking place in the library at the southern end of the house. In the front where he was, Patrick could count on the centerpiece of the old summer estate, a massive American flag flying and flapping in the wind at full mast on the lawn, to mask any noise he made. When he pulled the Mercedes around to the side of the house, that good ol' red, white, and blue covered every bit of sound he made getting out of the car and opening the back doors.

It took only about five minutes to lead his two children, both sons, to the disused barn on the outer edge of the property. The boys could walk, but not very fast yet. At what looked like three years old, their legs were still too short to keep up with his longer stride. Patrick had no compulsion to carry them—they were quite capable of quick, strong movement on their own and all they needed from him was his protection for the first few days of their lives, just long enough to go through the helpless chrysalis stage before maturing into full adults.

He couldn't have asked for a better, more secluded place than his mother's summer estate. The barn, three stories high with a loft, was nearly two hundred years old and hadn't been used in decades. But it was still sturdy enough to give him a dependable place in which to house and conceal his children. There was even a hexagonal marking in cracked and peeling paint on one side, reminiscent of an earlier time in which the family had taken such simple precautions against unseen evil spirits. That kind of forethought was so powerful and worked so well—in fact, Patrick had picked up on it by retrieving the key for the barn's oversized padlock yesterday afternoon. He hadn't understood why at the time, but now of course it was obvious. The evil spirits notwithstanding, Patrick figured that nowadays he could probably keep out most of what he considered evil by simply making sure he remembered to relock the barn's double doors when he left.

The front of the barn loomed while around the trio there was nothing but silence—no sound at all, not even the night insects. Both of Patrick's boys looked around with interest, taking in everything, learning at the astronomical rate that was so indicative of their superior species. But as with any species, some members would always be stronger, smarter, *faster*, than others of their own kind; before his brother could hone in on the nearly inaudible drone of the sleeping hornets' nest across the top of the door, the firstborn boy had thrown back his head and snapped it down with a swipe of his barbed tongue. Faster than most men could think, the nest lay decimated on the ground at their feet.

Proud and pleased, Patrick led his sons into the darkness of the barn and pulled the door shut behind them.

CHAPTER 10

"It's a beautiful day for a drive and this is certainly a pleasant-looking place," Laura said at her first view of the grand old mansion. "Right out of *Gone With the Wind.* But I'm guessing we aren't here on a social call . . . unless it's to visit a friend of yours?"

"Your sense of humor has always been tops," Press said dryly. "Welcome to the Garberville Psychiatric Institute."

"What are we doing here?"

"The telephone records at Goddard indicate that Dr. Orinsky's last call was made to this facility. To save a little time, I had the background of every patient here cross-checked, and only one guy came up with any connection to Orinsky. His name is Herman Cromwell—formerly *Dr.* Herman Cromwell—and it seems that he taught classes with Orinsky at Stanford."

Laura looked interested. "Really? Taught what?"

Press's answer made her forehead lift in surprise. "Microbiology."

She frowned and stared out the window, watching as they drew closer to the building. "From Stanford to here," she mused. "That's a pretty drastic change in career path. What the hell happened?"

"Ah," Press said. "That's the *really* interesting part. Whatever brought the fine Dr. Cromwell here is classified government information." As the car passed through the wrought-iron gates that marked the entrance to the grounds proper, the look he sent her was anything but comforting. "So classified, in fact, that no one on our team can get to it and tell us what it is."

Senator Judson Ross looked blankly at his son. "What did you say?"

"I said I blacked out after the fund-raising banquet last night," Patrick repeated. His handsome face was pinched and pale, and his worried expression had aged him ten years overnight. At the same time, the senator thought there was an aura of . . . *robustness* about his son that he'd never noticed before. For some reason, it made him vaguely envious. "I know something happened, but I can't remember any of it," Patrick continued. "My mind is just a blank. I went from walking off the platform after my speech to waking up in bed at the townhouse this morning—I must've been *driving* like that, for God's sake. And . . . and I don't think it's the first time that's happened, either."

Senator Ross rubbed a hand across his jaw as he considered Patrick's words. It was good that the boy had come to his father, good that he'd come *here.* This senatorial office in Washington was where the political man always did his best thinking, solving problems for his voters in Virginia and, ostensibly, for his country while settled comfortably on his custom-leather chair. His massive oak desk was flanked by the United States and Virginia flags, while carefully arranged photographs of himself and presidents adorned the walls. Ross's political rise had begun in the JFK administration, and the room reflected that accumulated power—men like Kennedy, Johnson, Nixon, and even Bill Clinton, showed it clearly in their images. Family life and problems—they weren't so hard. A man just had to approach them in the same way he had to deal with any piece of bureaucratic red tape: with an eye toward trying to untangle the mess.

Or at least make it into a more attractive knot.

"The drinks are always made strong at these fundraisers, Patrick," he said now. "You know that—it's just another way to get those wallets to open. You probably had a few too many and didn't realize it in the excitement. Next time you'll know to eat more so the meal will soak it up—we all noticed that you hardly touched your food at the table."

But Patrick only stared at him from across the expanse of the oak desk. Finally, he shook his head. "That isn't it at all. I think there's something wrong—*really* wrong—with me since I got back from the Mars mission. I'm not . . . *right* somehow."

Senator Ross sighed. "It was a long, stressful journey, son. A man doesn't recover from something like that overnight. Being separated for nearly a year from his family and friends, his girlfriend—that's damned hard. Reclaiming and reorganizing your life can take weeks, perhaps even months. It's a massive readjustment—"

"It's not *normal.*"

"But who knows what 'normal' is after an experience like that?" Senator Ross argued. "No one's ever done it before—you and Dennis and Anne were the first. And as far as I know, those two are fine." He paused and scrutinized his son's anxious face. "Tell you what. Why don't I call Doctor Swinburne over at Johns Hopkins? He's head of Internal Medicine there. We'll get you examined and see what he says."

His son stared at the floor. "It's not going to help."

Senator Ross choked back a sigh of exasperation. "Swinburne is the best man over at Hopkins," he said with false patience. "We need to shore you up, Patrick. If you think the trip to Mars was difficult, wait until you're in the middle of a Senate campaign."

The older man started when Patrick jumped to his feet. "No, no, *no!* Damn it, Dad—aren't you *listening* to what I'm saying here?" Patrick strode to the end of the senator's desk, then spun and went back, like an animal trapped in a cage. "Don't you understand? You have to help me—I'm having some kind of . . . of a breakdown or something. Would you just stop thinking about your fucking Master Plan and *help me* for once? For God's sake, I'm *scared*—"

"Stop it right now!" On his feet, Senator Ross put his full weight into slamming his open hand on the desktop; the sound was like a rifle shot cutting through Patrick's outburst. His son pulled up in his tracks and stared at him, trembling, his expression a mixture of disbelief and pleading. But Ross kept going—Patrick had to be reined in *now,* and he couldn't let himself be drawn into what was surely no more than a case of the jitters. There could be no more of these anxiety attacks or ridiculous little tantrums—what if he'd done this in public? Or, God forbid, at the fund-raiser last night? This kind of behavior could endanger everything, undercut way too many years of strategy and hard work.

"You stop acting like a child and listen to me, right *now,*" the senator ground out. "You are a *Ross,* damn it, and we can trace our lineage in this country all the way back to the people who came over on the *Mayflower.* The men in our family do *not* lose control, Patrick. Not *ever.*"

"But—"

Senator Ross cut off his son's protest with a wave of his hand, then came around to where Patrick was clutching the back of his chair. "The American people love you, Patrick. You don't know—you can't even *conceive*—how much this is true." He stared hard at the young man in whom he'd invested so many years of training and grooming, and whom he'd taught through hard-learned examples of leadership. "What I'm telling you is something you should already know. You could be *president* of this fine country someday, Patrick, and I'll be damned if I'm going to let anything stand in your way. The rest of it has to come from you." He gripped Patrick's shoulders, fighting against the urge to shake him and reset whatever was out of place in his head. *"Don't screw it up."*

For a long moment, Patrick stared at him, eye to eye and just a bit taller. When he spoke, the words were choked and barely comprehensible, obviously not at all what his son really wanted to say.

"Yes . . . Father."

It would have to do.

Senator Ross released Patrick and found a smile, like he always did in unpleasant situations where he absolutely had to keep up an agreeable face. "That's good," he said heartily and clapped the younger man on the back. "You know what you need? Some support." Smiling fully now, he turned Patrick and steered him toward the door. "Come on, m'boy. Let's take a walk through the gallery. There're quite a few of my illustrious colleagues who have been asking for your autograph, and it wouldn't do at all to disappoint your friends and future voters."

God forgive him, but he had to ignore the stricken look on his boy's face and push him on out the door.

"Wow," Laura said to Press in a low voice. "This is quite a difference from the way it looked from the outside, wouldn't you say?"

When they'd first arrived at the Garberville Psychiatric Institute, she and Press had been shown to a lovely reception area just off the main foyer. Appearances were apparently everything here, and the pattern of English tea-rose paper adorning the walls flawlessly complemented the high-grade reproductions of dark Victorian-era furnishings. They'd sat on an uncomfortable gold-brocade settee that matched a chaise longue across the room that hadn't looked very inviting either. There'd been no magazines there, and the pair had spent their time waiting and gazing at a sideboard and a glass-fronted china cabinet that held dainty porcelain figures that may or may not have been true antiques. Underfoot there was an expensive-looking Oriental area rug that stretched just a foot short of the walls in all four directions and showed the edge of the gleaming dark-wood floor.

Now, however, they saw the true face of Garberville.

Their "Special Government Agent" identification cards had gained them access to this room—small, with drab gray furnishings and dirty walls, overly lit by a double row of fluorescents screwed into the ceiling. A hard-faced technician—or perhaps she was an orderly—in a laboratory coat with food stains down the right side of it gestured to several chairs arranged haphazardly around an old stainless-steel table. Everything about the woman, from the way her fuzzy gray hair stuck up at the back of her head to the heavy pair of glasses that kept sliding down her nose, seemed to be an annoyance to her, and the presence of Press and Laura was just adding to her predicament.

"I'm going to bring Mr. Cromwell in now," she said curtly. "Please be brief. He's been acting very strangely of late and we've had to restrain him a number of times. If you get him overexcited, it will be on your conscience if we have to do it again."

She left the room with a slam of the door and Laura looked over at Press. " 'On our conscience?' What exactly are they doing to him here?"

"Oh, I think you have an idea," Press responded dryly.

She frowned. "Tranquilizers are not necessarily the best way to manage psychiatric—"

Before she could finish, the door bounced open again and the tech propelled a man in his late fifties or early sixties into the room with them. "No funny business, Mr. Cromwell," the woman snapped, "or we'll have to resort to measures." Her gaze lifted from her patient and fixed on Press and Laura, then turned into a glare. "You've got ten minutes," she snapped. Another slam of the door, and it was just the three of them.

"She called me 'Mister,' " Herman Cromwell said. The slightly skewed smile he offered them as he turned a chair around and straddled it never reached his intense, bright-blue eyes, destroying any notion that the man on the other side of the table was jovial. His head had been clean-shaven and his face was lined and cynical. "I guess the last time I heard that was in nineteen ninety-six. Before they put me here, of course." He frowned at them suddenly. "And who the hell are you two, anyway?"

"My name is Preston Lennox, and this is Dr. Laura Baker," Press began.

"Doctor, huh?" Cromwell peered at Laura. "What kind of doctor? Another psychiatrist? Or maybe they're going for something more medical on me this time. Let's see . . . they've tried behavior modification, but I just keep sticking to my story. So maybe you're some kind of . . . neurological specialist, a surgeon perhaps. Yeah, that's it, someone getting ready to split my head open—"

"I'm a molecular biologist."

Abruptly Cromwell's fingers came together, hard, like a man who'd suddenly decided it was time to launch a desperate prayer. "Yeah?"

"I'm here because—"

"I know why you're here," Cromwell interrupted. "You've come to hear my story."

Composed now, Cromwell was completely different from the crazy-eyed man who'd been led into the room here only five minutes earlier.

"Ralph and I were old friends," the former doctor told them. "I'm sorry to hear about his death." He lapsed into silence, but only for a second. "They never told me he tried to call, of course—that's to be expected. But I'm sure he did it because he'd found out something that had to do with my past. You see, I was doing research on the Mars meteorite."

"The one that was found in nineteen eighty-four on the Alan Hills ice field in Antarctica?" Laura asked.

"Exactly. I'm sure you're already aware that it wasn't recognized as being of Martian origin until nineteen ninety-three." Cromwell's gaze dropped to the table, but he kept talking; Laura had the eerie impression that he was almost . . . reading with his eyes closed. She wondered if he had a photographic memory. "There aren't a whole lot of Martian-traceable meteorites," he continued. "A dozen total, no more. The one I'm talking about here is called *ALH84001*, and it's the geologically oldest specimen that we have."

"Oldest?" Press raised an eyebrow. "How old is old?"

"Four and a half billion years," Cromwell answered, and Laura's mouth dropped open. "All the others range from a hundred and eighty million to about one point three billion years old, babies by comparison."

"Jesus," Press said. "I didn't know *anything* could exist for that long."

"Oh, you bet it can," Cromwell hissed. His face was suddenly creased with emotion. He inhaled and made a visible effort to collect himself, then continued shakily. "As I was about to say, *ALH84001* underwent extensive testing, of course. It was a complicated series—we used everything from a laser mass spectrometer and a highly classified means of carbon dating to extremely high magnification under a transmission electron microscope. It wasn't easy to get high-resolution images—the fossils we ultimately found were of primitive cellular life measuring only twenty to one hundred nanometers across."

"Everyone has heard about this," Press said. "It was all in the news."

Cromwell laughed, the sound on the edge of high-pitched. "No, not all, Mr. Lennox. Only part of it was released. It was what they left out that was the most interesting, you see. The part about how those fossils that we found weren't organic to the planet Mars."

Laura shot a glance at Press, who said nothing. A good soldier he was, but this was her arena. "What is the basis for that determination, Dr. Cromwell?"

Cromwell smiled at her ruefully. "Thank you for that sign of respect, Dr. Baker. But that title was taken from me." He looked away for a moment, his gaze fixing on the mesh-embedded windowpane on the outside wall of the room. When he turned back to them, the bald man's eyes were sharp and full of intelligence. "The research we performed on what we found led us to believe that carbon-based elements found in *ALH84001* exist only in the Magellanic galaxy." He leaned over the scratched surface of the table, determined to make his point. "That galaxy is over a hundred and seventy *thousand* light-years away from us."

"So what were these fossils doing on Mars?" Press asked.

"As I see it," Cromwell said softly, "Mars was colonized by an alien species several billion years ago."

Laura could feel Press's shock from across the table. "That's a very interesting theory," she said carefully. "But again . . . on what basis are you making these claims?"

Without warning, a fly buzzed across her field of vision. Laura blinked and jerked away from it while Cromwell began swatting wildly at it. Another strike, another miss. "The geologic history of Mars is quite common knowledge," he said, and leaned back on his chair. The exertion had made him slightly breathless, and now only his eyes, a luminous shade of blue, moved as they tracked the fly's progress in the air above the table.

"At the present time," Cromwell continued, "Mars is in its youngest state, of course, what we call the Amazonian Period. The planet itself is a little over four and a half billion years old, and in the first part of its history, the Noachian Period, it was a thriving environment. If it wasn't exactly like Earth—being farther away from the sun—it did have water, an atmosphere, and a hospitable climate. I believe the aliens that landed on that planet made it the hunk of useless rock we see today. They spread like a plague across its surface, and no doubt the life-form depleted its supply of water and raw materials. A technologically advanced species could easily have engineered the destruction of Mars's artesian aquifers and thus triggered the fault lines, which in turn resulted in the eruption of the Tharsis volcano, as well as the thousands of other volcanoes across the planet's surface." He looked at Press and Laura solemnly. "Surface buckling, artificially induced fissures in the landscape in search of water, on and on. We all know what a more powerful and so-called 'intelligent' life-form can do to its environment. So . . . *viola.* The end of a flourishing environment for Mars."

When no one said anything, Cromwell again folded his hands on the tabletop, that same strange gesture of supplication. "When I heard that the United States was sending a landing mission to Mars, I strongly urged the government to reconsider."

"Why?" asked Laura. "If what you say is true—and I feel obligated to point out that there is absolutely no evidence to back up your postulations—these alien colonists clearly died out millions, possibly *billions,* of years ago. On what grounds would you expect the government to cancel a project like this?"

Cromwell's cheeks flushed. "Don't you get it?" he demanded. "Grounds? I'll give you a reason, all right. For all of the beauty and life-sustaining atmosphere Mars probably had at one time, it would never, *ever* have supported human life. At its best, it would have always been a harsh planet on which only an extremely strong, hardy life-form could exist. A life-form that would no doubt be incredibly dangerous and harmful to humans!" Cromwell's voice had risen to a near shout. "A species that could very possibly go dormant and leave its own DNA on the surface—like spores—so that any attempt by another form of life would result in biological contamination!"

"Still—"

"Let me guess," Press said, cutting her off. "Uncle

Sam told you to shove your theory where the Martian sun doesn't shine."

"But you were insistent," Laura added, picking up where Press headed. It was just as well that Press had stepped in when he had; arguing with Herman Cromwell would accomplish nothing. "And in being so . . . determined, someone got rather annoyed with you. Do you know who?"

"Oh, I could give it a guess," Press said with a nasty grin.

"Senator Judson Ross, of course," Herman Cromwell said.

"Of course," Laura repeated. "Our nation's biggest proponent of space exploration since the nineteen sixties."

"It wasn't just Ross," Cromwell said flatly. "He was a part of it, yes. The clincher was apparently the Pentagon had strategic reasons for wanting to go to Mars. Strategic *military* reasons it wasn't likely to share with the lowly public. And the higher-ups definitely did not want some geeky college researcher stirring up public curiosity or opposition to their grand plans." For the first time since they'd sat down to talk to him, the older man's voice slid toward bitterness. "Got me fired from Stanford, and that was just the beginning. Oh, yeah. Couldn't jeopardize their little outpost of the future, or whatever crap it was they had designs for. They harassed the shit out of me, set me up at every public function, turned me into a laughingstock in front of my colleagues and friends . . . even my *family*."

"How did you end up here at Garberville, Dr. Cromwell?" Something in Press's voice was dark and unpleasant, and Laura looked at him sharply.

"I went to a conference at the Johnson Space Center," he answered, and again there was that longing look at the wire-sheathed window. "It's a biyearly thing, and I thought that there, *surely*, I could find someone with enough brainpower to at least listen to me. They didn't have to believe—all the figures and the research were there for them to read and decide for themselves. I went to a meeting there on the possibility of extraterrestrial life and got shouted down by some meathead whom I later learned was a Pentagon shill instructed to heckle." Cromwell looked at his hands, then unfolded his fingers. He wasn't a big man—average in everything but for his getting-on-in-years age. His voice held hints of both pride and regret. "I've always been a passionate man when it comes to my beliefs. We scuffled, and I . . . I was so angry. When I hit him, I broke his damned jaw."

"Those *fuckers*," Press whispered.

Laura cleared her throat. "What do you think Dr. Orinsky called you about on the night he was killed?"

There was no victory in the former doctor's gaze. "To say I was right," he answered in a small voice. "To tell me that those poor astronauts had doomed Earth by bringing home whatever aliens destroyed Mars."

Both Press and Laura jumped as Cromwell's hand shot out and snatched the fly from midair. He opened his palm and held it out, showing them the insect's crushed carcass.

"We will be to these aliens what this fly is to us," Herman Cromwell said softly. "I wonder . . . do you think God will take pity on the three who have brought about the destruction of his most complex creation?"

CHAPTER 11

Anne thought she would remember forever the expression on Harry's face as he touched a flame to the last of the three dozen candles she'd placed around their bedroom. Big ones, small ones, tall, short—all spilling scented, golden light across where she waited on the bed. She'd gone all-out on the ambiance, the decorations, on *herself*—money wasn't something they worried about in the Friedman/Sampas household, but they didn't throw it away, either. And she certainly didn't normally go for things like the manicure and pedicure she'd had this morning, not to mention the trip to the hairdresser and the facial.

The "good" linens were on the bed, the satin sheets and matching deep gold comforter she usually reserved for their anniversary and Valentine's Day. A new Chopin CD—sweet, unobtrusive mood music—played on the stereo. They'd been college sweethearts and nine years of marriage hadn't even put a smudge in their affection for each other; when Harry dropped the spent matchstick in the ashtray and turned to look at her, Anne knew, as she always had, that she'd gotten the best of everything.

"Surprise," he said. She smiled with delight when he reached to the side of the dresser and held up the crystal ice bucket they'd received as a long-ago wedding gift. Inside was a bottle of well-chilled Dom Pérignon, glistening in the candlelight. He set the bucket on the carpet next to the bed, then went back for the matching champagne flutes. He had a slightly comical fight involving the cork and a hand towel from the bathroom; then he was pouring expensive bubbly, trying vainly to look offended at Anne's laughter.

"I've missed you," she said suddenly. "This week . . . it's definitely been the longest of my life." Unaccountably embarrassed, her gaze dropped to the sparkling liquid in her glass. Funny how abstinence bred, among other things, awkwardness. She'd felt so poorly all week—dizzy, feverish, just *off*—and had been afraid about tonight, worried that she'd be too ill to finally break the quarantine. Beyond the required public appearances—the fund-raiser had been the worst—for today's pampering, she'd stayed close to home most of the time. Now that their special time was here though, she'd never felt better.

Harry sat next to her on the bed and stroked her cheek, his fingers warm. "You look lovely, you know. You get more beautiful each year. And this color, it really becomes you. It brings out the red in your hair." He smoothed the fabric of the forest-green silk-and-lace teddy, pressing it against the sleek line of her hip.

Anne's breath caught in her throat as his touch sent heat, unexpectedly fierce, racing through her blood. "Thank you," she managed. She reached past him and set her champagne glass on the nightstand, desire making her hand shake.

Attuned to Anne as always, Harry did the same. At last he stretched out next to her and took her in his arms.

After almost a year of waiting, he could finally, *finally*, make love to his wife again.

"If you're not going to listen to what we have to say, then why the hell did you solicit our help to begin with?" Laura whirled, then strode to the glass of the viewing booth and gestured angrily at the young woman imprisoned in the glass living quarters below. On the main floor was the rest of her team, monitoring Eve's every move; and the reports Laura had been getting from her top staff were disturbing indeed.

"I am listening," Carter Burgess said stiffly. "But you're not making any sense."

"The hell she's not!" Press exploded. "You used to be an intelligent man—when did you get a damned lobotomy?"

He drew in a breath to keep going, but Laura's voice, cold and brittle with anger, stopped him. "Then let me try again." Her words were grinding out from between clenched teeth. "What I am telling you, Colonel Burgess, is that during its polar nights, the temperature on Mars drops to nearly two hundred degrees Fahrenheit below zero, but at perihelion—when the planet is closest to the sun—the surface temperature along the Martian equator can be as high as a pleasant eighty degrees. The average surface temperature of the Red Planet, however, is approximately minus sixty-four degrees Fahrenheit, which is generally high enough that an advanced life-form might be able to suspend its life processes and go dormant, but *not* die. Once initiated into that state, it would most likely remain that way throughout the planet's change of seasons until a specific chain of events terminated that state."

Colonel Burgess folded his arms and stared out the window of the viewing booth, refusing to look at her. Frustrated, Laura strode to his side and grabbed the sleeve of his jacket. "Damn it, open your eyes! You're looking at living proof that alien DNA can successfully merge with human DNA! It's possible the samples Patrick Ross brought back onboard the *Excursion* were contaminated. If so, the contents—DNA-rich cells, larvae, spores, whatever you want to call it—would have been exposed to a perfect environment in which to revive: regulated warm temperatures, optimal humidity, and a suddenly rich supply of oxygen. If this happened, the revived DNA could have infected the astronauts."

Burgess turned from the window with a black expression on his face; the sinister effect magnified by the blank, glass eye. "This isn't the *X-Files*, damn it. You're dreaming up a far-fetched solution based on a lead you got from the interrogation of a certified nut case."

Now it was Press's turn to be enraged. "So you think Cromwell's a nut case, huh? It's pretty damned interesting he got slapped into a psychiatric institute after he warned the government—good people like *you*—about going to Mars in the first place. Besides that, you've got an NSEG doctor who was eviscerated by something unknown before he had the chance to record his findings, the blood he was working on is missing, and hey—in case you forgot—an unexplained seven-minute time gap while the U.S. of A.'s top space team was floating around another planet."

"We have *got* to perform blood-analysis tests on Gamble, Ross, and Sampas," Laura put in.

Colonel Burgess sighed, his face relaxing a little. "This is going to be very hard to explain to a lot of people—"

"I'm sure you're aware of the ten-day sexual quarantine that NSEG imposes on all interplanetary missions. The Mars quarantine ends *tonight.*" She put her hands on her hips, waiting.

"Keep thinking about it." Press sent the older man a disgusted glance. "And in the meantime, the three of them can fuck the human race right into extinction. Try explaining *that* to all your highbrow generals." His mouth pulled up at one corner. "Do you really want to be responsible for what might happen if Laura's right and we don't check them out?"

Burgess scowled and stared down at Eve. When Laura followed his gaze, she saw the half-human, half-alien woman staring with fascination at an old rerun of *The Dukes of Hazard,* drawn, for some reason, to the plight of the Duke boys and their souped-up orange Charger. Sitting inside her glass home and carefully painting her toenails with bright red nail polish, she looked like nothing more than a harmless, attentive college girl. But Laura knew, as did Colonel Burgess and Press, exactly what dangers were hiding beneath that perfectly creamy complexion.

Burgess turned away from the window. "Test the woman first," he ordered. "Then the others."

"Fine." Press and Laura headed for the door, bent on packing their gear and making up for wasted time.

Burgess's icy voice stopped them. "The *Excursion* mission was the best thing to happen to this country in more than thirty years," he said. "I believe in this country completely, and I believe what we did by going to Mars was *right.* If some son of a bitch from . . . say, *The National Enquirer,* were to get ahold of this bullshit and splash it across the front page at the supermarket checkout lines, there would be hell to pay." He paused. "No," he said softly. "There would be *more* than hell to pay." He spun without waiting for an answer and stalked out the door of the viewing room.

Laura stared after him. "Am I crazy, or did that hard ass just threaten us?"

For a long moment, Press didn't answer. "Once," he finally said, "on a covert op in Costa Rica, Burgess took out a guerrilla-controlled village. He did it by himself, with no backup, and he carried three hostages to safety. Trainers across the board—Army, WACs, SEALS, Jarheads, you name it—they all use the mission as an example of excellence."

"But you don't think it was." Laura frowned and rubbed her arms. For some reason, this story chilled her. Nonetheless, she grabbed the rest of their gear and followed after Press, listening intently to the rest of the tale.

Press shrugged as they made their way to the exit. "I . . . don't know. I suppose it depends on how you define 'excellence.' They say he killed everyone and everything that stood in his path. For Burgess, anything goes if it's for his God or his country. It's not my job to make judgment calls, but I can't decide if he's America's greatest patriot . . .

"Or just a psychotic with way too much power."

"Mmmm." Anne Sampas smiled contently and snuggled deeper against Harry's chest. "That was soooo nice."

"Wow," was all Harry said.

He stroked her hair, fingering the deep copper strands highlighted in the candlelight before his hand trailed down her shoulder to rest against her breast. God, how she'd missed him all those months. Not just the sex, but the tenderness, the *love.* The nights like this one, when she could go to sleep safe and warm in the arms of the man she loved. Everything she did—the interstellar missions, her work as an M.I.T. scientist—none of it would mean anything without this man at her side. This, of all things, was what made her complete.

"You were worth the wait," Harry said as he leaned over and kissed her. Their faces were flushed in the slowly lowering candlelight and perspiration shone along the fine line of his collarbone, a drop of it hanging there before falling on her arm. Anne lifted her mouth to meet his, then stopped, the pleasant rush of long-ignored desire stifled by a sudden wave of nausea and dizziness.

"Sweetheart," she managed. "I-I don't feel very well."

"Oh, hey," her husband said teasingly, "if that didn't do it for you, I'll be glad to try again."

"I'm *serious*!" The words came out as a series of gasps and she tried to push herself upright, then clutched at the sheets covering her stomach.

"Annie, what's wrong?" Alarmed now, Harry sat up straight and tried to help her up. "Was it dinner—something you ate?"

"My s-s-stomach," she cried. "Hurts—oh God, it *hurts*!" She twisted on the bed and felt Harry trying futilely to hold her down, sensed more than saw the change in his demeanor right before he abruptly let go of her arms.

"Your stomach—Jesus, I've got to call an ambulance, find someone to help—"

Unspeakable overwhelming agony cut through her lower body and she screamed and clutched at the bedpost for support, the pain giving her enough strength to pull herself up and free of the sheets twisted around her. Less than a minute ago she'd been at the height of ecstasy, belly against belly with her husband; now her abdomen was hugely distended, an oversized mound that would have more rightfully belonged to a soon-to-be mother of twins. Gaping with terror, she saw the surface of her belly undulate, as though something inside were stretching itself in readiness.

Another wave of torment, but she had hope, oh God yes, because there was Harry, clawing his way to the nightstand on his side and yanking up the telephone, panicked and clumsy but determined to dial 911. She would make it, she *would*—some kind of parasite or something, some freak of nature, they'd had sushi earlier in the evening, that must have—

She shrieked, a long, drawn-out howl that felt like it would never end, as her stomach split open from sternum to crotch. Blood splattered her body, the walls, Harry's face as he stood there with the telephone receiver gripped in one hand, paralyzed by what he was seeing, helpless to do anything to stop it.

Then it got worse.

Something *burst* from the gaping chasm in Anne's midsection. A tentacle, brown and covered in blood and mucous, waving in the air with the hypnotic grace of underwater plant life. Her cries now reduced to moans, Anne instinctively slammed her hands against the bleeding crater across the still-high mound of her belly, feeling the horrible tentacle slide against her skin as something so much larger and unspeakable still thrashed inside her.

Harry's paralysis broke. He backstepped and brought the phone back up, intent on getting his call for help to the outside world. When the tentacle, this part of whatever had taken control of her body, snapped toward him and wrapped around his neck, then lifted him clear of the floor as though he weighed no more than a bag of flour—

—Anne Sampas somehow found the lung power to scream again.

And again . . .

* * *

"Stupid piece of government-issued garbage!" Press raged. His foot was jammed so hard on the accelerator that he was practically forcing it through the floor, but the bucket of useless metal just wouldn't go any faster. Slow and ponderous, the damned Chevrolet sedan was taking the turns like an overbalanced flatbed, threatening to roll on nearly every one, even though he was trying his best to allow for its shortcomings. If he just had his Boxster, he and Laura would've been at the Sampas residence by now—

—and it sure wasn't any comfort to haul ass into the driveway and hear the shrieks of terror and pain coming from one of the upstairs windows.

"Grab the hydrochlorine," Laura shouted as they leaped out of the car.

Press leaned back inside the sedan and hit the trunk release, then was at the rear of the car almost before the lid had opened all the way. The canister, a double-tanked device with a high-tech aerosol nozzle, was heavier than he'd expected, but at least it had a shoulder strap. He slid it over his arm, then barreled toward the house after Laura. "Wait, damn it! Don't you go up there without me!"

For once Laura listened to him, waiting on the porch by the front door until he reached her. The door was locked, of course—no one as intelligent as these people would leave their house wide open—and Press shrugged out of the canister setup and gave it to Laura. He backed up two or three steps, then hammered at the lock with his booted foot. It took three tries to get through, just as Anne Sampas's screams began to fade.

"There!" Just inside the doorway, Laura pointed to her left. Press saw the stairway and went for it, taking the risers three at a time with Laura right behind him. They scrambled around the corner at the top and found themselves in a hallway; at the end was an open door where golden light and shadows flickered wildly and something dark flicked across the entrance.

"Aw, Christ," Press yelled—no stealth here—as he and Laura burst into the room. A tentacle waved in the air. He recognized it as a smaller but still lethally strong version of that ugly appendage so familiar from their previous encounters with Sil. Its end was wrapped tightly around the neck of the man it held aloft, presumably Anne Sampas's husband, his body limp, his face blue; Press knew instantly that for him, their help had come too late.

"Please—help!"

Press's hand instinctively went for his gun. Two shots, right on target into the meaty midsection of the thing waving in the air; Sampas's husband dropped to the floor with a thud that left no doubt that he was dead. The tentacle recoiled and wavered in the air, as if it couldn't decide how to deal with this new threat.

A choking sound came from the bed. Out of the corner of his eye, Press saw the woman who had been Anne Sampas. The gaping hole in her belly was the source of the horrible, snakelike thing hovering over her, as blood pulsed sluggishly from the grisly wound onto the golden bedspread beneath her. Her skin shockingly white from trauma and blood loss. "Please." Her voice was barely audible through the bubbling blood pooling in her throat. "Just . . . kill me. *Please.*"

Press shook his head—*no, he couldn't.* He heard a snapping sound as the serrated coil of flesh went for him. He recoiled and raised the Glock again, but something blue and misty abruptly filled the air in front of him—Laura had brought up the canister of hydrochlorine and triggered the spray nozzle. The brown-mottled tentacle spasmed and jerked wildly in front of his face and Press stumbled backward, nearly falling against Laura. On the bed, Anne Sampas gave a final howl of misery as her deadly offspring shuddered and dropped, then tried to pull its way back inside her body. Unable to look away, Press and Laura watched in horror as the defenseless woman convulsed under the thrashing of the thing within her—

—then died.

"Oh, *God,*" Laura choked. She whirled away from the carnage, then found a measure of control and hurried to squat next to the man on the floor. "He's gone," she said resignedly.

Press shakingly holstered his gun and he wasn't ashamed to find that his hand was shaking. It had happened so damned *fast.* No sirens cut through the serene Maryland night. There hadn't even been seconds enough for Sampas's husband to get his call through to the emergency line. And now here they were, standing in the candlelit bloodbath of what should have been a loving reunion.

Jesus.

"We're lucky to be alive," Laura said suddenly. He looked at her sharply. "Even at full strength we don't believe the hydrochlorine will be effective in stopping a mature alien. The only reason I can speculate that it worked now is because this is an—" She seemed to gag on the word. "An *infant.*"

What could he say to that cheerful news? "I'll call a clean-up crew," he said hoarsely. He offered Laura his hand as she took it and pulled herself to her feet. "They'll get over here right away." He waited until she would meet his eyes. "I'm sorry," he said gently. "But we have to get to the others."

"The only thing better than the smell of fine brandy," Dennis Gamble said as he inhaled deeply over his snifter, "is the scent of your perfume."

Jemila Asante smiled and raised one finely arched

eyebrow, in a pointed look. "As if you could actually smell it over the stench of that thing in your hand."

Dennis chuckled and hit the DOWN button on the limousine's window; in another second, his cigar was sailing away in the darkness. "Guess I can take a hint." He offered her one of the snifters and her expression softened, her long fingers resting against his as she took the crystal from him. "Oh, sweetheart," he said, "I am a wounded man and it's finally time for healthy healing." He lifted his glass and drained it, letting the brandy send a trail of warmth down his throat.

"Careful you don't drink too much, Mr. Astronaut," Jemila said coyly. A manicured fingernail trailed down one leg of his slacks, leaving a line of fire that completely overwhelmed anything the brandy could do. "I guarantee you'll want to remember tonight."

Dennis smiled, desire making him woozy. Or was it the brandy? God, he hoped not. He slipped one arm across Jemila's exquisitely coffee-colored shoulder. "When I say this man has waited a long time, I mean it was a *long* time. But the drought is almost over—"

Without urging, Jemila brought her face to his and kissed him deeply.

"—and not a moment too soon." Her mouth opened beneath his as he pulled her closer, then realized that the car had pulled to a stop. Home at last.

They parted reluctantly as the driver came around and opened the door for them, both men watching appreciatively as Jemila unfolded herself from the back door like a dark, exotic flower spreading its petals. While she waited, Dennis retrieved her purse and the nearly empty bottle of brandy, then tucked a fifty-dollar bill discreetly into the driver's hand.

"Thanks, chief. I can take her the rest of the way."

The driver grinned and tipped his hat, as Dennis led Jemila toward the house. Nothing fancy there, just an inconspicuous little place in the 'burbs. He'd leave the grandstanding and show to Patrick and Senator Ross. His thinking ran more to the unobtrusive, like Anne and her husband Harry but it was home, and he knew all its nooks and crannies.

By the time Dennis unlocked the front door, he and Jemila were pawing each other like a couple of horny teenagers crashed into the umbrella stand, on their way to ectasy. Dennis didn't care. "Oh, yeah," he groaned. "Alone at last!"

Whatever Jemila said in return was unintelligible as her hands began yanking off his jacket. Dennis didn't know if the wait had been worth it—eleven months had been a pretty fucking *long* time—but he couldn't remember the last time he'd had so much fun on a date. They stumbled up the stairs towards the bedroom, panting and moaning, leaving a trail of clothes in their wake—her shoes and his, the hated bow tie and cumberbund from tonight's tuxedo, more pieces that he couldn't identify along a staircase lit only by the night-light in the upper hallway.

"Wait," Jemila gasped as they reeled into the bedroom. "Just a minute."

"What?" Dennis's voice was a croak and he tried to hang on to her. "I've *been* waiting—"

"Silly man," she giggled and pushed him backward until he fell on the bed. "Just let me use the bathroom."

Oh, jeez—of course. Women always seemed to want to do that, didn't they? She scampered away and he grinned and used the time to yank off the last of his clothes, the trousers of the expensive tuxedo sailing off into a darkened corner. He set up a ghost of light from the dimmer switch connected to the stained-glass lamp on the dresser, then . . . what else? Music—that'd be the ticket right now. On one wall was a small bookcase with a stereo cassette player. Dennis rummaged around in his tapes until he found something he thought would be good—D'Angelo, dark and moody, *sexy*. He popped it into the player and hit the button just as Jemila threw open the bathroom door. When he turned, she was standing there, naked and waiting, and for a single, amazing moment, Dennis thought she was some dark Egyptian goddess.

"Are you ready?" she purred.

He couldn't even answer as she glided across the room into his arms. Twisting, turning, her hands were everywhere on him and Dennis thought he would explode from the heat. Somehow they were on the bed, in the inferno that had become his bedroom. Finally, Jemila was under him, those endlessly long silken thighs, open and welcoming him, so sweet, soft and warm, and—

Then her body went stiff beneath his.

Dennis froze and pulled his lips from hers. "What's wrong, baby?"

Jemila's expression should have been sensual and full of passion; instead, it was a cross between amazement and fright as she looked at something over his shoulder as she tried to form words that wouldn't come out. Dennis twisted around, at the same time the overhead light was snapped on and found himself gaping at four black-uniformed men.

"What the *fuck*—who are you?" he demanded. Reflex made him jerk the side of the bedspread over himself and Jemila.

The first of the men who barged into his bedroom held up an identification badge. "Federal agents," he said flatly. "Dennis Gamble, I'm afraid you'll have to come with us."

"Who put you up to this—Patrick Ross?" Dennis

snapped. "If this is his idea of a joke, it's not funny. Now get the hell out of my house!"

"This isn't a hoax, Mr. Gamble," said the same man. He jerked his head at his three comrades and Dennis watched with a sort of detached horror as they unshouldered their weapons—the standard federal-issue M-16s—and leveled them at him. Cowering behind his back, Dennis felt the whimpering Jemila's taut breasts hitch against his skin.

"Aw, Jesus," Dennis said. "What's going on here—what did I do?"

None of the men answered; instead, their leader strode to Dennis's dresser and began opening drawers; in a few short moments he held out a pair of jeans and a shirt. "You'll need to put these on," he said simply.

Dennis started to stand, then glared at them. "At least turn your backs."

All four men continued to stare at him with black eyes. Finally, the first one gave a small shake of his head. "I'm sorry, sir. We can't do that."

Dennis started to say something, but fell silent. Defeated, Dennis stepped out of the folds of the bedspread and yanked it quickly back over Jemila—he'd be damned if these bastards were going to get a free look at her. He dressed without a word, telling himself that these men were only following orders but unable to stop himself from sending them murderous glances. When he was ready, he turned back to Jemila still huddled on the bed. "I'll be back in no time," he promised. "Get this straightened out and we'll start over, fix everything up just right." Another furious glance at the agents still waiting patiently. "And next time, we'll find somewhere *private*."

She gave him a brave smile but he could see tear tracks on her cheeks. "Okay," she said, and what a woman, she even managed to keep her voice steady. "We'll try it again."

"You just curl up and relax," Dennis told her. "Hell, fix yourself some popcorn and watch a movie downstairs." He grinned. "Or better yet, draw up a nice hot bath and wait for me there." That earned him another trembling smile.

Dennis tenderly touched her cheek, then spun around and faced the federal agents. "Let's get this over with." He started to step past them and they did a vague quick-shuffle that somehow planted him in their middle as they left the bedroom and descended the stairs. The bastards were making him feel like some kind of criminal.

"This is no way to treat a national hero," he told them icily as they guided him to a black van parked outside. No mistaking this for a government vehicle, right down to the transmission antennae sprouting like metal weeds all over the roof. "Come on, fellas," Dennis entreated when they opened the back door and gestured at him to climb in. "What's this all about? I know you boys can talk—somebody speak to me."

Nothing, and damn but he was getting angrier by the minute. Finding another two agents waiting in the third seat didn't help matters—for God's sake, had they sent enough men to do their dirty work? Or did they think he was that dangerous?

"You know," he railed, "I'm a personal friend of Senator Judson Ross. You ever watch the *X-Files*? By the time I'm through, I'll have all of you investigating radioactive sewage on Russian sea tankers!"

But nothing Dennis Gamble said could stop the van from speeding off into the Washington, D.C. night.

"Can't you go any faster?" Laura demanded as she broke the connection on her cell phone.

"Not in this bucket." As if to prove his words, the tires slipped and sent the sedan sideways when he took a turn too fast and he had to fight to bring the Chevrolet back under control. "Piece of crap!"

Laura didn't comment on his driving. Instead, she said, "Burgess left a message that he's got Dennis Gamble in custody and he's undergoing tests."

"That's two out of three. We're getting there."

Laura twisted on the seat and glanced out the rear window, making sure the backup cars were still there. After what she'd seen at the Sampas house, she wasn't looking forward to the next encounter, and she definitely wanted to even the odds a little. "How much farther?"

"Two blocks up from Georgetown Commons. We're almost on it."

Homes and small buildings blurred past the window as Press focused on navigating the streets. This late at night, the sidewalks were mostly deserted and traffic was almost nonexistent. Along the sidewalks, lights from a thousand windows were nothing more than wavery bright lines crossing Laura's vision. She cleared her throat. "Let's hope he's not with his fiancé."

Press spun the wheel, making her grab for a handhold. "Reality check, babe. Where else would he be after eleven months of forced abstinence? I just hope we're in time."

"How much far—"

"You already asked me that," Press said grimly. "And we're here."

They threw open the car doors nearly simultaneously and were already headed up the walkway to Patrick Ross's townhouse by the time the other vehicles screeched to a halt behind them. The tri-level townhouse towered above them, the windows dark, no sound filtering through the door.

Laura grimaced. "Oh, this doesn't look good, Press."

Press hammered on the door. "Open up!" he

shouted. He tried the handle for good measure, but of course it was locked. "Federal agents—open the door *now*!"

He waited a few seconds, then stepped to the side and motioned to one of the other agents with a jerk of his head. The townhouse door was made of steel and two men stepped forward and set themselves in position in front of it, one on either side of a handheld battering ram. They steadied themselves against the coming motion, then gave the ram the set-up swings—

One—

Two—

WHAM!

A single blow at the lock area was all it took to send the door slamming into the darkened interior of the foyer. Press stepped over it and inside, slapping at a light switch to the right of the doorjamb. "Patrick Ross?" he yelled. "Are you here?"

No answer. Laura followed as he sprinted up the stairs, intent on finding the master bedroom. God, Laura thought as she saw Press tug his Glock 9mm free of its holster, let us be in time. Please let's not go through this twice in one night.

The townhouse had only two bedrooms, and one was a small room at the top of the stairs that they quickly realized Ross used as a home office. The master bedroom was at the end of the hallway, and the door there was closed.

This time Press didn't bother to knock. He shattered it with one kick and dove inside. Without hesitating, Laura went in after him.

"Oh, my God," she said in dismay. She threw a hand out to support herself against the side of a beautiful golden-pine armoire.

They both stared around the room, gazes probing the corners on the far side of the neatly made bed with its luxurious Southwestern coverlet, touching behind the matching chair, and finally tracking along the dresser and framed photographs arranged next to old college football trophies and sports memorabilia. Everything was neat and clean and in its place.

And utterly empty.

"Christ," Press whispered. "Where the hell is he?"

CHAPTER 12

Even in the summer, nights in the Blue Ridge Mountains could be chilly.

But the fire would take care of that.

Patrick fed another log to the fire, watching as the flames licked along its side. He didn't need the heat, but his fiancée's body temperature tended to be on the cool side. Most of his clothes were already off, so he certainly wasn't in any danger of overheating.

At least not yet.

Patrick turned from the fire and reluctantly went back to the bed where Melissa waited, snuggled beneath a heavy flannel blanket. He climbed under the covers and wished he could find the words to tell her how beautiful she looked, so much so that it made his heart ache. Her eyes looked like transparent amber in the soft light, her hair shone with orange-gold highlights reflected from the blaze across the room, skin as smooth and pink as an unblemished peach, and those lips . . . dusted with the slightest hint of gloss, begging to be kissed. There was no doubt a part of him wanted her very badly.

And that was the part Patrick most feared.

"Melissa," he began, but she reached up and pressed a finger over his mouth.

"Shhhh," she said gently. "It feels like I've been waiting forever to get you alone. All the interviews and the autographs, the screaming girls. All that . . . *hoopla*, finally gone. And as for tonight . . ." Melissa smiled. "Tonight, Patrick Ross, you're all mine."

He tried to say something, but she leaned forward and kissed him warmly. His lips parted of their own will. He felt and tasted her tongue—sweet, like peppermint candy—brush the inside of his mouth. For a long moment, he lost himself in her flavor and the sensation of her kiss, then fear flared in his gut and made him pull away, rougher than he intended as his fingers dug into her upper arms.

Melissa sat up, bewildered. "Patrick, what's the matter?"

"I . . . I don't know." He couldn't, *wouldn't*, look her in the eye. "I think we should, you know, hold off."

"Tonight? For heaven's sake, why?"

Fidgeting on the bed like a nervous schoolboy, Patrick said the only thing he could think of—the *truth*. Surely Melissa, of all the people in the world, would listen to him. "Because I just don't feel that well."

She ran a hand experimentally over his forehead, as though checking a child for a fever, then leaned forward and trailed her lips across the line of his jaw. "There, there." Her voice turned low and silky. "Then let Missy make you all better." Before he could stop her, she wriggled out of his grasp and ducked beneath the sheets.

"Melissa, don't—"

His protest died in mid-syllable as her mouth closed around that most sensitive part of his body and desire blasted through him. He made one last attempt to push her away—

—then Patrick had no choice but to just surrender to everything he felt inside him.

It took only a quarter of an hour, and he never even heard Melissa's screams.

"I demand an explanation," Dennis Gamble said furiously. "You don't just break into a man's house in the middle of the night, drag him off to Monroe Air Force Base without saying why, keep him there for *hours.* And why the hell are there five, *five* guards with loaded rifles aimed at *me*? I'm not armed and I haven't done anything to anyone." He sent a scathing glance toward a couple of the guards who'd been among the raiding party at his home. "Just ask these jamokes!"

"Please calm down, Mr. Gamble." The words came from a white-coated female biologist and were spoken with the air of someone suffering through an unwanted ordeal. Shit, this woman had no idea what an ordeal *was.* He felt a sting as she withdrew what was hopefully the last of the syringes of blood they'd been taking from his arm. Fucking vampires, that's what they were. "We'll have the results in just a few minutes," she continued as she passed a stinging pad of alcohol over the puncture in his arm. "You've waited this long, what's a few more minutes? Hold your finger here."

"A few minutes?" Dennis choked out. His finger dug savagely into the pad on the crook of his elbow. "I have been here for nearly *four fucking hours.* No one will tell me anything, my night is ruined, and my girlfriend is probably going to break up with me because of this. Damn it, I want to know *why* I'm being tested. The NSEG doctor said I was fine!"

From across the room, the stiff military man whom the others had referred to as Colonel Burgess gazed at him placidly. "Just sit tight, son. We'll explain everything later."

"Don't call me *son*," Dennis blared. "And *you* sit tight, you damned jarhead. I haven't been laid in eleven months and you meatheads have probably ensured it'll take another month to get my girl to talk to me again!"

Leaning against the wall was a dark-haired, suave-looking guy who'd introduced himself as Special Agent Preston Lennox—*"Just call me Press"*—when they'd first brought Dennis down to the blood-testing lab. Now he unfolded his arms. "Come on, Burgess. The man's entitled to a reasonable explanation."

"You're damned right I am," Dennis said hotly. "And you can start by telling me what's with these guards. What the hell is going *on*?"

When Burgess stayed stubbornly silent, Press tilted his head. "It's a . . . precautionary measure, that's all. I realize it's a pain in the ass and we screwed up your evening, but if you'll relax and hold on just a little while longer, the computer will analyze your blood and we'll know everything we need to."

"About *what*?"

Press made a game attempt to hide how troubled he was. "I can't really say, not just yet. But in a few minutes . . ."

"Fine," Dennis said sullenly. He made himself lean back on his chair, but couldn't stop his hands from worrying at each other. "But my patience is getting really, really thin."

"Then why don't we pass the time with a few questions," Colonel Burgess suggested. "You can start by telling us what happened during that seven minutes when the *Excursion* lost contact with Mission Control."

Dennis scowled at him. "Is that what this is about? We've been over this a hundred times with the

NSEG, and I don't have anything to tell you that I didn't already tell my superiors."

"Which is?"

"That I don't remember. I must've blacked out. Patrick said the life-support systems failed—maybe we were shorted on oxygen or something. If I knew what happened, I'd tell you. In fact, I'd tell the NSEG and the *world*, but I don't *remember*."

Dennis couldn't decide whether Burgess believed him or not. Instead the colonel asked another question. "When did you last speak to Dr. Anne Sampas?"

"Annie?" They'd spent so much time together he had to stop and think for a second to recall that she was no longer in his life twenty-four hours a day. "That would have been at the NSEG fund-raiser a couple of nights ago. She was there with her husband; we all sat together at Senator Ross's table with him and Patrick and Melissa."

Burgess looked at him oddly and it took Dennis a moment to realize that it was because the man had one glass eye. No wonder this bastard was so creepy. "Did she act peculiar that night?"

Dennis drew himself up, not at all happy about where this conversation was headed. "She seemed fine to me," he said slowly. "What's this about? Did something happen to Annie?"

"You tell me."

Dennis was off his chair and standing before he even realized it. "Enough of this shit!" he yelled. "What happened to Anne Sampas? You tell me right now or I'm walking out that door and you fuckers can just shoot me if you want to stop me. *What the fuck happened to Annie?*"

"Anne Sampas is dead, Dennis." Press crossed his arms. "I'm sorry."

Dead?

"But . . . she was just there," Dennis said in bewilderment. He sagged back onto the chair. *"Damn."*

Before anyone could say anything more, the telephone mounted on the wall next to the door began to ring, the sound more like a rude buzz than a ringing bell. Burgess's expression had turned murderous at Press's admission, but the young agent ignored him and turned instead to answer it.

Dennis didn't know who Press Lennox was talking to, but there was something about the way the guy was looking at him, a set to his expression of thinly disguised suspicion . . .

Seven minutes in space, still unexplained.

And now Annie was dead, and he clearly remembered Melissa saying Patrick hadn't been feeling well.

Oh, this was getting worse all the time.

"Press, is that you?" Laura Baker tucked the telephone receiver between her ear and shoulder, fighting to keep it from sliding off as she flipped through the computer printouts in her hands. Spread on the stainless-steel autopsy table in the center of the medical examiner's laboratory was what remained of Dr. Anne Sampas. Despite the streaks of blood across her skin, the woman's green eyes were clear and staring at the ceiling—for God's sake, why hadn't the Medical Examiner closed them? Instead the moron was blithely poking away at the chasm in the dead woman's belly, not a thought in the world to Anne Sampas's now sightless eyes.

"Yeah, what's up?"

Irritated, Laura turned away from the corpse, focusing instead on the printed information in her hands. "You know, of course, that Anne Sampas's blood work indicates the presence of recombinant alien/human DNA. But it doesn't match with the substance we found in Dr. Orinsky's wounds. Anne Sampas did *not* kill Ralph Orinsky—it was either Ross or Gamble." Press didn't say anything and Laura could picture him, standing in the lab at Monroe and staring at the healthy young black man perhaps only a few feet away. Was he wondering if Gamble was going to undergo some unspeakable transformation? She certainly was. "Press," she said urgently. "Please—be careful."

"Yeah," he said at last. He hung up, leaving her listening to a dial tone and shaking her head.

Laura put the receiver back on its hook and turned to the medical examiner, Mark Lundquist, a youngish guy with premature lines across his forehead and a perpetual squint. He was still energetically moving flaps of skin and dead tentacle tissue around the cadaver's abdomen. The scene reminded Laura of something she'd seen in a science-fiction movie once, where an android had been busily examining the dead shell of an alien parasite. This time, it was the host that had ended up as the dead shell.

"Close her eyes, would you?" Laura snapped. Lundquist looked appropriately ashamed as he cupped one hand and drew the dead woman's eyelids down. "How's it going?" she asked, a little more gently.

"Well, I've examined the torso and pelvic regions. There isn't any sign of external alien incursion. All physiological changes occurred internally, from the cellular level out. Their biology clearly has a protective mechanism that avoids external detection, a very advanced ability to adapt to whatever surroundings it encounters. I'm not sure if it camouflaged itself behind her cells and made itself a part of them until it was . . . well, fertilized."

He sounded both excited and exhausted, and in a way, Laura could understand that. All she had to do was remember back to the days when she'd first become involved in a project like this. And wasn't it funny that the results had once again turned deadly? "There are obviously some fundamental differences in our species, Dr. Lundquist. Human cells place very definite limitations on what we can and cannot do; their physical makeup has an entirely different set of rules."

"It's just so . . . fascinating." He looked over at her, his face full of an enthusiasm that she just couldn't share. Suddenly he glanced from her to the body of Anne Sampas, his expression changing to one of distress. "I-I'm sorry, Dr. Baker. I hope this, the, uh, victim—Dr. Sampas—wasn't a friend of yours."

Laura shook her head, thinking that perhaps there was some hope for this young man after all. "No," she said softly. "I'd never met her." She fell silent for a minute. "But a whole lot of people had, Dr. Lundquist. An entire country, as a matter of fact." He nodded respectfully, and after a pause, Laura squared her shoulders and nodded too, ready to continue.

"All right," Dr. Lundquist said. His voice was more matter-of-fact as he reached up to adjust the overhead microphone for recording, then snapped on a pair of disposable rubber gloves. "Let's find out if there was any alteration to the cranial cavity."

Laura braced herself—she'd always hated this part of an autopsy the most—as Dr. Lundquist first brushed the corpse's hair forward, then lowered the bone saw to the midpoint of the skull. Even the sound—that high-pitched whirring, the grind of the saw cutting into human bone—she detested it. So much so that—

The body screamed.

No, not true—Anne Sampas was as dead as she'd been when they'd shrouded her body at her home and brought it here earlier this evening. Something else was . . . *wailing*, and between that and the scream of the bone saw and the terrified shrieks of Dr. Lundquist, Laura didn't know who or what was making which noise.

As she grabbed for the vibrating saw in Lundquist's hands she saw something hideous and black spew from Anne Sampas's mouth. Long like an eel, the ribbon of flesh twisted and slid back down, then twisted again, all the time making that ear-rending, nightmarish noise. Some kind of alien afterbirth. The third time it lurched upward, Laura jabbed forward with all her might and met the slimy limb end to end with the bone saw.

Tarlike sludge and pieces of pulverized alien flesh flew everywhere, splattering Laura and Lundquist, the body, the walls and ceiling. Lundquist reeled away, retching, but Laura held her position, pressing her mouth shut and grinding away at the stuff bubbling from Anne Sampas's mouth, grinding and

grinding and

grinding . . .

Until it was simply no more than dead, black slime melting down the walls of the M.E.'s laboratory.

"Why are you looking at me like that?" demanded Dennis. "Who were you just talking to?"

"No one important," Press answered. But Dennis knew he was lying, could see it in the set of the man's jaw and the way his eyes had narrowed when they focused on him.

"Relax, Mr. Gamble," said one of the biology technicians moving around the lab. At least this one hadn't jabbed him with a syringe. "It'll be just a few more seconds and we'll have everything we need to know."

Dennis ignored the biologist and turned his attention to Colonel Burgess. "About Annie," he said, "what was the cause of death?"

Burgess stared at him for a second. "We don't know," was all he would finally say.

Shit, Dennis thought. Another liar—this place is infested with them. "Come on, give me some information here—how did she die? She was my friend and I have a right to know." When Burgess just stared at him without answering, Dennis felt his fists curl up in frustration.

"The sequence is almost complete," said the biology technician from her place at a computer console a few feet away.

Dennis glanced at her, then began to frown. "Wait a minute," he said slowly. His eyes felt red and sore, itchy from exhaustion. Fury was making him sweat, making water collect along his forehead and under the arms of his shirt. "I think I get it now. I don't know what happened to her, but I think I've figured out why you're taking my blood. You fuckers think *I* did it—"

"Data retrieval is on line," said the biologist.

To Dennis her voice sounded flat and dangerous, like some sort of automated assassin. That's probably what all these men were, Lennox included—assassins. Well, they could jam their guns up their backsides if they thought Dennis Gamble was going down without a fight for something he didn't do. "I did *not* kill Annie," he snarled at the same time he sprang from the chair. He registered with a sort of detached, careless alarm that the guards in the room, every damned one of them, had instantly leveled their weapons at him. And what *were* those anyway? Not all the standard issue M-16s, but some kind of spray-nozzle rigged canisters that reminded him of flamethrowers. "I'm *leaving*."

"Halt," ordered the guards' leader. His finger was twitching against the trigger of a rifle rather than one of the spray canisters. "You freeze where you are or we'll fire—"

"Now just hold on, Dennis," Press said hastily. He held out a hand in an imploring gesture, planting himself bodily between Dennis and the guard. "If you'll just stay calm—"

"I said I'm *leaving*—"

"Wait! The computer says he's normal," the technician suddenly blared. "He's normal—there's no sign of infection!"

For a single, endless moment, no one moved.

"Infected with *what*?" Dennis shrilled.

Press gestured at the guards and they lowered their weapons, sending him nervous, slightly ashamed smiles while Burgess, that rat-souled son of a bitch, had the balls to give him a fatherly pat on the shoulder. "Go on home, son," he said. "Get some rest."

"I told you—I am not your *son*. And I deserve some fucking answers!"

Burgess seemed unaffected by Dennis's outburst. "You'll have them in due time. We'll be in touch."

" 'We'll be in *touch*,' " Dennis sneered back at him. "That's the best you can come up with after all this shit?" It was all he could do to keep from spitting on the military man looking impassively back at him. "How close did you come to killing me just now, you bastard?" Burgess didn't reply and finally Dennis gave up, sent them all a disgusted look, and headed for the door on the other side of the laboratory.

"Hold on a second, Dennis," Press said suddenly.

He turned back and glowered at the special agent. "What?"

Press's gaze was calm and cool. "Do you have *any* idea where we can find Patrick Ross?"

Dennis hesitated, then said, "No."

Press studied his fingers for a minute. "You're a longtime friend of Patrick's," he said quietly. "And I know you wouldn't want anything to happen to him. So if you hear from him, please—let us know."

Dennis gave him a mistrustful look. "Yeah," he said. "Sure I will. You'll all be the *first*." He stalked out, not believing or caring about the desperation he heard in Press Lennox's next words to Burgess—

"We have to find Ross."

Did he know where Patrick and Melissa were? You bet he did.

Was he going to tell those assholes?

In a fucking blue moon.

CHAPTER 13

Patrick stretched and smiled, feeling a pleasant shaft of sunlight creep through the part in the cabin's curtains and cross his face. Warm and satisfied—God, he felt *great*, like he was on top of the world. It was a brand-new day. Even the political ambitions of his father didn't bother him this morning, not here in the privacy of the family's cabin in the mountains and lying next to the woman he loved. His smile widened and with his eyes still closed he reached out one arm, intent on pulling Melissa's sleeping form closer to him.

Wet.

His eyelids flew open and he jerked upright as he saw her, or rather, what was *left* of her.

"Missy?" Her name came out of his throat as a painful rasp. "My God, did I . . ." Patrick's voice trailed off as he tried to reconcile the memory of his sweet, beautiful Melissa, his high-school sweetheart and the woman who would've been his wife, with the silent, blood-drenched person lying beside him. What had happened? His last memory was of them making love, joined together and him hot and pleasurable inside her. He'd been climaxing, and she right along with him, and then—

Nothing.

Another blackout, another piece of his life gone that could not be explained. So many of those lately—twice the night of the NSEG fund-raising banquet, and that hadn't even been the first. And each time waking at home or, like here, somewhere safe, knowing nothing about the lost hours except his own dark suspicions that he must have somehow done something unspeakable. And now, finally, the undeniable proof.

Patrick sobbed and lifted his dead fiancée into his arms. He rocked her for a while and stroked her hair, not caring about the blood and ragged flaps of flesh from the horrible, inexplicable hole in Melissa's stomach, mindful only that she should have been warm and full of life and she wasn't. Whatever had happened, it was most certainly of his own doing. After a time, his crying dried up. He just sat there, numb and disbelieving, without a clue about what to do now.

Staring into space and thinking only about old memories—so many good ones—Patrick almost missed it when something moved at the foot of the bed.

"Who's there?" he demanded suddenly. He felt hot and feverish, and he hoped to God he was dying. Somehow he didn't think he was going to be that lucky. The response to his voice was a ghastly, liquid-sounding cry that made Patrick's eyes widen and clutch Missy's body closer to him in a belated gesture of protection. He strained forward, trying to see—

—but couldn't believe it when he did.

A *creature* of some kind was sitting on the floor

down there, something brown and black with a multitude of soft, flailing limbs and a mewling, babyish wail. Something less than human but with the vague bone structure of an infant . . .

The child of his union with the lovely, dead Melissa.

"No!" Patrick shrieked. He let go of Melissa's body and flung himself out of bed, registering too late that he'd pushed her too roughly and now, adding to the horror of the thing that was hissing and trying to waddle toward him, the girl he'd loved his entire life was sliding off the bed like so much unwanted meat. It was too much—*way* too much—and the best that Patrick Ross, America's greatest hero, could do in this moment of complete and utter madness was to scream and retreat to the cabin's bathroom, and barricade himself inside.

It wasn't so hard to deal with.

He climbed in the shower and watched the smears of Melissa's blood on his skin melt away under an onslaught of soap and hot water. He washed his hair, scrubbed his nails, and after he'd toweled himself completely dry, brushed and flossed his teeth. Then he stepped out of the bathroom, stoically ignoring the gurgling noises coming from the gnarled baby-thing still on the floor at the foot of the bed. When he was fully dressed, he took a deep breath and went back to the bed, carefully averting his eyes as he covered Melissa with a clean sheet, wishing he'd moved a little faster when her blood soaked through the cotton before he could turn away. The crimson stain on the fabric reminded him of a crushed heart.

Then Patrick went across the room and looked for a long time at the object hanging above the fireplace before finally taking it down and inspecting it.

The shotgun had been his Grandfather Ross's, a Browning Superposed over/under shotgun that had once literally helped put the food on the table. It was a little dusty but everything else about it looked, at least to Patrick's unpracticed eye, in working condition. He knew where the shells were, and when he retrieved them from their corner in the back of one of the kitchen cupboards, he stood and watched the grisly creature watch him, fancied he could see it growing and changing even as each long minute passed, becoming more and more the human form behind which it would hide, as he himself had done.

When he was through looking at it, Patrick went out onto the porch and closed the door behind him, then sat down on the old creaking porch swing his father had put up when Patrick was just a boy. The sun was out, dappling the lush greenery of the trees around the cabin and the wildflower clusters that lined the fence that surrounded the property. He could hear birds singing somewhere out of sight, summer insects buzzing and doing whatever insects did in the cooler temperatures of mid-morning.

The baby-beast inside sort of reminded him of an insect.

Patrick sighed and kicked absently at a loose board on the porch. No matter what was inside of him or what had been born because of him—that monstrosity in the cabin—he, the *true* Patrick Ross, was not a killer. The things he'd done were at the hand of something that had control over him—for God's sake, he couldn't even shoot that sniveling little blot of flesh that had destroyed Melissa with its birth. Yet there was no doubt in his mind that these things—the blackouts and the life-form in the bedroom and *Melissa*—would continue if he didn't take charge of the situation. And Patrick Ross, by God, was a take-charge kind of guy.

He turned the gun around and put both barrels in his mouth.

* * *

Dennis would have rammed the fence if he'd realized what he was looking at when he stomped the brakes and ground his Explorer to a stop outside of Grandfather Ross's mountain cabin.

Instead, he climbed out and waved away the dust kicked up by the tires, wishing he hadn't done that because now he'd have to get the Ford washed. He tried the gate but it was locked, one of those annoying little push-pull latches that for some reason, he—a man who could steer a spaceship, for crying out loud—always had to fight with. He was fumbling with it when he heard the familiar creaking of the porch swing; he'd sat on it countless times over the last five years and recognized the noise instantly, as he also recognized Patrick. His friend was sitting on the swing, and all Dennis could see of him was his back, and he was mildly surprised that Patrick hadn't turned around when he'd heard the noise of the truck.

"Hey, Patrick!" he yelled. "Wait'll you hear what I had to go through last ni—"

The blast of a gun tore apart the back of Patrick's head.

The noise blotted out everything—the birdsong in the trees, the myriad sounds of summer in the forest, Dennis's own *heartbeat.* For a short span of forever he couldn't make himself move or breathe, then—

"Oh, shit—Patrick! Patrick, no, you didn't—"

—adrenaline slammed through him and he vaulted over the waist-high fence as though it was only two inches high. He made it to the porch so quickly that the swing and Patrick's body were still swaying

creak

creak

creak

gently beneath the force of the blast. Beneath Patrick's legs was the old Browning over/under, covered in blood and pieces of something that Dennis couldn't bring himself to acknowledge.

"God," Dennis choked. Instinctively he reached a hand toward his friend, although he had no idea if he could actually bring himself to touch Patrick's body. His fingers were only an inch from Patrick's hair when Dennis finally understood what he was seeing and he yanked his hand away.

Patrick's head was . . . *healing.*

"Impossible," Dennis whispered. He backstepped once, then couldn't stop himself from leaning forward and watching in unwilling fascination as the vast damage to his best friend's head began to disappear beneath a frenzy of regeneration. Such a strange sight—the flesh-and-bone matter knitting together, the pink-gray brain morphing back like some kind of repulsive video game—

Dennis ran.

Thinking back on it later, he would remember seeing Patrick sit up on the porch swing and look straight at him, injury-free and oblivious to the blood soaking through his shirt and the pieces of what should have been his skull lying all over the porch—he'd somehow grown *new* flesh, not reused the old. Dennis thought he might have even said something to Patrick—

"How?"

—though he couldn't recall for certain, but Patrick had looked right through him, hadn't heard a word. No recognition, no acknowledgment, no . . . *humanness,* not quite plugged into the world yet.

He went over the fence with a lot less grace than the first time, tumbling to the outside of it and landing hard on his hind end before clawing his way up and into the driver's side of the Explorer. He churned road dust for a quarter-mile and the vehicle skidded from one side of the road to the other in his haste to get the hell out of there.

But that was all right. He needed the dust; maybe concentrating on seeing through it would obscure something else . . . like the sight of his best friend coming back to life and staring right through him as though he hadn't been there.

There was one thing he'd seen that hadn't healed in Patrick though, and no amount of spinning of tires or beating up dust or tears of regret would take the memory out of Dennis's mind. He just couldn't shake the impression of *deadness* that had remained in Patrick's cold, cold blue eyes.

The old Patrick Ross's time had come and gone, and now the greatest and latest of American heroes was a changed being. Not quite a man anymore, but redefined, *more.* A healthy, excellent moving vessel for the life-form that now inhabited his body, and oh, what a body that was—a new, improved version that would carry the seed of a new species throughout this warm welcoming new planet. All the right memories were there, the language and human functions, but now they had merged with the skills and resources, the *superiority,* of something so much bigger and older . . . better educated.

He was still Patrick Ross inside, oh yeah. Space explorer, astronaut, superb American citizen—he even *liked* himself once again. No more doubts about himself and what was happening to him, no more worries about trivial details like Melissa or stupid NSEG fund-raisers. This Commander Patrick Ross was bigger and better, and he could conquer the world.

All he needed was a few weeks.

"Hey mister, you lookin' for a date?"

It was a dirty neighborhood in the northwest part of the city where the darkness was split by the gaudy, buzzing shine of multicolored neon. Only a few blocks over were high-rent office buildings that housed men and women with six- and seven-figure incomes—D.C. was funny that way. The prostitute peering through the driver's window was thin and pretty, painfully young. The main thing was that she was healthy, and the Mercedes SL drew her like it'd drawn all the others so far tonight:

Like flies to sticky, deadly honey.

CHAPTER 14

"I can't believe I'm here," Dennis Gamble said. "I don't think I'm even describing what I saw very well—and you probably don't believe me anyway." He paused and looked at them helplessly. "But I knew this was something that . . . not just anyone should know. And because of Annie's death, I just didn't know where else to turn."

"You made the right decision," Laura said soothingly. She offered him a glass of water, then watched as he drank gratefully. "And you'd be surprised at what we'll believe."

"Why don't you tell us again what happened?" Burgess asked from his spot over by the viewing window. Laura shot him a look—

Be patient!

—but he didn't see it. His gaze was locked on the laboratory floor below, tracking every move the biology crew made as they tended to Eve and kept ongoing records of her vitals.

Dennis, however, seemed to have lost any animosity he'd had toward the colonel. "It won't be different this time," he said. "I saw Patrick commit suicide, and the only way he could've done it was by sticking the business end of his grandfather's shotgun in his mouth and squeezing the trigger. I was right there when the back of his head just . . . *exploded.* It was like when you drop a bottle on the floor and it shatters—his hair, blood, his b-brains—" For a second Dennis choked up, Laura offered the water glass again; this time, he waved it away and stubbornly kept going. "It went all over," he finally continued.

"But you say he's alive now?" Press was standing to the side, his face dark and troubled. "With no wounds to show where he was injured—nothing?"

Dennis shook his head and held on to the side of his chair like a man afraid he was going to fall off. "He was more than just injured. He was *dead*—the whole back of his skull was blown away." He stopped and blinked for a second, as though trying to shake away the recollection. "God, I was so scared—who's ever seen anything as crazy as that? It's like he just sort of . . . grew another one."

"Well," Laura said slowly, trying to be mindful of Dennis. "We've always known that the alien species had the ability to regenerate living tissue—"

"This isn't exactly a chameleon's tail we're talking about," Press reminded her. "This is the brain of a man."

"But with the characteristics of an alien about which we know next to nothing. A species that is quite possibly billions of years old and could have developed a sort of nano-physiology that enables it to 'think' in some manner with virtually every cell in its body. Clearly it has successfully merged its DNA with that of its host—Patrick Ross—and can now control it in every respect. They've become one creation."

On his chair, Dennis Gamble lowered his face to his hands. "Aliens," he said bitterly. "I still can't believe it. I remember Annie warning Patrick about little green men when he went down to the surface of Mars. 'Watch out for little green men,' she said." The astronaut laughed, but it wasn't a happy sound. "At the time, Patrick said they'd most likely be red. Guess he didn't realize he'd be predicting the future." He studied the floor, as if certain that the answers could be found somewhere on the sanitized white tiles. "If they knew there were aliens up there, why the fuck did they send us?"

"The NSEG was warned," Press said flatly. "They chose to ignore it."

"You're way off base," Burgess cut in harshly. "There was never any solid evidence to support that theory."

Laura stopped the argument with a pointed clearing of her throat. "Nevertheless, we believe there may have been hostile DNA in the soil samples that Patrick collected and brought back on board the *Excursion*."

Dennis raised his head. "You know," he said after a few seconds' lag, "I think something did happen up there. But I can't remember exactly what—it's like a bad dream that you don't recall when you wake up. You know it was there, but now it's just a . . . fading, terrible echo in your head. That's what this was like."

Burgess pulled a tiny bottle of Visine from his pocket and unscrewed the cap. A quick flick of his wrist put a drop in his good eye. "I'm sure it *was* terrible," he agreed in his tone, insufferably condescending. It was clear that he had heard, processed in his mind, and already dismissed Dennis Gamble's tale. "The question is, how do we proceed from here?"

Press rubbed his chin. "I've got surveillance agents on top of every possible place Ross might go. Maybe Dennis here can give us a few other leads."

"How long?" Burgess asked.

Press shrugged. "It could take hours to find him," he answered. Then, more ominously, "Or days."

Laura's fingers tapped her clipboard nervously as she gazed at the three men. "That's not good. If he's reproducing, we have the potential for offspring—"

"This son-of-a-bitching alien has control of a man who was just voted by *People* magazine as 'America's Sexiest Man Alive.' " Press snorted. "And we learned the alien mindset the last time we went through this—breeding is their main objective. I think we can assume he's out there reproducing."

"Wait," Dennis said. "I don't understand—what I saw was frightening, sure. But he didn't *do* anything—"

"Oh, he's done plenty," Burgess said. "The bodies are piling up by the day."

"You're saying Patrick is a murderer?" Dennis asked in disbelief.

"Not Patrick," Laura reminded him as gently as she could. "It's what's inside him—it controls him and makes him do things we all know he would never want to on his own."

"But who has he killed?"

"The two we can prove so far include his fiancée and Dr. Ralph Orinsky," said Colonel Burgess.

"He killed *Melissa*?"

An entire range of emotions played across Dennis Gamble's face and Laura sent a dirty look toward Burgess. "How good of you to break the news so gently, Colonel."

Burgess only shrugged. "I'm not here for niceties, Dr. Baker. Let's just get on with it."

She could think of nothing to say in response to such a lack of feeling, so she focused on finding and slipping a binder from its place next to one of the computers. She could feel all three men watching her as she flipped through the pages, then she verified what she'd been thinking. "These creatures go through their first juvenile stage in less than two weeks," she told them. "Then they enter the chrysalis stage—"

"Chrysalis stage?" Dennis interrupted. His face looked ashen, as though he'd absorbed just about all he could take. "You mean like a . . . butterfly?"

Laura didn't respond right away, then she nodded. "I suppose you could make that comparison, since it *is* a cocoon phase. I think we'd all agree that what emerges isn't nearly the same lovely work of nature that mankind is used to seeing. The problem is . . ." Her voice trailed off.

Press snapped to attention. "What?"

Laura looked over to Burgess, wanting to make sure the colonel was fully listening. She took a deep breath. "The problem is that this information is based on Sil and Eve, not on Patrick Ross's offspring. We've already seen a massive deviation in the sense that the alien DNA literally *invaded* the cells of two human beings of its own volition. It's clearly the stronger cellular material, and introduced in this manner, it functions entirely differently."

Burgess glowered at her. "What are you try to tell us, Dr. Baker?"

"That we have absolutely no basis on which to assume that if—or maybe I should say *when*—the alien that Patrick Ross has become successfully breeds, it's going to take two weeks for the offspring to reach maturity. We might be safe in predicting a chrysalis stage, but rate of changeover within that period might be only *hours*."

"Shit on a stick," Press said crudely. "We've got

to issue a public warning before this goes too far—''

Burgess's voice cracked across the room. ''What planet are you on, Lennox?'' He yanked a handkerchief from his pocket and swabbed at his eye. ''If you think I'm going to allow you to start a full-scale panic, you're crazier than I've always thought you were. Patrick Ross was—*is*—a national hero. The President's approval ratings are through the roof right now because of his endorsement of the Mars exploration program, and he'll go berserk if we publicly accuse Ross of murder.''

''I don't give a flying fuck about the President's approval ratings!'' Press yelled back. He looked ready to leap on top of the older man. ''If you don't use public communication to pull this man in right now—radio, television, APBs, and plastering his photograph all over everything—a lot more innocent people are going to die. And it's going to be on your head besides.''

But Colonel Burgess's return gaze was frosty. ''No respect for the chain of command has always been a problem with you, Lennox. The most I can do on my end is to discreetly contact his father. I've already done that, and let me tell you—he was not at all pleased to discover that we're looking for Patrick, especially when I chose not to disclose why—especially the part about the murders. He made it quite clear that Patrick has probably gone off by himself in an attempt to relax and get away from the constant crowds. As I recall, he specifically said he wasn't his son's 'babysitter.'

''As for the rest of it, you have my orders—you will *not* involve the media in any way at all. Use whatever resources are necessary to bring Ross in, but do it without attracting any attention. Do I make myself clear?'' He turned his back and headed toward the door.

"Colonel Burgess, wait." Laura stepped in front of him, resisting the impulse to grab him by the collar and drive her facts home. "I don't think you fully understand what we're dealing with here. You've had access to the records, read all the files—this man is thinking like Sil did. He has a biological imperative to mate—instinctively, that's his entire function. Sil was uneducated and a complete stranger to human ways, yet she managed to do just that *and* give birth before we were luckily able to stop her."

Burgess's face remained impassive. "Do you have a point here, or do you just like telling me things I already know?"

For a moment Laura couldn't speak as all her thoughts went a sort of hazy red. "The point, you stuffed-up old *fool*, is that Patrick Ross knows everything about this world that Sil didn't. He doesn't have to learn to drive a car, count money, or *fit in.* He already knows how. We are running out of time to stop him—*if we're not already too late.*"

The colonel stepped around her and pulled open the door. "Then tell Lennox to earn his million and find the son of a bitch."

Residents in the Washington-Maryland area are being warned by local law enforcement that a serial killer may be on the loose. Over the last few days, six victims, all female, have been found, ranging from two well-known young women who frequented the upper echelon of the Washington, D.C. social circuit to those the police termed as northwest-area prostitutes. The Medical Examiner's Office reports that all of the bodies were horribly mutilated. There is apparently no motive for the killings and no connection between the victims. The police department is advising all women to take extra precautions until the killer is caught. Travel with a companion at all times and avoid areas where you might be alone. Above all, authorities are warning that you should proceed with extreme caution if you are approached by a stranger.

"How much for a room?" Patrick asked the hotel clerk.

"Twenty an hour," the guy grated, never taking his eyes from the television broadcast. The sound was on too loud but that was good; the man probably wouldn't remember his voice.

Patrick glanced at the screen and recognized the photographs showing there as the two women from the Watergate Hotel the other night. He smiled, then put sixty dollars on the counter. The man's gaze flicked to the money and he reached out a grimy hand and snatched it up; an instant later he slid a set of keys toward Patrick and his date.

The old elevator screeched as it rose. Patrick and the woman climbed out of it on the fifth floor. This place was as seedy as they came, but it made no difference to Patrick as long as the key he held in his hand—Room 505—would open the right room and give him the privacy he needed with this prostitute. The room itself was dingy and probably not very clean, but Patrick didn't bother to turn on the lights. This woman was taller than average with platinum-blond hair billowing around a square-jawed face. Her lips were full and pouty and she smiled as she grabbed his hand and pulled him toward the bed. "You look like someone I've seen on television," she said. "This ought to be real good."

Her hand was hot around his, but it felt . . . *wrong.* Patrick stiffened and backed up before the hooker could wrap her tanned arms around him. "Hey," she said, but her voice had lost an edge of confidence it'd had only moments before. "What's wrong, honey?"

He studied her, trying to fathom what was missing here. He felt no desire to touch her, no imperative to breed with her. He didn't even—

Patrick's eyes narrowed but he smiled as he extended his hand to touch that gorgeous head of white-blond hair. She returned the smile, obviously relieved, and leaned toward him so he could stroke her hair; when she was close enough, Patrick twined his fingers in it, then gave it a good, hard yank.

It came off in his hands.

A wig—

—and suddenly all sorts of explanations and protests were coming from the mouth of the man who'd duped him into coming up here. "Hey, come on now. You're a handsome guy, and ain't I a good-looking piece? I mean, fun's fun, right? I'm as good as any girl—better even." The guy reached for the clasp on Patrick's slacks. "Just let me show you. We'll start right here, and I promise you'll forget about the whole man/woman thing inside of ten seconds, okay? It's all just fun, right?"

"Fun," Patrick agreed as he, too, reached out.

He didn't care about the sixty bucks, he thought as he slipped out the back entrance of the hotel less than two minutes later. But it was a damned shame to lose a good three hours' worth of privacy in that hotel room.

"I don't like this," Laura said. "And I don't like not knowing what the hell it means."

She was standing before the main monitoring system on the laboratory floor, staring across at the habitat and its occupant. Inside the glass-walled sleeping area, Eve was thrashing on her bed; her eyes were closed and she might or might not have been sleeping, but they couldn't tell that from the equipment readouts. In fact, Laura thought they were lucky that the alien woman hadn't unwittingly yanked every one of the electrodes off.

"See what I mean, Dr. Baker?" asked Brea. "It's all in our reports. Every so often, all her signals go berserk. Heart rate, blood pressure, respiration—even her temperature."

"You know," Vikki began. "Ah, never mind."

"What?" Laura asked.

The younger woman's cheeks turned pink. "Never mind. It's probably a stupid idea—no basis in fact whatsoever."

"Let's hear it anyway. I'm open to anything right now."

Vikki's face turned even redder. "Well, the way she's moving, kind of bucking like that. It's . . . it's almost like she's dreaming about having an orgasm."

Laura considered this for a moment, then frowned and turned back to watch Eve. She'd quieted in these last few seconds and her vitals, although still high, were slowly sinking back to normal. An orgasm?

Yeah, that's exactly what it had looked like.

Patrick watched the woman on the stage very carefully.

Another tall one—he seemed to prefer them that way, although he didn't know why. This girl had long chestnut-colored hair, and the way she was tossing her head back and forth during her sexy dance around the silver pole in the center of the stage made him pretty sure it was all her own. Her outfit was gone as she stripped down to a red-satin G-string. Slender and lithe, the gal had generous breasts with big dark nipples, but Patrick wasn't stupid; plenty of gays went for silicone implants nowadays. At least the fabric that dipped between the inviting vee of her legs was smooth and tight-fitting, but in this day and age, that didn't mean anything either.

Just in case, Patrick leaned forward across the narrow bar that surrounded the round platform on which she danced. It wasn't long before he caught her eye, and her gaze went quicker still to the hundred-dollar bill folded lengthwise in his fingers. He gestured with it and she did a slinky little triple-step that put her swaying hips only two feet from his face, twisting and turning like a snake to give him the best possible view of everything. He waited until her twisting had slowed and she was facing him, then reached forward and motioned with the money. She thrust out her pelvis obligingly and he slipped the hundred-dollar bill, along with his first two fingers, far down the front of the tiny piece of fabric she wore. She quivered and he pulled his hand away and looked up at her, feeling a hot surge of desire as she gazed at him and licked her lips, gave a little nod of her head that promised more when her dance was over.

No mistakes this time.

"Special agents, huh?" The room clerk looked at Press and Laura with keen interest. "Since when does some fag hooker getting hisself offed warrant a visit from bigwigs like you?"

"I'd just like to know if you saw the guy he went upstairs with," Press said with exaggerated patience.

The look the clerk gave him said clearly that he thought Press was an idiot for even asking. "They come and go." His dirty fingernails tapped the counter and he gave them a nasty grin showing teeth coated with the residue of what was probably a week's worth of meals. The T-shirt and jeans he wore surely hadn't seen a washing machine in a month. "All day long. Know what I mean?"

"I think we can figure it out," Laura said dryly and glanced at Press. "Let's go. There's absolutely nothing here that will tell us anything about him." She shot a withering look at the desk clerk, who just returned it with a sneer. "We're better off out in the field."

She waited until they were outside the ratty little hotel before she exhaled and gripped Press's arm. "We've got to find him, Press. We've *got* to. We have no idea what's he's doing, what the maturity rate of the offspring is if he's already mated, nothing. Because Anne Sampas was a woman, we can't even use what happened to her as a reliable model for what Patrick might be doing, and obviously we killed the offspring from that birth. For God's sake, Ross could be fathering twins or triplets or worse.

"Press, every hour that passes could put us closer to it just being too damned *late.*"

Another shallow grave in the darkness of the pasture beyond the old barn.

Patrick didn't recall how many graves he'd dug back here—three or four, or perhaps it was ten—and he didn't care. There were other graves, too, scattered around the property, but they and their numbers were also inconsequential. The only things that mattered were waiting for him in the barn right now. Beyond them was the soul-deep urge to mate, and beyond that . . .

Nothing.

He tamped the dirt in place with his foot, then picked up his flashlight and scanned the dense brush around him. After a minute, he found what he was looking for and held out his hand; the child, this one a girl, was already close to three human years old and she came to him eagerly, wanting nothing more in the world than to be close to her father and protector. When Patrick led her to the barn and took her inside, his daughter joined her brothers and sisters—nearly a dozen of them—in waiting for the next wondrous stage in their lives. He'd brought them plenty of food and water, made sure they wanted for nothing. Now it was just a matter of time. Meanwhile—

—the rest of the world awaited.

Chapter 15

"If what you told me the last time we were in this laboratory is true, Dr. Baker, then the people of this planet could already be in dire danger. That was two days ago and Lennox doesn't even have a lead on Patrick Ross—no one has the first suggestion as to where to find this man, the body count is rising, and more women turn up missing every day. We're wasting valuable time and Lennox hasn't been able to make headway."

I am not a violent woman, thought Laura Baker as she endured Colonel Carter Burgess's speech, but if I could drop this man into a pond full of piranhas, I would. Him *and* his "Pentagon Three" cohorts, who had also decided to grace her lab with their presence this morning. Aloud she said, "Maybe that's because you and your high-powered committee here won't let him use the media to reach the public. If he could do that—"

Burgess's cold gaze stopped her in mid-sentence.

"We've had this conversation before. As I said, we're wasting time."

"Dr. Baker," said one of the generals, "you mentioned during our previous visit that you believed Eve has telepathic abilities." To Laura, the man's round face looked innocent and bland, completely untrustworthy in a way she couldn't really identify.

"Well . . . yes, there's some indication of that." Why did she suddenly have a very bad feeling about where this conversation was headed?

"Can we send her after Patrick Ross?" Of course the question came from the second of the group—these three strange men seemed to run in the same unspoken cycle. Maybe they were all connected somehow, little governmental cyborgs on the same transmission frequency.

Laura blinked at him, then turned her head and saw Eve watching them from her habitat. The outside walls of the alien woman's living space were quartz glass and nearly thirty yards away from where she and Burgess's nasty little entourage were talking, and all the intercoms were off. But was it possible Eve could hear what they were saying anyway?

Who knew?

Laura had no choice but to answer. "It would be complete foolishness to take Eve out of this controlled atmosphere. You must remember that before Colonel Burgess contaminated everything by coming in here with Press, Eve's only knowledge of the outside world came from television. This included contact with males. From a psychological point of view, her human side would tend to view what she sees on the screen as a fantasy—that is, something that doesn't really exist. Despite the unfortunate previous intrusion of Colonel Burgess and Press Lennox and the presence of yourselves in here today, Eve has never physically *touched* a man. To show her the rest of the world and therefore allow her to do so is potentially lethal."

One of the men started to say something, but Laura cut him off. "There is also the very real danger of her escaping. If this were to happen, we would have two aliens to deal with instead of one. We already know that the aliens have a biological imperative to reproduce. You can bet that they'll also have an inborn drive to find each other to do so." She gestured at the data scrolling continuously along the monitor screens on the main console. "It's quite clear that human DNA cannot and will not be the victor in any sort of cellular match against the alien DNA. An infant born as the result of Eve mating with Patrick Ross could very well end up with all the human DNA completely repressed—a 'pure' alien, if you will. The resulting offspring might be unstoppable."

"I don't believe you answered my question, Dr. Baker," said the second general quietly. His eyes suddenly reminded her of a snake's—small and flat, and completely devoid of warmth. "Can we send her after Patrick Ross?"

Laura gritted her teeth. "In so many words, sir, I believe I did. The answer to your question is *no.* We cannot 'send' Eve after Patrick Ross, because she cannot be allowed outside the walls of this laboratory. To release her would be so hazardous as to be utterly out of the question."

Silence while they considered this, then Burgess asked the question that Laura had been dreading:

"Can she tell us where he is without leaving the facility?"

Laura bit her bottom lip, but she had to tell them the truth; any cursory glance at her notes on the computer would show a fabrication instantly. "We have seen a . . . spiking in her biorhythms that could possibly indicate the existence of a rudimentary connection to something we can't identify," she admitted. "There isn't any way to tell for sure because half of her alien genes are dormant, intentionally repressed by genetic manipulation when we created her. Whatever connection she may have right now isn't controllable or deliberate. Tracking another person—or another alien—would be out of her league."

"Dormant is nothing but a technical term for asleep," Colonel Burgess said levelly. "I suggest we simply wake them up. I assume you have the means to do so."

A question, not a statement, and again Laura had no alternative but to be truthful. "We do have certain equipment," she said with reluctance. "The lab cyclotron could be reprogrammed to bombard her with radiation. In all probability, this would stimulate the alien genes enough to revive them. But . . ."

"What?" The third general, right on cue.

"Well, for heaven's sake," she exploded. "Isn't it obvious? Doing this will reawaken in Eve everything we've worked so hard to suppress—the alien side of her, incredible physical strength, her mating drive. We repressed all of these impulses so that we could maintain control over an alien life-form that is completely capable of besting us. Did any of you actually *hear* what I told you just a few seconds ago?" Laura gestured angrily at the female life-form still standing at the glass of her enclosure at the other end of the massive room, still watching them with extreme interest. "Colonel Burgess, have you ever stopped to think that when she 'wakes up,' as you so handily put it, she might just be a wee bit disturbed by the fact that we've kept her imprisoned in a damned glass box for her entire life?"

For a moment no one spoke; then Burgess and the first two men looked to the third member of their group. "We appreciate your concern, Dr. Baker," said the third man. His voice was quiet, but suddenly Laura knew who truly had the say-so in this room. "But the results in this matter—the opportunity to locate and eliminate Patrick Ross—are worth the risk." His sharp eyes scanned the laboratory, recording everything, no doubt already planning the upgrades. "We'll tighten security, of course."

"Oh, of course," Laura mimicked. She slammed her clipboard on the countertop. "You know this isn't a laboratory animal we're talking about here, and the process you're demanding isn't just an unpleasant little prick in the arm with a syringe. This process is irreversible. This life-form is half human and the radiation is going to *hurt.*" Frustration made her dig her fingers into her arms. "She has human feelings—"

"Please," interrupted Colonel Burgess. "Spare us the 'alien rights' agenda, Dr. Baker. Use the . . . what did you call it? The cyclotron. Do whatever it takes."

She glared at him, wanting very badly to slap that lop-eyed, power-happy leer right off his face. "And if I refuse?"

Burgess lifted his chin knowingly. "That is obviously your prerogative as a civilian employee, Dr. Baker. You know, of course, that there are other staff members in the facility who have skills more or less equivalent to yours." The colonel spun and stepped into place behind his three colleagues, who were already headed for the exit. He didn't bother to turn around to say his last words:

"Either way, Dr. Baker, it's going to happen. It's only a matter of who's in charge of the procedure."

Before Colonel Burgess and Press had come into the laboratory and corrupted the atmosphere, there had been a certain innocence to Eve, a simplicity of thinking that was charming and unexpected in a fully grown woman. That quality had disappeared when Eve had gotten her first scent of a man, and if there was anything left of it at all, buried somewhere deep inside the lovely girl who stood before her now, Laura was convinced that what she was about to do would destroy it forever. What was worse, she, with her degrees and her education and all her damned *science,* didn't know how to tell Eve what she was about to ask. All she could do was stand in front of Eve and stare at the floor, struggling to find the words.

"It's all right, Laura. You don't have to be afraid. I know . . . what they want." Eve's face was open and accepting. *Resigned.*

How had she known? There was no other way to explain it but that she must have heard every horrid word of that argument between Laura and Burgess and his cronies. "I-I'm sorry. This isn't at all what I'd intended, but I have no choice." She touched Eve's arm, trying somehow to convey her emotions. The skin was warm and pleasant, the effects of whatever had caused her last "spell" long gone.

"I understand," Eve said, but the words sounded rehearsed, or worse, like something she'd learned from a television soap opera. Her next statement just made that all the more likely. "You have to answer to your superiors."

"You wouldn't be agreeing so readily if you knew how painful this is going to be," Laura said, more harshly than she'd intended. Eve said nothing, and Laura's voice softened with defeat and regret. "But . . . you'll save human lives. And I'll be in charge of the procedure, so I'll be as careful as possible."

Eve nodded complacently. "That's good. And I want to help you find him."

Laura swallowed and gave the young woman a nod of her own, then hurried out of the habitat and back to the control room to set up the cyclotron. There were so many possible repercussions to doing this, so many things that could go wrong. Even the life-form's last statement—

"And I want to help you find him."

—worried Laura, because simply put . . . she was afraid Eve would do exactly that.

"Are you comfortable?"

An inane but automatic question, and when Eve nodded, Laura checked the straps—wrist, across the upper chest, hips, and ankles—a final time. Uneasiness was running along her spine like a tingle of electricity and her hands were jittery on the buckles. With everything tight, the doctor stepped back and gave it a visual check, hating everything she saw.

The device into which Eve had been fastened looked like a parody of a dentist's chair, or perhaps the absurdly padded seat of some deviant's torture mechanism. The whole thing had been designed in white, and combined with the bright overhead lights shining off the glass enclosure—yes, another one—around the cyclotron and Eve's painfully white medical grown, there was a sort of unearthly radiance coming from this part of the room.

"Yes," Eve said. She didn't bother to elaborate.

"All right." Laura's voice was halting. "I'm going to power up. You'll hear a high-pitched sound . . . with your ultra-sensitive hearing, it might even hurt. I've set the machine to radiate for ten seconds, then it will shut down. If you can, you should try to keep your eyes shut. I don't . . . the sensation is probably going to be very much like a huge, sudden sunburn."

Eve said nothing and Laura realized belatedly that Eve had no idea what a sunburn felt like. She'd never *seen* the sun or felt its warmth. No matter what Eve thought, Laura would never, *ever*, be able to think of this young woman as a laboratory rat. For an instant she hated Carter Burgess and his compatriots more than ever. But if she didn't do this, Burgess had the power to put someone else in charge; she had no doubt that he'd handpick someone with a level of compassion matching his own, and then what would happen to Eve?

"Are you ready?" Laura asked, feeling even more thwarted. Again, no response. Laura looked up from the controls and saw Eve staring up at the white metal device looming over her as though it were some kind of sanitized metal monster. The female life-form looked small and helpless, in awe of this thing that was about to change her forever. For a heartbreaking moment, Laura wondered if Eve had ever wished she could be fully human. Now she was doomed to go in exactly the opposite direction.

Let's just get this over with, Laura thought. "Here we go." She snapped four switches to the ON position and turned the control key, then typed in her password when the computer demanded it. For a timeless moment nothing happened, then the screen flashed, giving her one last chance—

"RECONFIRM REQUIRED: BEGIN CYCLOTRON PROCEDURE NOW? NO/YES

Laura set her jaw and hit *Y*.

Light filled the laboratory, accompanied by a piercing whine that was shockingly loud. Several of the women around the laboratory clapped their hands over their ears instinctively; Laura only stared down at the cyclotron and Eve and wondered what in God's name it was like to actually be the *target* of the machine that was making this unearthly racket.

Then again, in view of what was happening to Eve, maybe she didn't have to wonder at all.

The alien woman's skin was as fresh and unblemished as always . . . on the surface. Beneath it, everything seemed to *wrench* and grow suddenly translucent, as though she were blistering six layers down, cooking from the inside out, right down to the yellow-orange glow that suddenly surrounded her. Laura had garbled thoughts about microwaves and moths cooking in the coils of insect zappers, then a scarlet drop of blood—startling in all that brightness—leaked from the corner of Eve's left eye and trickled down her cheek. If the device hadn't cycled itself out and shut down, in an abrupt cessation of function that was exactly the opposite of its start-up operation—Laura's fingers would have found the emergency shut-off switch.

For a moment, there was absolute silence in the laboratory. Then Eve groaned, her voice several octaves deeper than before and carrying a strange, echoing quality that made the skin along Laura's neck quiver.

Right on cue, all the normal sounds rushed back in to fill the void. Around the room, people began to talk—

"Check the settings on the monitor—"

"Did you record the blood-gas levels while—"

"The thermostat control on this doesn't—"

—and Laura hurried to the cyclotron and pulled the lock release, then yanked open the hinged door. "Are you all right?" she asked anxiously. At each corner of the machine, the female guards watched Eve warily. "Eve, answer me!"

Nothing.

Eve felt like she was dreaming awake.

There were things about her that she knew weren't normal compared to full-blooded human beings, but sometimes she had trouble accepting that she herself wasn't fully human. She looked like them, talked like them, felt the same emotions, no matter what her keepers believed. She knew, too, that the people who watched over her, including Laura, also believed she had the potential to be dangerous. This was the thing she'd had the most trouble understanding. She felt no inclination in her to hurt anyone, or even to escape. In that regard, she wanted only to come and go as she pleased, like the people outside her glass home. Why could she not go out and visit the world and come back at the end of the day like they did? And mating . . . even now, after having been exposed to the two men whom Laura had accused of "contaminating" the laboratory, she felt no real urge to do anything. They'd smelled . . . good, touched her inside in a way she couldn't identify, but the only result was a sense of yearning that soon went away and a few nightmares she couldn't remember when she woke up.

All that was changed now.

Eve was still human, but that part of her had been . . . reduced. No, *overpowered* by a darker and so much larger core of herself that she'd never known existed. Her body was filled with a new set of sensations like power and frustration, restlessness, and . . .

Desire.

Someone touched her on the shoulder, and Eve's eyes flew open; she knew the touch, the scent—Dr. Baker—but the scene she was witnessing wasn't taking place anywhere near this laboratory. Her eyes moved from side to side of their own accord, back and forth and back again, like she was experiencing REM sleep without closing her eyelids. Laura's touch again, this time on her cheek as the doctor wiped at Eve's face with a lab towel. But that didn't break her concentration, nothing in this room mattered, because—

"I'm connected, Laura." To Eve's ears, her own voice sounded hoarse and far away, as though she were talking through a length of long, rusty pipe. "*I can see everything he sees.*"

Patrick stares at his reflection in the rearview mirror, satisfied with what he sees: clear blue eyes, clean face, neatly combed hair. No one could know by looking at him that anything is different—he has no blood on his hands or his clothes and he is thinking clearly and concisely. His driving has been perfect, his shirt is tucked in, even his shoes are shined.

He is perfectly human.

Dismissing his reflection, Patrick spends a moment listening to the newscaster prattling monotonously on the radio station—

> *"Authorities are still baffled by the recent disappearances in the Washington area, and so far the perpetrator of a number of grisly killings continues to elude—"*

He reaches over and turns the knob until the announcer's voice is cut off and the sounds of the morning fill the car: the traffic passing on the street, people talking on the sidewalks and outside the tiny stores that are so common in this area, the hissing of the automatic doors in the small supermarket across the street. He looks over there now and sees a young woman headed toward the store, then she stops to smile and talk to a little boy playing on a coin-operated mechanical hobbyhorse out front. They are fifty yards away but he can hear them as clearly as if he is standing there with them—

"My mom's inside and I ran out of money," the child explains to the woman. "It's a quarter."

The woman is pretty in a homespun way with shining light-brown hair and hazel eyes. Her skin is clear with a fresh-scrubbed look that reminds him of farms.

And of Melissa.

And he did so love Melissa.

"Eve?" Who—oh, yes. Laura's voice, cutting into her mind and forcing her back before she could meld completely with the man-thing to which her mind had become connected. "Eve, stay with me," Laura said sharply. "You have to talk to me, tell me what you see."

Eve blinked and tried to refocus, this time without becoming so deeply immersed. "He's in . . . Maryland, I think. There are little shops everywhere around him. The human part of him likes them because they're different from where he's been the past couple of days. They're *cleaner.* Little stores with odd names and other things, too—Kookooroo, McDonald's, Benetton. There's an ad for Camel cigarettes at the corner of Rogers and Elm." She cocked her head to one side, straining unconsciously. "He's driving his best car. It's a midnight-blue Mercedes, very expensive. He . . ." Eve stopped, her eyes widening as she understood what Patrick was about to do.

"What?" Laura prompted. Sometime during the time that Eve had kept her eyes closed, Laura had picked up a cell phone and was now relaying their conversation into it. "What do you—what does *Patrick* see right now?"

"There's a . . . woman," Eve said softly. "She's across the street by the Mayfair Market. She reminds him of his dead fiancée."

"Oh, shit," Laura said. "Dennis, are you there? You need to listen to this." She repeated Eve's words into the telephone at rapid-fire speed, then made sure he'd heard the name of the supermarket correctly. "Elm Street is where? In Haverford? All right. No, nothing more just yet."

Eve didn't know or care who Dennis was, only that she could maintain her bond with Patrick Ross. It was hard, so hard, to do that *and* keep track of Dr. Baker here, to do what the doctor wanted, to pass along the information. Being in Patrick's head was so . . . *fulfilling.* It let her see the things outside the lab in a way that the television could never do. How tawdry and simplistic the overly loud programs and commercials seemed now, when compared to the beauty of the day and the sun and the sound of everything beyond the lab.

"What's happening now?" Laura shook her arm slightly, forcing Eve's attention back to her. "Stay with me, Eve. You know we need your help." The person on the other end of the phone must have said something because Laura gave a ghost of a smile, then said, "Yeah, I know he drives like a maniac. If I were you, I'd buckle up. You never know what that man might do." She hit the END button and turned back to where Eve was still strapped in. "Eve? Can you tell me what he's seeing?"

Patrick steers the Mercedes into a space at the far front of the parking lot that's out of the main flow of traffic, shaded from the harshness of the sunshine by the lush growth of an oak tree that might be half a century old. He climbs out and heads toward the store, noting that the child is still on the mechanical horse, although the contraption has once again stopped its motion; the little boy looks at him and maybe even recognizes him—another woman coming out of the store certainly does—but the kid inexplicably backs away when Patrick starts to approach him. Some people, Patrick notes wryly as he pauses to help the middle-aged woman who has just dropped half her groceries because she saw him, have an innate sense for survival, and some clearly don't. He wonders if the child will be alive in five years when his new species has taken over this planet.

"The inside of the Mayfair Market is the antithesis to the green, sweet-smelling morning outside. Bright fluorescent lights reflect off everything and leave no room for hiding. The floor is made of slick tile and the sounds are an unpleasant mixture of hard rubber tires squealing beneath the weight of metal carts, voices over the intercom, and customers and staff members yammering at each other, all floating over the scent of old meat and slowly rotting vegetables.

"Patrick follows the woman for a while, watching the way she moves, letting his craving work up while he enjoys

the game of choosing his next consort. She is so lovely, even when engaged in the mundane things of human nature; in the liquor aisle, she examines the shelves and finally selects a bottle of Sutter Home Wine to add to the small shopping basket she picked up by the front door. She goes through the store slowly, aisle by aisle, someone who doesn't have a list but is in no hurry. He paces her along the corridors like a big deadly predator, watching her scan toiletries, coffee, beans, and pasta sauces. Finally she pauses in the cereal section—Cocoa Puffs, Apple Jacks, Fruit Loops—

Wheaties.

Patrick makes his move.

"Hi."

She looks up warily but her expression melts into disbelief when she sees him. She looks from his face to the Wheaties box she holds in her hand, then back again. "Oh, my God," *she says. Her hand grips the cereal box a little tighter. "It's you!"*

Patrick gives her a falsely embarrassed smile. "Yeah, just me."

The woman giggles nervously, sounding like a shy highschooler, then offers him the Wheaties box. "Will you autograph my cereal?" She giggles again.

Patrick drops the embarrassed act and gives her a smile full of charm. "Can I tell you a secret?" She nods and it's clear she has no clue what to say. Patrick leans closer. "Wheaties—I hate these things. I think they taste like cardboard." He motions toward the back of the store. "If you want something autographed, let me show you what they're going to put on the shelves this afternoon . . ."

Laura's cellular telephone rang, and Eve heard the tension in the doctor's voice escalate as she tried to answer the questions from the other end. It was only a few, slow heartbeats before Laura's hand touched her arm and tried to bring her back a little, pull her out of the head dream that being inside Patrick's mind had become.

"Eve, I've got Press on the phone. He can't find Patrick. Where—"

"He's in the cereal aisle," Eve said faintly. "No—wait. I see boxes, lot of them, the stockroom maybe. Now he's taking her outside." Her eyelids openly slowly. Beads of heated perspiration slipped down her temples and across her collarbone, the sweet moisture collecting beneath her breasts and elsewhere that couldn't be seen. She smiled languidly, unable to stop herself.

"Eve?"

All that alarm in Laura's voice, but it was far, far too late; the radiation had done its work, performed its magic—so many new and wonderfully *dark* feelings were awakening inside her, such *hunger*, and there was nothing to do but sit back and revel in all of them. When Eve spoke again, her voice was lower than she'd ever heard it, filled with anticipation and anger and, yes, jealousy.

"He wants to mate with her."

"Damn it," Laura hissed from beside her chair. "What the hell have we done to her?"

"It's okay, Laura. I want to help." An automatic response as Eve tried to find her place in the world again, in Laura's world. Nearly the same words as she'd said earlier, but this time Eve could only half believe they were the truth. No—they had to be. Laura Baker was on her side, fighting to keep things bearable for her, or at least as good as they could be given the circumstances. It was the circumstances that bothered Eve, how unfair that she must be the one to endure an existence like this. But nothing could be done about that. She was what she was; Patrick Ross might be the master of deception, but Eve had never been outside these walls, and besides, she could never, ever lie to Laura.

"I can't see anything," Eve said abruptly and opened her eyes. "He can sense that I'm tapping in, and he's too strong—he's blocking me. The connection is gone."

She could never lie to Laura.

Could she?

Patrick drags the woman who reminds him of Melissa through the stockroom. She is terrified and struggling but his hand is over her mouth and she is too weak, her movements like a moth caught in the mouth of a bat, and he is vaguely disappointed by this. Even the single scream she managed before he stopped her was small and ineffective, does not even turn a head toward the stockroom to where he had coaxed her. He would prefer to mate with someone strong and fierce, someone like himself. He would prefer, too, that his mate not die every time in childbirth and leave him with no choice but to find another and to care for the offspring alone.

But he will take what he can get.

The parking lot in the back of the Mayfair Market is deserted, all the spaces taken and marked "Employees Only." *He pulls her through the rows of parked cars, searching for just the right one, knowing he will never be able to take her around the front and to the Mercedes. At last he spots it at the far end—a Chevrolet Econoline van. It is easy to hold the woman with one hand and wrench open the back door with the other; it does not matter that it is locked. It takes barely a hard twist to make the handle turn. He forces the woman inside without ever removing his hand from her mouth and begins ripping at her clothes.*

But something's wrong. Someone's . . . watching *him somehow. He can feel danger closing in, is sensing somehow through a presence in his mind that his enemies are about to drop on him. The thing in his head is pulling him away from his prisoner, insisting that he focus on himself and the need for self-preservation rather than on the urge to mate; he must let his hostage go, too, for by killing her he will place himself in a position of greater potential harm.*

He releases the woman who looks like Melissa but keeps his hand on her mouth. "I'm going to let you go," he says in a deadly cold voice. "Head directly back to your car. Don't stop anywhere and don't go back into the store. No one will believe you anyway, and if you scream, or if you stop and talk to anyone, I will find you. And I will kill you." He takes his hand away and the young woman is already nodding her consent—

yes yes yes yes yes

—and clawing at the door. In another instant she is gone and Patrick can see her through the window, leaving the Mayfair Market behind and heading toward the front parking lot at an outright run.

The tickle in his head grows louder and he slicks his hair back, then straightens his tie, working to make himself look normal. He concentrates on the feeling of someone inside his head, closing his eyes and reaching for it, trying to backtrack along the lines of neural and telepathic communication—

And suddenly, there it is.

A white laboratory, an extraordinarily beautiful woman in a sweat-soaked hospital gown strapped in some kind of glass-enclosed device. Inside his brain, he sees her eyes open, clear blue, and stare into nothingness, stare at him. *For a brief flash he is inside her head, a role reversal, and she instinctively scans the room so that he will know where she is. It is not hard to figure out because stenciled on the cinderblock wall to one side of her are the words* BIOHAZARD 4—MONROE A.F.B. *He learns, too, that she is like him, but not like him; she is everything he has been looking for. She is . . .*

"Eve."

He says her name out loud and knows that on the other end—

—she hears him.

He senses immediately that she cannot come to him. Thus it is his responsibility, his need, *to go to her.*

"Patrick."

"Eve," Laura said sharply. "Are you okay?"

For a few seconds, Eve didn't answer. Instead, she

ran her tongue across her upper lip, feeling how the flesh there was still tender and swollen from the dose of radiation. She was feeling other things now, too: emotions, sensations, *abilities.* Finally, she looked at Laura out of the corner of her eyes and nodded. "Yes, Laura. I'm fine."

But she couldn't keep the chill out of her voice.

"This is it—Press, pull over or you'll miss it!"

"Damn it," Press snarled. He practically stood on the brakes, jerking the wheel of the sedan to the side as he did and cussing the Chevrolet when it tried to roll. A hair-raising four seconds later, he slid the car to a stop in the fire lane in front of the Mayfair Market and he and Dennis Gamble jumped out, neither bothering to shut the doors behind them.

Their entrance to the supermarket was like a textbook example of everything that could go wrong on a criminal chase—carts in the way, people screaming and dropping shit all over everywhere; even the assistant manager who rushed up to meet them got knocked into a display of green beans and ended up on his ass when he ran full tilt into Press.

"MOVE!" Press bellowed. *"GET OUT OF OUR WAY!"* It was amazing the message that a full-throated man could send. Of course, the Glock 9mm he held in one hand probably had something to contribute to the way the folks scattered.

"The stockroom," Dennis hollered at no one in particular. "Where is it?"

"Back right corner of the store," said the guy in the manager's coat. His voice was shaking and he was still on the floor, but he pointed behind Press and Dennis toward the area beyond where a few customers cowered with the cashiers and baggers. "Double metal door with an orange stripe by the fresh-fish counter."

God bless 'im, Press thought. At least he didn't ask

us any stupid questions. "Let's go," he said, and Dennis followed him on a zigzagging course through the aisles until they got to the door the manager had described. No niceties here; and they burst through with a shout, Press with his handgun aimed and ready to fire. But the stockroom was empty and silent, a gray expanse of boxes below poor lighting fixtures set in a ceiling that was too high. Their only hint to where Patrick might have gone was a lighter line at its other end where a sliver of daylight, nearly painful in the gloomy room, revealed that the outside door had been left open.

But outside, the parking lot was silent and empty, the neatly aligned cars nothing more than lumps of sun-washed color. Nothing moved anywhere. Except—

"There," Press whispered and pointed to a beat-up van in the back row.

"Oh, yeah," Dennis agreed. The vehicle was rocking up and down and there was no mistaking the familiar motion.

"We have to stop them before he finishes," Press said grimly. "Otherwise the woman he nabbed is a goner and we're in for a real mess. Come on."

The trek down the row of cars took barely five seconds, but it felt like forever. The van was bouncing harder now, and Press ground his teeth and reversed the Glock, then smashed the butt of the gun against the window of the driver's door. A woman shrieked inside as Press reached through and unlocked it, then yanked open the door, the Glock already turned to firing position. "Freeze," he yelled. "Don't move anything!"

"Don't shoot, man!" cried a voice from inside. "We're *sorry*!"

Dennis peered around Press's shoulder, then put a hand on his back and tugged at his jacket. "That's not him," he said. "I think it's just a couple of kids from the grocery store."

Press glared into the back of the van. Now that his eyes had adjusted to the interior light, he could finally see them—some slick-looking guy of about nineteen putting it to one of the cashiers, and her probably underage, too. He should have realized it from the condition of the van—rusty and covered with school and smart-ass bumper stickers. He snapped the Glock toward the ceiling of the van. "Find a fucking motel, you idiots."

He and Dennis whirled back toward the parking lot but it was just as empty as before, except for a lone woman at the far end hurrying toward her car. Press frowned when he saw her and was about to call out when, incredibly, Patrick Ross stepped out from between two cars about twenty feet to their left.

"Freeze, asshole!" Press barked. The Glock was in place and aimed almost without his being aware of it, his arms extended and steady in front of him. He'd had enough screwing around on this job—no pun intended. He was bringing this bastard in or blowing his head off. No more in-between.

"Whoa," Patrick said. He stood where he was, respectfully eyeing the weapon pointed at his face. "Hey, why don't you put that thing down before one of us gets hurt?"

"Want to place bets on which of us that'll be?" Press said icily. "Now put your hands up, hero. And keep them there."

But Patrick was anything but concerned. Instead of complying, he turned his head and looked to his friend. "Dennis, what the hell is this? Who is this guy—and what are you doing with him?"

Flustered, Dennis blinked at Patrick, then at Press. The agent knew exactly what was wrong, too. "Don't get close to him, Dennis. Yeah, he's looking real normal right now, but remember what you saw on the porch at his cabin."

That brought Dennis back to reality, making him take a step backward. "Look, Patrick," he said with a helpless gesture. "Come on—you can't deny that there's some really weird shit going on with you."

But Patrick couldn't have looked more innocent. "I don't have a clue what you're talking about. What kind of shit?"

"Don't tell him anything," Press cut in. He motioned with the gun. "Didn't I tell you to get your hands in the air? You're coming real close to pissing me off."

This time Patrick obligingly lifted his hands, the model of compliance. "Whatever you say. Am I right in assuming you're some kind of . . . police officer? Federal agent?" He gave them both an affable grin. "Boy, the NSEG must be really aggravated at me to go through all this grief."

Dennis's mouth turned down. "Knock it off, Patrick. You told me yourself you weren't feeling right. You need to go in for tests and find out what's wrong."

"Sure, no problem. I give up, don't shoot, and all that jazz. I'll be happy to go back to the lab and take your tests or whatever they are." Patrick smiled even wider. "Just lead the way."

Press frowned and wondered how Patrick had known about the lab, then dismissed it. Hell, it was all NASA- and NSEG-related, wasn't it? He jerked his head toward the front of the store. "Car's parked out front, standard black Chevrolet sedan. You know the type—"

"Sure," Patrick said. "General government lack of imagination."

"You go on ahead of us." Press's tone was cold and unemotional. "If you bolt, I'm going to shoot you in the back of the neck where your spinal cord meets your brain stem. Then I'm going to shoot you again in the skull, just for good measure. In case you haven't figured it out, I don't care who you are or who you know, and I'm *not* fucking around." Dennis looked at him, dismayed, but Press ignored him. "Got the picture?"

Patrick nodded, but still didn't seem worried as he turned and began walking. His steps were measured and careful, as though he were making every effort not to upset the two men following him, hands in full view while he smiled the entire time. "Bit testy, aren't you?"

"Just go toward the car, hotshot. When you get there, you ride in the back passenger side."

Patrick turned his head slightly, until Press and Dennis could see one blue eye glittering above that frozen grin. "Aren't you afraid I'll bite you on the back of your head or something?"

"Oh, jeez," Dennis said, sounding miserable.

"Not a bit," Press replied. "We've got an unbreakable glass barrier over steel bars. And, of course, the handcuffs. And you can bet I'm going to use them."

Patrick shook his head in mock sadness. "America's greatest hero, taken away in broad daylight by government agents in handcuffs. For this, I walked on Mars?" He glanced back at Press again. "You did see the Mars landing, didn't you?"

"I'm sorry," Press said blandly. "I must've been watching America's greatest game.

"Baseball."

CHAPTER 16

"What the hell is the matter with her?" Brea demanded. "The printouts are going wild—everything is escalating." She held a pencil against the line of text scrolling across one of the monitors, then glanced at another screen. "Pulse rate is a hundred forty and rising, and she isn't even on her feet, for Christ's sake. And look at the spikes on the EKG!"

"This is all screwed up since the radiation therapy," Vikki complained. She peered across the lab, then made a sound of disgust. "Oh, for—look at her now."

"What?" Brea followed Vikki's pointing finger and saw that Eve, sitting in the garden area of her glass habitat, was caressing her breasts through her shirt. Brea scowled. "This isn't good, Vik. It's clearly an indication that she's experiencing an increase in sexual impulses that never existed before the cyclotron procedure."

"What do we do?"

Brea chewed her bottom lip, then jumped as noise reverberated throughout the lab—

WHAM!

Everyone was suddenly on high alert—the female guards, the techs, the biologists—all gazes locked on the glass habitat, where Eve had risen and gone to one wall, then raised her fist and begun pounding on it. "I guess we wait and see for now."

Vikki ran a hand through her short brown hair. "Think that quartz glass will hold?" Her voice was shaking.

Brea considered this and finally nodded. "Yeah. They knew what they were up against when they designed it—they lost the first once like that, remember? They won't make the same mistake a second time."

"God," said Vikki as they all watched the alien woman slam the side of her fist methodically against the walls of her cage.

WHAM!

"I sure hope not."

"Don't think I've ever been in here before," Patrick said as Press and Dennis guided him down a long, tiled corridor. "What is this place?"

Press scowled and gave Patrick's back a little push to keep him going. "If you've never been here before, then how did you know we were going to a lab?"

Patrick shrugged, dismissing Press's slight shove. "I just figured it would be, that's all. Where else would the NSEG do a bunch of tests?"

Press said nothing, but it nagged at him. It could've been in a doctor's office, or a hospital... hell, it could've been in a fucking traveling van for all Patrick Ross knew. Well, it didn't make any difference, because they were here now.

"Wow," Patrick said. His voice was open and pleasant, a buddy making a comment on the upkeep of a friend's lawn. "You guys sure haven't skimped on the manpower, have you?"

"Standard operating procedure," Press said as they hurried down the corridor. They passed at least a dozen armed guards, male and female alike, all outfitted with portable canisters of the toxic hydrochlorine as well as everything from the customary issue fully automatic M-16s to SWAT H&K MP5A3s.

The astronaut's sharp blue eyes flicked toward the canisters. "What's the other stuff they're carrying?"

"I don't have any idea," Dennis said. He looked more alarmed than Patrick. "Press?"

"Never mind," Press said briskly. "Let's just get where we're going and be done with it. Then we'll find out a lot more about each other."

"Oh, this is bad," Brea said. *"Shit!"*

"What's happening?" Vikki's voice was shrill. "Was she eating something? *What is this?"*

Eve was slumped against the other side of the habitat's glass wall, gasping for air.

"I think she's faking it," said one hard-edged woman. Her rifle was at the ready, the barrel pointed at Eve although the glass was bulletproof.

"I wouldn't be so sure—her face is pretty red."

"She's choking!"

"I thought she was eating something. I think I saw it."

"I'm telling you, it's bullshit. This babe's never so much as coughed."

"But look at her!"

Brea could no longer tell who was speaking, and she rose from where she had crouched next to the glass and hurried back to the control console. A quick flip of her finger sent her voice over the lab intercom. *"Med Alert, BioHazard Four. Repeat: Med*

Alert, BioHazard Four." That done, she hit another switch at the top right corner, this one marked in red. In the center of the main wall of Eve's habitat, the outside set of steel bars across the entrance rose with a hiss of hydraulics.

"What are you doing?" demanded Vikki. "You can't—"

"Shut up." Brea faced the guard at the second console. "Open it," she commanded.

"Sorry, no can do." Just her luck, the guard with the turnkey was the one who believed Eve was faking an attack. The woman, tall and muscular with nearly black eyes, looked completely unaffected by either Eve's illness or Vikki's near hysteria. "Dr. Baker's strictest orders. No one goes in without her present in the lab."

"She's choking, you metal-brained woman. See if you don't end up watching the time tick away in a silo under northern Minnesota if Eve suffocates because you wouldn't open the fucking gate!"

For a long moment, Brea thought the guard still wasn't going to obey, then the woman reluctantly pulled the turnkey from her uniform pocket. It seemed to take forever for her to insert it in the keyhole, then twist it; finally, the inside set of bars hummed up. "I still don't like this," the guard said.

"You're not the only one!" Vikki's brown eyes were huge and terrified, and she'd taken a position behind the three guards hovering near the habitat entrance. "No one's ever been in there without Dr. Baker being here."

Brea ignored her and dashed inside the habitat. Eve was writhing on the floor now, soundlessly clawing at her throat and leaving long, red welts where her fingernails dug into the skin. "Eve?" Brea grabbed the alien woman by the shoulders and tried to stop her twisting. "Eve—what's wrong? If you can't talk to me, I'm going to have to try to clear your airway! Be *still*!"

And just like that, Eve obeyed. She went limp and Brea found herself supporting the weight of Eve's shoulders, heavier than expected, and staring into wide, vastly intelligent and not at all friendly blue eyes. She felt Eve's hands close around her upper arms—

Then Brea was thrown out of the entrance to the bio-environment. She wasn't the biggest of women, rather short and a little too round; her body acted like the world's clumsiest bowling ball as she landed on the guards clustered around the entrance and they all crashed on top of the cowering Vikki.

And as they all came tumbling down, Eve just . . .

. . . walked out of the habitat, and then out of the laboratory.

"Bring him in here," Laura directed. She watched Patrick Ross carefully, noting the confident body movement, wary of the man's apparent lack of resistance. There was something wrong here, something she'd missed. Press had told her over the cellular that Ross had surrendered without a fight, even to the point of showing up when they hadn't had any idea where he'd gone, and more, expressing a willingness to come to the lab for the tests. What was she overlooking?

An instant before stepping inside the blood-work laboratory, Patrick Ross hesitated. "Say," he said mildly, "would anyone mind if I used the bathroom?"

Press glanced at Laura and Dennis, then jerked his head at the two heavily armed guards flanking Patrick. "All right. But make it quick."

It was so . . . easy.

I'm free, Eve thought. That's what this is—the

freedom to walk where and when I want and not be stopped by a wall made of something nearly invisible. *I'm free.*

Two people in the lab area had tried to grab her, but no one had used their weapons; a few snappy punches—the moves learned from action and adventure programs on television—had made it immediately clear how ridiculously *fragile* these human beings were. Either that or she was like Superman or something, another character from a television show. Was he real? If so, she'd sure like to see him in person.

She pushed through a door and found herself in a long corridor, unbroken by any doors or exits. It was either keep going or return to the lab, so she went forward, marching down the hallway with a purpose she'd never had while trapped inside the bio-environment. The corridor turned right at its end and Eve did too, then came up short when she found herself face-to-face with a male guard. She'd never been within touching distance of a man before and she froze for a precious two seconds, long enough for the sight of her to register on his angular face.

"Hey," he said in surprise. "Hold on a second. You're not supposed to be—"

Eve smiled and stepped up to him, hearing his words fade off in mid-sentence. He smelled . . . *male,* and that was good. She would have liked to pull off his clothes and see what was underneath—that would have been even better. But he was a guard and someone who would, if he could, stop her from leaving here. And that, of course, was bad.

Still smiling, she gripped the lapels of his flak jacket and tossed him fifteen yards back in the direction from which she'd come. He landed hard and maybe he was hurt; this was not something about which she was concerned.

Belatedly, however, Eve realized she should have been.

She was hardly another thirty feet around the corner when she heard shattering glass—the cover on the alarm in the first corridor, back where the guard had landed. Obviously, she hadn't hurt him very much.

Alarm bells began screaming everywhere.

"Whoa, man!" Patrick exclaimed as he pushed through the men's room doors. "Listen to that racket—what do you think's going on?"

Both guards had snapped to attention. "No idea," said the first gruffly. He grabbed one of Patrick's arms and steered him back toward the testing facility. "Let's go, Commander Ross. We need to get you back to the blood-work lab pronto."

"Sure," Patrick said with a good-natured grin. He took two steps with the man, then reached up with his other hand and rammed the guy's head into the wall as hard as he could. His other escort barely had time to register the smear of blood on the white wall, much less level his weapon, before Patrick had a one-handed choke hold around the man's windpipe that instantly crushed his trachea. "Pathetic," Patrick said. The agreeable expression never left his face as he tossed the body behind him and stalked away.

Somewhere in here was Eve, and he was going to find her.

"Damn it!" Laura flared. "I just don't believe this—I *knew* something like this would happen!" The three of them had burst from the blood-work laboratory at the first wail of the alarms, and now she turned back, snatched the receiver off a phone by the door, and rammed a finger against one of the buttons on it.

"What the hell is going on?" Press demanded.

"Listen to me," Laura barked into the telephone, paying no attention to him or Dennis. "Ten minutes, and no more. *Ten minutes*—if you don't receive a cancellation telephone call from me within that time, you trigger the tether mechanism. Absolutely *no one else* has the authority to tell you not to do so. Do you understand?" She waited for a second. "Good."

"The tether mechanism?" Dennis asked with a bewildered expression. "What's a tether mechanism?" He looked up at the ceiling as another round of sirens went off, ducking his head as though something big and horrible was going to swoop down on them.

"Eve has escaped," Laura said. There was a bitterness to her tone, an *I-told-you-so* undercurrent that was present but not directed at her two companions. "I never wanted to put her through the procedure that reawakened her alien genes. Only a fool wouldn't have seen this coming."

"Burgess—" Press began.

Dennis's suddenly frightened voice cut him off. "You know what? Patrick should have been back by now."

"Come on," Press said. "We're wasting time. We all know Ross has probably whacked his guards by now and taken off." He slammed a fist into his open palm. "The tricky little bastard set us up."

Laura's eyes widened. "Wait a second—you're right! He's never been in this facility, only Dennis has. Orinsky did all his testing in another building."

"Somehow he knew Eve was here," Press told them grimly as the three of them raced down the corridor and back toward Laura's main work laboratory and Eve's bio-environment. "He must've had a connection right back to her when she was tracking him. He knew she'd find a way to break out of her cage and he wanted to be here when it happened. We played right into his plans, right down to the fucking ride and the clearance we provided to get him here."

Laura halted at a junction in the corridor next to a door marked STAIRS. "All right then. Dennis and I will check downstairs for Eve—she might still listen to me. You have to find Patrick and stop him from coming into contact with her. We have no facts at all about true alien physiology—for all we know, reproduction between two advanced aliens could happen simultaneously, like cellular division. Or a nearly pure mating could result in multiple live births—we could be overrun. We have *got* to stop them!"

"Oh, don't you worry," Press said, clenching his fists. "Mating season ain't about to begin."

The gunshots were, perhaps, like bee stings. Eve had never been stung by a bee of course, but she could imagine the pain—localized and hot, but generally not lethal. The wounds along her arm and rib cage smarted just enough to really piss her off. She took out her irritation on the two guards who'd fired at her by cracking their heads together. She found the sound actually quite pleasant, reminiscent of a lone person clapping their hands very sharply. She stepped over their bodies and kept going, her only direction being forward, and her only goal:

Patrick.

Eve had never been down here in her life, but when she found the stairs, instinct took over. Up, she thought. Up and away from this hellish hole of a prison they think they're disguising with layers of white paint. She tried the handle of the door marked STAIRS—UP and found it locked; when she peered at it, she saw one of the cardkey readers that were so prevalent around the facility. She'd never seen a cardkey up close, though; the staff in the bioenvironmental laboratory weren't allowed to bring them into the lower level.

Eve looked at it and cocked her head. She had no card, nor was she likely to find one quickly enough to get her out of here. The only thing left to do was to simply break it.

No problem.

"Sir—Mr. Ross!" The sentry rushing toward him had an open, friendly face. His voice was frantic with worry. "Please, sir. You can't come this way. We have an emergency on our hands, an escapee. If you could just go back where you came from—"

Patrick gave him a reassuring smile, then punched him in the face. The guy went down brutally hard, his feet jerking forward and out from under him as his head snapped back. He hit the floor with a thud and a clatter of the metal weaponry he wore. Patrick stepped past him and kept going, using one fist to ram his way through a lock now and then as was necessary to maintain his pace. Sooner or later this weaving path would send him down toward the laboratory where Eve's living quarters were and he'd finally get to meet his mate. His *destiny.*

Patrick smiled wider, practicing this oh-so-important human trait.

He was getting really good at this smiling stuff.

Laura was right, Press thought spitefully. She *should* have known better than to agree to "grow" another alien, should have known they'd end up in a situation pretty much like the first one all over again. He'd thought she was smarter than that . . .

Then again, that wasn't it at all. She *was* smart—much more so than him. It was probably the one thing that she had that he didn't that assholes like Burgess had found and played like a fucking harp: *compassion.* No doubt they'd used that line about "If you don't do it, we'll find someone who will. And that person won't have near the heart that you do.

Don't *you* want to be in charge of the experiments?" And, of course, in the end all their inferences hadn't meant shit, because she'd been forced to do something to her test subject that she'd never wanted to anyway.

And Eve—or Sil, as Press was still privately calling her in his head—where the hell was she now? Probably somewhere off in a closet with Patrick Ross, the two of them screwing their brains out in some kind of weird alien-sex thing that would really put everyone in a bind.

Another corner up ahead in these seemingly endless turns and angled corridors—this place was like a damned rat's maze. If it weren't for the signs posted on the walls, he'd have been lost two turns after he'd left Laura and Dennis. And here was another one, making Press pause and listen before he crept around it. He couldn't hear anything beyond the background hum of white noise that always moved in to fill the space between his heartbeats in the high-tension times of assignments. This was when he was at his best and he felt like his senses had heightened enough that nothing in the world could best him. Still, he went around the juncture cautiously—he would never be called a fool—

—and came nose to nose with Eve.

For a single, breathless moment, she seemed not to even see him. So close he could touch her, the alien woman's flesh was bubbling and distorting beneath its surface, as if something inside were trying to re-form itself and escape. Her blue eyes burned into Press's like shards of arctic ice, but she made no move to attack him.

Press found his voice around what felt like a lump of sandpaper in his throat. "Eve, you have to—to go back to the cage. You can't stay here, and you can't leave. We can't let that happen." His Glock was out though he had no inclination to fire it; he wanted instead to move back and away, but he couldn't take his eyes off the hideous movement that was churning along wherever the woman's creamy skin was exposed.

Still, Eve stared at him, not moving, not speaking. Her only acknowledgment of his presence was a deep, sudden inhalation that finally put a stop to the revolting undulations. Abruptly she just seemed like a woman to him, young, frightened and beautiful, like some country college girl lost in the big city. Blond hair, clear blue eyes and full lips in a heart-shaped face that didn't have a single imperfection—it was hard to believe that this gorgeous gal could be anything like the creature he *knew* she was.

Eve must have sensed a change in him, some sort of shift in his pheremones or something. Instead of fighting or running, she smiled and licked her lips, then ran the fingers of both hands up and down the buttons on her shirt in a stripper's move that she had no way of knowing about. Her technique, however, was much more direct. No fancy music here, just the sounds of fabric tearing and plastic buttons hitting the floor as she wrenched open her blouse and revealed flawless breasts.

Speechless, all Press could do was shake his head and stumble backward when she would have reached for his free hand. He had an idea, all right, of what she planned to do with it and he wanted no part of her—the memory of Stephen Arden's mutilated body was enough to smash down any jolt of desire this life-form might be able to generate in him. Stephen had been a Harvard Professor of Anthropology and part of the team that hunted for Sil before she'd convinced him to have sex with her. Thanks, but Press preferred his lays to be human. "Eve—"

"Freeze!"

Thank God—the backups had finally arrived. He might be tough and good at what he did, but experience was a bastard and he had no real desire to face off with an alien by himself. At least this time the troops consisted of more than an extra two or three guards so scared they were crapping in their pants—the guy leading them was as true a hard-ass jarhead as Burgess if Press had ever seen one. "We've got you covered, lady," he announced in his gravelly voice. "If you so much as move a muscle the wrong way, you'll be splattered all over this floor. Your choice." And no doubt she would be, too—beyond the full auto M-16s, every last man and woman was wearing a hydrochlorine canister as a shoulder pack.

Eve turned her head and glared at the squad's leader, but he didn't back down, holding her gaze like a watchdog focused on its upcoming target.

"Eve," Press said to pull her attention away from the knot of solders. "These guys mean business. Even if they weren't here, you've forgotten something really important." He gestured vaguely in the direction that he thought would take them back to Laura's laboratory. "Down in the lab is the tether mechanism. Remember that? You take one step off these premises or you kill one person, then Laura or someone else is going to trigger that thing and you'll be dead. You don't want to go down that way, do you?"

Eve's gaze flicked from him to the row of guards staring at her, their fingers so very close to squeezing their triggers. He could see in her eyes that no, she didn't want to "go down that way." He was willing to bet she was thinking that now she had too many things to do with her life, an entirely new realm of it to explore and find a way to expand to its fullest. And Press would have to be stupid not to think that her prime objective was still to find and mate with Patrick Ross. He was, all told, damned glad it wasn't himself, and let's not forget that no one in Monroe

A.F.B. had any intention of allowing that coupling to happen.

Lulled by the presence of the backup squad, Press must've let his defenses slip just a hair too much, because abruptly Eve had him. He struggled but he couldn't get free, couldn't get his gun arm up and between them—hell, if he squeezed the trigger now, he'd probably blow off his own big toe. Shocked, he realized that she was kissing him—full mouth to mouth, and all he could think of was the way the now-dead Sil had had that wonderful tongue . . . yeah, the one that had shot down the throat of a rejected mate and eviscerated him from the inside out.

Press heard the sound of weapons shifting and just as quickly, Eve let him go. He swayed backward to get farther away, but she didn't reach for him again. The smile she gave him was odd—part girl just experiencing her first kiss, part woman who wanted so much, much more. "Magically delicious," Eve said softly, then held out her wrists. She didn't look at him again as the soldiers leaped forward with handcuffs and hustled her back down to the bioenvironment level.

It wasn't until she and the squad were out of sight that Press sagged against the wall and gasped for air, and realized that he'd had the muscles of his throat locked in what would have been a useless attempt to stop the alien woman's tongue.

Too late.

Patrick's long-legged gait pulled up short and he stopped in the middle of one of the never-ending hallways. He knew immediately what had gone wrong—Eve had been overpowered and returned to the BioHazard 4 area, where they kept her imprisoned. He didn't know why, but he was certain that she'd made the decision to surrender based on all the circumstances—she was not afraid of any of the people around her and most of their weapons would do little to harm her. Something else must have weighed heavily in the decision, something over which she'd had no control and also deemed too hazardous to combat.

This changed everything. She would not be able to meet him, and even as strong as he was, he'd have to be a fool to try to fight his way down there. At this point he was only one, and there were others—his children—to take into consideration. They needed his nurturing and his protection until they had fully matured and could mate and take care of themselves. While he doubted that anything existed on this base that could kill him without taking out everyone else and most of the building, it was not inconceivable that he would be captured and, like Eve, locked in a facility from which it would be difficult to escape. He couldn't let that happen.

Patrick whirled and went back the way he'd come, intent on finding a stairwell that would take him up and out of here. Always in tune, he heard Dr. Baker and Dennis long before they would have seen him, heard the elevator doors open in response to the plasticized slide of her security card.

"Go on, Dennis," Laura urged.

The elevator was only a few feet from an L-shaped bend in the corridor, and Patrick sidled up to the edge of the wall and watched them. He could smell Laura from where he crouched, a not unpleasant mixture of perfume and laboratory chemicals over the starch of her cotton lab coat. She was an extremely attractive woman, with her strawberry-blond hair and blue eyes, and exceedingly intelligent—that, especially, made her a good choice. Slender and in good health . . . yeah, she'd do in a pinch.

He watched Dennis step into the elevator, then Laura started to follow. Before she could get all the way inside, the elevator doors began to close. Before *that* could happen, Patrick shot around the corner and yanked her out of the elevator.

"Laura!" Dennis cried, but it was too late. The doors were closing, and they weren't the forgiving kind found in downtown civilian office buildings. They might not crush your hand if you didn't get it out of the way in time, but they'd retract only a half inch or so, just enough to let you get free; if you wanted them to open again, you needed that security card. "Shit! Let me *out*!" Alas, pounding on the inside of the doors, as Dennis was doing now, would accomplish nothing. Another two seconds and his former friend's shouts faded to nothing as the elevator descended.

When Patrick turned, Laura Baker was already backing away. He grinned and began pacing her, step for step; it wouldn't be long before she realized that the corridor came to a dead end twenty feet behind her. "What's the matter, Dr. Baker? I'm not going to hurt you."

"Just . . . stay where you are," Laura said shakily. "Don't come any closer. I mean it."

That almost made Patrick laugh. A great act, but she was defenseless—not even a pistol in her pocke, much less anything that would really work. She might have some measure of influence over Eve, but Patrick felt no such compulsion to obey her orders. Speaking of Eve—

"So where do you keep Eve? I've gone through so much trouble, I'd really like to meet her."

"That's not going to happen," Laura replied. Her gaze flicked over her shoulder and registered the wall only a few feet away. There was a shadow of panic on her face, then she forced it away. That was good—Patrick liked strong women. Very much. "You should turn yourself in," she persisted. "It'll be easier for everyone." Despite her predicament, the doctor's voice had turned calm and rational, persuading.

"I don't think I want to do that." Now there was nowhere left for her to go and her back was pressing against the wall as though she could melt right through it. He was in front of her before she could try sliding to the side and making for the one possible escape, the stairwell door about eight feet away and on which Patrick had smashed the security-lock mechanism. He put an arm on either side of her, then leaned forward and pinned her in place. "It's about time we got to know each other better. Don't you agree, Dr. Baker?"

"Let me *go*!" she tried to yell, but Patrick's head snapped forward and his mouth locked on hers. So good—not perfect, but not bad, and he pushed his tongue out and tried to force it between her lips. Nothing doing—Laura Baker had her lips and teeth clamped together as firmly as she was able; in the meantime she was struggling against him like a wet fish in the hands of a fisherman.

"C'mon," Patrick said urgently against her mouth. Her response was a hard twist to the side that nearly got her free—desperation could do that sometimes. He threw his weight forward and heard her grunt as air rushed out of her lungs, but she still wouldn't open up. Such a lack of cooperation, and at this something inside him shifted and got indefinably *darker.* His tongue pushed out and probed again, but this time it was different, elongated and two-pronged, like a snake's tongue tasting the air, searching along the line of Dr. Baker's lips for a way inside. Still no good, and the best the dual prongs could do was make the tiniest of openings.

But Patrick's bag of tricks wasn't empty yet; a third branch unfurled from the center of his tongue, this one studded with tiny barbs and stingers. Laura's eyes bulged and her efforts to break free went to the point of frenzy as this spiked appendage wavered in the air, then swung toward the crevice its brethren had managed to create. Teeth still locked, Laura somehow managed to scream, but it certainly wasn't going to do her any good.

Something crashed behind him and before Patrick could look up, he heard—

"Alien bastard."

Patrick's head jerked around and his tongues retracted instantly. He'd hardly closed his mouth before something invisible and full of stinging pain hit him full in the face.

He howled and let go of the woman, who dropped to the floor and rolled away with another scream. Horrible red blisters erupted across his forehead and cheeks, his nose and sensitive lips, the backs of his exposed hands. He tried to wipe the mess from his face and only made it worse when whatever it was that Press had sprayed him was ground into his eyes by his own fingers. Enraged, Patrick swiped the air around him but Dr. Baker was long out of reach. He managed only a malicious, runny-eyed glare toward Press, then spied the door to the stairway and vaulted toward it.

By the time Patrick was on the next level up, the welts and blisters along his skin had already started to heal.

"You all right?" Press demanded, squatting next to Laura.

She struggled upright and nodded. "Don't let him get away—"

"I'm on it," he said and swung the canister back onto his shoulder.

"Wait!"

He paused and looked back, his eyes asking the question he didn't have time to vocalize.

"Don't bother taking that," Laura told him. "The

hydrochlorine only works once—Patrick's alien cells will have already adapted to it. By now he's not only healed, he's *immune* to the stuff." She stared at him, her eyes huge and blue. "Press, you don't have *any* defense against him."

"Shit," Press said. He tore the canister strap from his shoulder and threw the entire stupid setup against the wall, where it hit, then bounced to the floor with a painfully loud clang. His hand slid beneath his jacket and came up with the heavy steel of the Glock 9mm and his expression was like granite. "Sometimes you just have to do things the old-fashioned way." A last glance to make sure Laura was okay and the corridor was clear, then Press kicked open the door to the stairway and ducked inside.

He took the stairs two at a time, keeping a solid grip on his old friend the Glock. One landing up and caution took over as he heard footsteps not far above; he checked the clip as he climbed more slowly, wondering if bullets would even work on this son of a bitch. Another six stairs and the footsteps grew louder still. Press crouched as a figure turned into his line of fire.

"Freeze!" he bellowed. "Don't make a fucking move or I'll blow your brains all over the wall!"

"Put the weapon down, mister," said a cold voice. "You're just a bit outnumbered here."

Press never forgot a voice and he'd heard this one only an hour before. One of the M.P. squad leaders running patrols throughout the facility, he and his comrades had been introduced to Press and Dennis at the outside gate when they'd brought Patrick into the facility. As he lowered his gun, Press spun and looked back down the stairs—nothing. "Damn it all," he snarled. "I was going up the stairs and you guys were coming down—where the fuck did he *go*?"

The squad leader threw a glance to his left and Press followed his lead. There, across the twelve-foot expanse of the landing, was a three-by-three-foot window covered in narrow steel bars in a crisscrossed pattern. The bars were twisted and curled outward in the center of the window, as though someone had shot a mortar shell right through them.

Patrick Ross was gone.

CHAPTER 17

"Man," Press said with a reluctant amount of admiration. "Look at this—he blew through this gate like he was a tank and it was paper."

He and Laura and Colonel Burgess were outside the buildings that made up the BioHazard 4 complex, watching as a maintenance detachment scurried around with tools and rolls of fencing and worked to repair the huge rip in the front security gate. Above them was the sentry tower, heavily manned but apparently as useless as anything else had been in the efforts to keep Patrick Ross from leaving the base.

"What's that supposed to be?" Burgess asked with a sneer. "Another excuse? We had him in custody, under guard, and *you* let him escape. Do you think you could get any more incompetent than you already are?" Press started to retort but Burgess turned his back and gestured furiously at the men measuring out lengths of cyclone fencing. "Hurry it up," he shouted. "Get this damned thing fixed!" He whirled and faced off with Press again, his cheeks red with anger. "I can't believe I offered you a million bucks to do this job, Lennox. You're not worth two cents!"

Again Press opened his mouth to reply, but this time Laura beat him to the punch. "Fuck you, Burgess," she cut in. The older man's jaw dropped and Press felt himself start to grin, tried to hide it because he knew it would only make things worse. "If there's an imbecile anywhere on this base, you're it."

Carter Burgess's face went a nice shade of plum. "What did you say?"

"Are you deaf as well as foolish?" Laura spat. "This is all *your* fault—none of it would have happened if you hadn't forced me to put Eve into the cyclotron. Patrick never even knew she existed until she made that telepathic link, and she never had that until your cyclotron order. Why don't you be a man and face up to the fact that you just fucked up big time?"

Burgess took a step toward her, but Laura stood her ground. "Now you listen to me, Dr. Baker. You just watch what comes out of your mouth. You have no idea who you're talking to, and if you ever speak to me like that again, I'll shut your trap for you—"

It happened before he consciously sent the command to his brain: Press's hands were twisted in the folds of Burgess's military dress shirt tightly enough to cut off the colonel's air supply and *really* give his complexion a reason to change color. "I think the person who ought to watch what the hell he's saying is right here," Press growled. His nose was an inch away from Burgess's and he could smell the man's aftershave, something inexpensive and sharp. Funny, Press would have expected even this jackass to have better taste. "You threaten Laura again and I'll kill you. No fancy method, just a good old hand-to-hand elimination job where I rip out your lungs by their roots." He released Burgess with a shove that made the man stumble backward. "Get it?"

Carter Burgess glowered at him. "You don't want to go there, Lennox."

Press's return grin was nasty and much more menacing than anything that Burgess could have come up with. "Maybe I do."

For a long, frozen moment, the three of them stared at one another and no one moved. Finally, Burgess broke the standoff. "Let's just knock it off. Everyone's upset and anxious, but we need to keep our heads clear and not muck things up further by losing our tempers. Remember, we still have to find Patrick Ross." He paused and looked away, staring at the nearly mended fence but seeing something else. "I may know a way," he said at last. "I'll be in touch, and if you come up with any leads in the meantime, let me know."

Press and Laura watched him move off to his sedan and talk to the driver, then climb in the back seat. A few tricky maneuvers and the driver had turned the vehicle around and sped away from the base.

"Thanks," Laura said when the car was out of sight.

"Aw, he's nothing but a marble-eyed, goose-stepping son of a bitch."

She looked at him, then burst into laughter. "I've missed you," she said with a nostalgic smile. "You always made me laugh."

Press swung back to her instead of starting back toward the lab. "I've missed you, too."

They gazed at each other and Press took a chance and touched her cheek. It'd been a long time since he'd felt the softness of her skin and the feeling was better than his lousy memory had let him enjoy. "Laura—"

"Gamble's waiting in the lab," she said gently. "Let's go."

Press dropped his hand and nodded resolutely, following her back to the BioHazard 4 laboratory. Losing Ross was his fuck-up of the day, but he wasn't at all sure it was the biggest one in his life.

It was a beautiful office and, of course, one that Carter Burgess could never hope to have for himself. Funny how that was—the quirk of fate that let one man be born into the arms of a centuries-old southern family with political ties as unshakable as their family fortune, while another man—himself, for instance—was born the son of a World War II army mechanic and a WAC. All those carefully framed photos of Senator Ross with various Presidents and here, on the prime corner of the huge desk, was a portrait of the man himself and his astronaut son, Commander Patrick Ross. What a terrible waste. But Judson Ross would get past it because, Burgess believed, the man was a survivor like himself.

The senator just needed a little time to get a handle on things.

"The proof is incontrovertible, sir," Burgess said. "Your son was infected by alien DNA while he was up in that capsule. I'm sorry, Senator."

Spread on the desktop in front of a disbelieving Judson Ross were a dozen photographs, all in lurid, unforgiving color. Dr. Ralph Orinsky, the two young women from the Watergate Hotel, a half dozen others; at the last minute Burgess had decided to remove the photograph of Melissa, thinking that something like that would be a shock for even a strong man when he knew the victim.

"My God," said Senator Ross in a tortured voice. "You're telling me my son did these . . . these horrible *things*?"

"Yes, sir. We have matching blood types, DNA

matches, and a witness. We had your boy in custody, but he injured a number of people when he engineered an escape attempt." Burgess gave him a sidelong glance. "I'm afraid that two of those men are in critical condition. Generally speaking, they aren't expected to recover."

The senator scrubbed at his face with his hands. "You're sure it was my son?" he repeated.

Burgess stepped forward and put a hand on the desktop. "Listen, Senator. You can rest assured that we'll deal with this problem quietly. Patrick will receive medical treatment—the best doctors the United State government has, as well as the most expensive the private sectors have to offer. You know what that means, what we're capable of—treatment and cures that the public generally doesn't even know exist yet. And all top secret—the last thing this country and the President needs right now is anything that would tarnish the Ross family name."

Burgess heard a scraping sound and saw Ross bend slightly to the side. A moment later, he pulled a bottle of Old Grand-Dad from the drawer along with a crystal shot glass. His hands were shaking as he poured himself first one slug, then another; he looked like a man who was drowning and just wanted to anesthetize himself as he went under. The alcohol must've burned on the way down, because he swallowed hard and it was a long time before he could finally speak. "What do we do?" he asked mournfully. Senator Ross's face reminded Burgess of a sad old dog, shriveled and sagging at the edges.

Colonel Burgess cleared his throat. "There are two imperatives, Senator Ross. First and foremost, we have to find Patrick and bring him in immediately. There can't be any more deaths and any more . . ." The senator looked at him expectantly but he broke off, unwilling to tell the elder Ross any more than was absolutely necessary. "Any more problems," he finally finished. "Second, we have to neutralize *any* possibility that this situation leaks to the media. That would be extremely damaging in far too many areas. Not only would the Ross family name be destroyed, the NSEG's integrity would be suspect and the President's favorability ratings would plummet. We can't allow any of that to happen. I have to tell you . . ." He hesitated, then decided to continue. Of all things, the senator had a right to hear his next words. "The generals are very concerned."

His statement had the effect of a rifle shot on Senator Ross. Lines of anxiety appeared like crevices in his skin and there was a sharp flash of fear in his eyes. "The generals?" For an instant, no more, his face went blank while the knowledge worked its way a little deeper. "Jesus Christ, Burgess—they'll kill my boy, won't they? Or have him killed!"

"Senator—"

"Those fucking Pentagon bastards will have Patrick assassinated to protect themselves! To keep it all nice and tidy and *quiet*!"

"Senator," Burgess tried to cut in. "I assure you that we have no intention of—"

"I've seen what they can do!" Senator Ross shrieked.

"Senator, please. You don't—"

"Don't you let them kill him, Burgess!" He was rising from his chair, already shouting and with his voice still climbing. "That's a direct order, damn it. Don't you—"

"We won't—"

Ross suddenly lunged around the side of the desk and clutched at Colonel Burgess's jacket. "Please, Carter, *please*. He's my son, my only child." Blubbering now, and this kind of display of emotion in such a powerful man made Burgess's skin crawl. "I'm begging you," Senator Ross sobbed. "Don't let them do this—don't let them take my son away. He's my only boy!"

Burgess barely stopped the sound of disgust in his throat as he forced the senator's hands to let go, then straightened his jacket. God, the man was drunk—how much of that bottle had this fool pumped down even before Burgess had walked in here with the horrible news about Patrick? To know that this man, who was in charge of so many things for the American people, had been sitting here and knocking back whiskey as though he'd been in a back-street bar instead of a senatorial office was appalling.

"If you want to save your son, Senator Ross, I suggest you help us find him." Burgess's voice was cold and comfortless. "It's the only way the boy will live."

"She's incredibly beautiful," Dennis Gamble said. "How can she be so dangerous and look like this?"

He was standing right outside Eve's bio-environment, staring at the woman inside. He felt vaguely like a voyeur but if Eve resented being looked at, she showed no sign of it. Instead, she came to the glass to look back at him, studying his face curiously before letting her gaze travel up and down his body. After a second's hesitation, Dennis gingerly lifted his hand and pressed it against the glass. Eve did the same, placing her palm against his on the other side. Then, inexplicably, she made a repulsed face and pulled her hand away; without even looking back at Dennis, she spun and returned to the living area of her habitat to sit in front of the television. For her, Dennis Gamble no longer existed.

"Damn," Dennis said. "Would you look at that? It just figures—the way my luck's been running, I can't even attract an alien. I thought you said she and Patrick were attracted to anyone."

"They are, for the most part, " Laura agreed. She was about twenty feet away, working at a computer console while Press leaned off to one side, his watchful eyes taking in everything around the lab. Laura's voice was more relaxed than it had been in days and the reasons were all around her—security in the BioHazard 4 laboratory had been tripled since Eve's near escape. A sole guard had even been assigned to stand by the tether mechanism, and her only job was to trigger it if something went wrong.

"Then what the hell's wrong with me?" Dennis asked as he walked back over to the computer area. "She was looking at me, then suddenly she pulled away like I had leprosy or something."

"I'm not trying to scare you, Dennis, but to her, you do." She tapped a few more things into the computer console, then sat back.

He frowned. "What are you talking about?"

"Some people carry a genetic code in their DNA that gives them a predisposition toward a certain disease," Laura explained. "It doesn't mean that they have the disease, or even that they'll ever get it. However, for certain types of illness there is a distinct probability that the disease will appear in their offspring. People with certain types of bone-marrow disease, for instance, will generally get blood tests either before they marry or before they decide to have children."

Dennis was silent for a minute or so. "I don't think I have anything like that," he said slowly. He shot a troubled glance back at Eve's glass habitat. "Unless she can . . . I don't know. Smell something on me that I don't know about."

Laura turned back to the console and rapid-fired a series of keystrokes into the computer. Windows flashed on the screen, then the speaker gave a bleep. "Let's take a look at your chart," she said serenely. "Obviously you were in excellent health when you were chosen for the Mars landing expedition, and you maintained that health throughout your training. The periodic physicals and ongoing blood monitoring would have revealed any change." She studied the text scrolling by on the screen. "Nothing here," she murmured. "Wait—"

"What?" Dennis asked anxiously. Even Press turned his attention away from whatever mental security calculations were going on inside his head.

"Ah," Laura said and sat back. "It's right here on your chart. Not to worry—you don't have a thing wrong with you. There is, however, a predisposition in your family history on your father's side toward cancer. So far, you've escaped any problem; however, these aliens can—how should I put this?—*read* us in some way that we don't understand yet. Things that take intensive medical testing for us to discover, they detect immediately, and as you just saw, sometimes without even physically touching the person."

"That's a pretty good skill," Press commented.

Laura nodded. "Oh, you bet. If I remember correctly, you and I talked about it in our encounters with Sil." Her gaze on Press was clear. "I know you think I'm the world's biggest idiot for agreeing to be a part of this project and for helping the military to re-create—what did you call it? 'Sil-Lite.' " She actually smiled. "But I saw so much potential for good there—what if we could breed a tamer, calmer version of a creature that would help us diagnose diseases we can't even find with our best medical equipment?"

"Wow," Dennis said. "That would definitely be a bonus."

"So this is why Dennis wasn't infected along with Ross and Anne Sampas up on the *Excursion*," Press said. "Because the aliens can sense that he might have cancer?"

"Not exactly," Laura said. "What they can tell, apparently, is that any *children* he has in the future might, and since their prime imperative is to mate and reproduce, Dennis is not a suitable father. On the surface this 'preference' seems innocuous, but it's not at all insignificant. Instead, gentlemen, it is our key. Our *weapon*. Why? Because the alien DNA can't cope with the genetic flaws that exist in human DNA. It's defenseless against them."

Press gave her a smile that was full of misgiving. "You mean like in *War of the Worlds*?"

Laura looked at him blankly but Dennis's face lit up. "That's a classic science-fiction movie that started out as a novel written by H. G. Wells. The story is that Earth is invaded by aliens and nothing we do to fight back does any good—guns, bombs, nothing. What finally does the bastards in are the tiniest things we have. Our germs. So you think that's our answer—our germs?"

Now it was Laura's turn to smile. "I suppose you could put it that way, although technically I can't say that the cause of every disease can actually be traced to a bacteria or a virus, which if I'm understanding you correctly, seems to be the miracle cure in your movie." She tapped a key on the computer and Dennis's medical history disappeared from the screen, and was quickly replaced by a flowing stream of data—more information about Eve and her body chemistry. Laura looked at the two men, her expression gone completely serious. "I just know that turnabout is fair play. The alien DNA infected us, and now it's our turn to do the same to it."

Home, sweet home again, Patrick thought as he pulled the car into the driveway of his mother's summer mansion. There were lights on in the house—the servants again. It was always possible that his father might be here tonight, but the big car the old man rode around in was nowhere to be seen, which also meant nothing, since it could be parked in one of the garages or his driver might have taken it to town on some errand. Tonight there was no breeze to rattle Old Faithful on the pole and cover his noise; then again, regretfully, Patrick had no new offspring to bring to the barn anyway.

Without a child to lead, the walk across the back grounds took half the time. It was late and dark and still, with not even the far-off barking of the neighbor's dogs to break the silence. Lost in his own thoughts, Patrick literally didn't realize the padlock on the barn doors had been busted until he moved to insert his key into it and saw it on the ground next to the crowbar that had shattered it.

Alarm shot through him and he grabbed for the handle of the barn door. Before he could enter, a voice from the shadows stopped him.

"I knew you'd be here."

Patrick whirled and saw his father standing there. The older man looked smaller and slightly shriveled, as if the last four or five days had sucked away a good portion of his life force. They stared at each other until Judson Ross looked away, his gaze scanning the darkened fields between the barn and the house. On the other side was an orchard, a small stream, and a large, fenced pasture where they'd ridden horses when Patrick was a teenager. The animals were gone now, the pasture choked with weeds and wildflowers.

"The best part of your childhood was spent here," his father said wistfully. "Do you remember? So many wonderful summers we had, the three of us. Until your mother died, of course. Then everything changed."

Patrick waited and said nothing.

"I dropped myself into my work," Senator Ross continued. "And the bottle, too—I'm quite aware that I drink too much. I guess the work and the liquor helped me to ease the loss." His head turned back toward Patrick. "But it didn't do much for you, did it?"

Patrick frowned but stayed silent. What did the old man want?

"Patricia always loved it here," Judson Ross said softly. "And she loved you, too—so very much. She was a much better mother than I've been a father. But you know all that, don't you?"

Something inside Patrick . . . *stretched.* There was no way to explain it other than that there was a defeated part of him that reached out and tried to resurface. He felt pain suddenly, but it wasn't really physical. A twist in his heart and his mind and suddenly Patrick was standing in front of his father and blinking as tears started to fill his eyes. Now that he wanted to say something, nothing would come out.

His father dropped his gaze to the ground, and he had never seemed more ashamed. "They told me what happened in space, Patrick. How you were infected by something up there. And all the while, I'd been in my office, thinking about power and a seat in the Senate and when my only son comes to me for help, I turn him away. I should have listened."

Finally, *finally,* Patrick felt he could speak. "You never listened," he whispered. "Never."

Senator Ross lifted his chin. "But I'm listening now," he said fiercely. "And I'll do whatever it takes to make this right, to fix it."

Patrick shook his head. Suddenly his mind was a jumble of images, some he couldn't understand, others he didn't want to see. Everything inside his head seemed undercut with a sort of shiny, golden-brown fog . . . where it wasn't tinted red. Like blood. "No," he rasped. "You can't, not now. It's too late—if I go with you, they'll kill me—"

"Absolutely *not,*" Senator Ross said. For a moment he sounded like his old self again: strong, secure, in charge of the world. "There is no possible way that

I'm turning you over to any of those military-minded Pentagon bastards. Until I make all the arrangements for you to go to Johns Hopkins for treatment, you'll be plenty safe here—this property's always been in your mother's maiden name. They won't even know where to look." He held out a hand. "Come on, Patrick. Let's go back to the house and make a pot of coffee, sit down and talk about what's happened and what needs to be done. We'll walk through this together, just like we used to handle problems when you were a boy."

Patrick stared at his father's hand, a part of him wanting so badly to take it. But another part, a *darker* part, would never allow that. He should turn away now, walk out of range of this man who had once been a part of him but who was now forever separated. Instead he felt frozen in place, pulled in two different directions by unseen forces whose power at the moment canceled one another out and left him stuck in the middle, staring at the hand his father had extended. It promised so much—warmth, love, *help.* "I've done . . . terrible things," he managed to say at last. "They can't be undone—"

"It doesn't matter," Judson Ross said stubbornly. "You're still my son. You'll *always* be my son, no matter what." He took a step toward Patrick, then another. His hand, large and warm, closed around Patrick's elbow and urged him forward. "Come on, son. I'll take care of it, I swear. Everything will be all right."

Patrick shivered and tried to shake his head—

no no no

"I know I haven't been the father I should have been," Senator Ross said levelly. "And I understand if you're reluctant to listen to what I have to say—I probably would be, too. But if you won't do it for me, then remember your mother, Patrick. Your mother would want you to go on and be healed, to do the right thing for yourself. If nothing else, Patty, do it for her."

That internal yearning again, wanting so much—

"*Help me,*" Patrick said raggedly. "Oh, my *God*—"

He sagged but his father was there, for the first time in years, to carry Patrick's weight. So much time spent on his own, making his own way without anyone's help and with no one but friends—usually Dennis and Melissa—to talk to about what to do with his life and the future. Now his old man's arms were around him, strong and sure, and the elder Ross was turning Patrick back toward the house and steering him away from the barn. "It's all right, son, it'll be fine. You'll see. Let's go back to the house and then—"

His father's touch, so warm and . . . *human,* sent a sudden chill down his spinal column. Something within him screamed a warning—

—and was smashed down.

Forever.

Senator Judson Ross's face contorted in agony and blood welled from his mouth as a tentacle, beautifully studded with dozens of barbs, rammed all the way through the middle of his torso. The tentacle twisted and churned, and its work was done in hardly more than a heartbeat; glistening with the crimson lifeblood of his father, the extra appendage drew back into Patrick's body and dropped the corpse on the ground. Marking its wake was only the blood-splattered tear in the center of Patrick's once-white shirt.

Patrick stepped over the body of his father and turned back toward the barn. There, clustered around the open doorway and staring at him with pride from the darkened recesses, were his children.

Patrick smiled, and went to them.

CHAPTER 18

"Colonel, may I remind you that this situation has gone on far too long for comfort. Each day that passes makes it more difficult to maintain the utter secrecy for which we've been striving throughout the duration of this project."

Ah, yes, Carter Burgess thought. Another dressing-down from my superiors. And I'll warrant that Preston Lennox thinks he's the only one who keeps getting reamed out over this farce.

The second of the generals picked up where the first one had left off. "A leak to the media could open a Pandora's box unlike anything this government has ever seen. It would not be difficult to trace it internally and find out that not only had we suspected life on Mars, but that Herman Cromwell, lunatic though we thought he was, predicted that a human sent to Mars would be exposed to undue risk. Even worse, an investigative reporter with a tantalizing lead, the right connections, and enough bribe money could in all probability work out a path all the way to the fiasco with the first alien woman, that 'Sil.' "

Colonel Burgess frowned. "There have been no reports or indication that anyone found out—"

"You're wearing blinders if you believe that, Colonel," said one of the others in a flat voice. "And I don't believe you're a stupid man. Questions have already been raised about Patrick Ross. The NSEG office is fielding calls from civilians who have been complaining about his strange behavior, most from women he's apparently approached and tried to pick up. There's always some bimbo trying to make a fast buck by talking to the tabloids, and the fact is, we should have been giving thought to the matter of silencing these so-called witnesses all along. We can try to discredit them, but for the most part, now it's too late."

"I've informed Senator Ross of our dilemma," Burgess said when the trio looked at him expectantly. "My hope is that he'll be able to help us locate his son."

"When we do, Preston Lennox will have to kill him," said the general who was usually the quietest. "Such a shame to be forced to eliminate a national hero." The others nodded in agreement, but they all knew there was no alternative.

"I'm afraid it's Press Lennox that I'm worried about," Burgess said coolly. He waited, but it wasn't for long.

"How so?" asked the first general. "Do you think he would—"

"He's a loose cannon," Burgess said matter-of-factly. "He blames the military for this entire project and its results, and he deeply resents what he perceives as an irresponsible repetition of our first mistake with Sil. And we all know how much he resists authority." He gave them time to let that digest, then hit them with the final blow. "When this is over," he said smoothly, "don't be surprised to see the whole sordid story on the front page of *The New York Times.*"

The second of the group looked doubtful. "Preston Lennox is an excellent covert agent who has always been highly dependable and efficient," he said. "He's uniquely qualified to terminate the alien, and the simple reality of this is that there isn't anyone else with both his level of skill and his previous experience with just this sort of creature. There simply isn't anyone else who can do this job." He studied Burgess's unyielding face, then sighed. "If you still have misgivings, we'll just have to deal with them when he has accomplished his assignment of exterminating the alien threat."

Burgess almost smiled. But no; it would never do to have these men, all of whom thought they were so intelligent and cagey, realize that they'd played right to where he wanted them. "I have a suggestion."

"And what's that?"

He didn't know which of the men had asked the question, and he didn't care. What mattered was that his chance was finally here. Nobody manhandled him like Lennox had. As far as Burgess was concerned, Press Lennox was the King Asshole and the colonel had ways, eventually, of dealing with people like that; Lennox was about to get dealt with. "We'll use the Oswald-Ruby gambit. Or, to quote a cliché, kill two birds with one stone. Preston Lennox will take care of Patrick . . ."

They stared at him, waiting.

"And I'll take care of Preston Lennox."

He wanted to see them go into the changing stages of their life.

There was one of those massive Wal-Mart stores

not far away, so Patrick went there, digging around until he found what he was looking for in the automotive department: four portable electric lights, the kind that clamped onto the hood of a car so you could work hands-free. One for each floor; the barn had been abandoned, but no one had ever bothered to disconnect the simple electric lines that offered the occasional outlet for power tools. Within an hour, the inside of the dank and musty barn was lit well enough to see whatever he needed to.

Now Patrick was watching the last of his current offspring enter the chrysalis stage. Patrick himself had been denied this great experience, but he wasn't jealous. His childhood had, of course, been spent as a human, and now he viewed that earlier time as a primer for the learning that he had put to such good use after his visit and his . . . *enlightenment* on Mars. While the thought of the chrysalis stage was intriguing, it was also a time of complete and utter helplessness, which was something that Patrick could not abide. That was why he was needed here in the barn, to assure that these children came to full growth. When that happened, they could go on their way, and he would go on his. And they would all, obviously, continue to breed—the males would find the strongest of the human females, and the females would chose the strongest of the human males. *Ad infinitum*, until his kind ruled Earth.

No frightened boy here; his youngest son was quiet and content, reassured by the presence of his parent as more tentacles than Patrick could keep track of pushed from everywhere on the child's exposed skin. Long and graceful, they extended up and up and up, into the shadows between the beams overhead where the gleam of the portable lights couldn't reach. Somewhere up there the willowy appendages must've met and attached, because not even a full minute passed before his son was lifted up with them. Fastened high among the rafters, the boy stayed soundless as the final walls of his chrysalis enveloped him.

Satisfied, Patrick went to the stairs at the back of the barn and began to climb. One flight, then another, and finally he was on the fourth and final level of the barn, the loft. Along the way, he inspected the results of his handiwork of the last week or so, walking among his children and touching, where he could reach, each one to feel the sweet life within. Weak they might have been, but perhaps he should be more grateful to the human women who'd given their lives to become their initial living incubators. Now those children, like their youngest brother downstairs, had been wrapped snugly away and hung here and there to await rebirth into adulthood. So many women, so many children.

At least three dozen. Maybe more; it was hard to see way up in the roof rafters.

It wouldn't be long now.

"Jesus," Dennis said as he stepped inside the room behind Press. "I thought we were at a medical facility. This looks like some kind of illegal arms manufacturer."

"Nah. It's not nearly big enough." The room was small, barely ten by ten and painted that oh-so-attractive shade of dull military green. Press began inspecting the weapons stored neatly in racks along the walls. "Besides, they don't make 'em; we just stock 'em. That's why it's called the 'Emergency Armory.' "

"You sound like a commercial."

The special agent gave a short laugh. "Yeah, that's me. Number One Fan of Uncle Sam." Next to a rack of M-16s, Mossberg 590 shotguns, and SWAT H&K MP5A3s, he saw half a dozen Kalishnikov rifles; he picked one up and peered at it, then put it back in its place. Speaking of Uncle Sam, where—and why—the hell had a U.S. Air Force base come up with this Russian shit? There was even an entire shelf of ammunition. So much for buying American.

"What's this thing?"

Press glanced over his shoulder. "A Tartex land mine. It'll pretty much wipe out this room if you drop it and it goes off."

"Shit," Dennis said nervously. He set the mine back in its slot on a shelf, handling it like it was a paper egg, then eyed the supply of olive-drab hand grenades next to it. "Can't we just call in the National Guard?"

Press shook his head. "Sorry, pal. No can do—this is strictly a solo mission."

Dennis made a sound that Press thought was a moan. "Man, I'm a lover, not a fighter. How'd I get involved in this?"

"Lover, my ass," Press said with a wicked grin. "You ain't been laid in eleven months, remember?"

"Yeah, and no thanks to you, hotshot. And I *do* recall, thank you very much. Right down to that up-and-coming moment of golden truth when your army boys burst in and ruined it all."

"Big talk."

Dennis scowled at him, but without real animosity. "Okay, so I used to be a lover." He gazed around the room again, taking in the kind of armor that they'd never had on the *Excursion*. "But I'm sure as hell no kind of soldier."

"You'll be doing your country a good turn," Press said. "Helping out more than anything you ever did up there floating around in space. Hell, you never know—maybe once we've got him captured, they'll award you the Congressional Medal of Honor. Hell, I'll even recommend it."

"Whoopee," Dennis said, but Press thought he sounded anything but enthused.

"This looks about right." He plucked a small, high-tech tranquilizer gun from a stand and inspected it closely, then snagged a box of darts. "Perfect, except that it only holds one dart at a time, plus there's only one of these shooters in here—not much call for this kind of thing lately."

Dennis came over to see and his mouth dropped open. "That punk-ass little thing? What are you trying to do—make it take a nap? No offense, but where are the bazookas? This looks like something my grandmother would hide in her purse at the bingo hall!"

Press smirked. "Hasn't anyone ever told you that size doesn't matter?"

"The hell it doesn't," Dennis retorted. He scanned the rows of weapons, then stepped over and plucked a long, serrated machete from its place on the wall. "You can have your wimpy little gun, but I'm taking this for good measure."

Press stopped, watching as Dennis fastened the handle of the machete to his belt loop. There was no doubt that the guy was a cutup, a smart-ass, and a continuously horny bastard to boot. But there were other qualities here that Press was discovering. "Dennis," he said pointedly, "you don't have to come with us, you know. You're not Special Ops, and you're not under any kind of obligation—"

"Oh, you are so wrong," Dennis interrupted. He looked at the floor and Press knew he was trying to hide the pain on his face. "I've got *so* much of an obligation. Patrick was my best friend, and despite what he's become, he was a great guy. You've seen all the horrible things he's done now, but you never knew him when he was okay. He would've never done anything to hurt people, would have never, *ever* harmed Melissa—he worshiped her." Dennis's words had grown thick and he stopped for a moment, then continued in a quieter voice. "If he could stand outside himself and see what's he's become, know what's he's done . . . he would want us to end it for him."

Eve sat and watched the activity outside her habitat, noting with detached interest the tripled guards, the woman stationed by the tether mechanism, and down at the far end, Laura and that special agent, Press Lennox. They were doing something over there that had to do with filling tranquilizers that would be shot out of a pistol—as if such things could stop her. Or Patrick . . . especially him.

Sometimes Eve wondered if the good doctor had as much of a handle on her as she was reported to have on Patrick. Here she came now, a determined look on her face, and confidence—false, Eve could feel it—in her step. She motioned to the sentry to raise the outer gate and the person obeyed. A smart fox, though; the female guard retracted it only enough to allow Laura to duck inside the exchange hallway. When the gates behind her had been lowered back into place, she gestured for the guard to open the inner set.

"Dr. Baker," Brea said, "we strongly advise you not to go in there. There's been a definite shift in Eve's personality. She's unpredictable at best, and at worst she's got the strength of ten men." The young woman's eyes were wide and frightened, her face bisected by the white strip across her broken nose. Both eyes were rimmed in bloody-looking purple, all thanks to the results of Eve's little choking act. After patching her up in MedLab, Laura had wanted her to stay home for a few days, but Brea had refused. "I guess we all know how devious she can be, and now she's refused to cooperate anymore with the laboratory monitoring."

"I have to agree, ma'am" said the guardswoman by the tether mechanism. Again, it was one of the women who had been there during Eve's first outbreak. Beyond a few nasty bruises, she was fine, although her opinion of the life-form was clearly leaning toward a preference for termination. Brea seemed to regard the female soldier with more respect since the incident. "Even with this"—the guard gestured at the main switch—"the fact is that thing in there could kill you before the toxin would kill her, and there's nothing I could to stop it."

Laura stood for a moment, considering. Finally, she said, "It's okay. It's worth a reasonable risk if she cooperates."

Brea stared at her. "And if she doesn't?"

"Then I'll get the hell out of there. Go on—open it."

Brea shook her head and activated the switch for the external gate. Before Laura stepped inside, she glanced back at her staff members. "If she takes me hostage, trigger the tether mechanism. Do *not* negotiate, and do *not* open this gate for her, under any circumstance. Understood?" They all nodded, faces creased with apprehension.

The external gate came down with a clang, but Laura had to gesture again before her reluctant crew would raise the inner one. Then she was inside Eve's habitat and she could see the alien woman on the other side of several glass walls where, at the far end, she was amusing herself in what they called the exercise area. This small section had a few basic pieces of exercise equipment—a treadmill, an exercise bicycle, one of the Total Gym systems that used body weight as resistance. There were no weight plates, barbells or dumbbells, nothing that could be thrown or used as a weapon. As it turned out, they needn't have bothered with anything but the treadmill, which Eve seemed to use only as a way of releasing pent-up energy. She was on it now, dressed in a sports bra and a pair of spandex bicycle shorts above thick cotton anklets and her Nikes. Her long, lean body was lathered in sweat as she pounded along the rubber surface at a good ten to eleven miles an hour, the treadmill's motor screaming and at its performance limit. Her hair was plastered to her forehead but she wasn't breathing hard at all; there were no more electrodes taped to her body.

When she saw Laura, she flipped the OFF switch and let the treadmill wind down, then stepped off it. "What are you doing in here?"

Laura studied her, noting the fine muscles and the immediate cardio recovery despite the long, vigorous run on the treadmill. Such beauty . . . such *danger.* She hesitated, then went for it. "I came to ask for your help again," she said slowly. "To find Patrick. On our own—"

"No."

"Eve—"

"If I came to you," Eve said coldly, "and asked you to help me destroy the only other one of your kind in the world, would you agree to help me do it?" Her mouth twisted as she watched for Laura's reaction. When nothing came, her expression changed once again, this time to fury. "We're back to that lab-rat thing again, aren't we? That's me, an experimental little *nothing* to be poked and prodded and thrown out when I'm just no fun anymore."

"That's not it at all."

"Sorry, Dr. Baker. You'll have to find Patrick without me. I won't help you this time. Good luck, though—you're definitely going to need it." She turned her back and started to step back on the treadmill, but Laura's next words stopped her.

"Eve, you have to understand that if you refuse to cooperate in this laboratory I can't guarantee that the program will continue," Laura said. She tried to keep her voice bland, but Eve wasn't a stupid woman. Still, this was a last resort—

Eve whirled. "You're threatening me!" she said incredulously. "Do you think I *care* what you do to me?" One hand gestured angrily at her living quarters. "This is all nice and bright and cheery, but in case you've forgotten, it's a *prison.*" Laura saw the color change in Eve's skin as her face took on a faint shade of red. "You want to kill me, Dr. Baker?" she hissed and took a step toward her. "Then do it . . . if you *can.*"

Laura locked gazes with Eve and her heart started pounding. For the first time in all these months, there was nothing at all human in Eve's eyes—sure, the blue color was the same, the shape was the same, but there was something else there, too. Something she couldn't put a name to and that was unbelievably menacing.

The tables had turned.

Fear or not, Laura still told Eve the truth. "No," she said as evenly as she could. "I don't want to do that. I never did."

Heart thundering, unwilling to turn her back, Laura edged out of Eve's exercise area and left the life-form staring after her, then hurried out of the habitat.

She would never go in there again.

CHAPTER 19

"Are they ready?" Press asked. He and Dennis watched as Laura carefully injected a bright blue gel-based substance into the emptied shells of the tranquilizer darts. The two men were holding a couple of spray canisters filled with the same material, which Laura had substituted for the failed hydrochlorine toxin. "Do you think it will work?"

Laura's eyes crinkled as she concentrated on the last of her task, then she straightened and packed up the filled tranquilizer darts. "I can't give you any assurances about that," she admitted. In theory . . . yes, it ought to be extremely efficient." She gave them a faint, tired smile. "In practice, I'm afraid it hasn't been tested yet."

"Well, it's the best shot we've got," Press said and held out his hand for the weapon. Laura gave it to him and he inspected it carefully, making sure he knew how to load it now so he wouldn't end up dying while he tried to figure it out when he was in the field. Single shot—too bad these things didn't come semi-auto.

"That other stuff didn't work," Dennis said.

"That's not entirely true," Laura pointed out.

"It didn't *work*," Dennis said stubbornly. "Otherwise Patrick would be . . . ah, shit." He looked miserable. "Well, he'd be dead, that's what, and he's not. So what if this stuff doesn't work either? Then what?"

Press had no answer for Dennis and he looked to Laura. Her eyes met his, then cut to Dennis. Finally, she spoke.

"Then we'll be walking onto a battlefield with a water pistol," she said softly.

Dennis started to say something, then frowned as he eyed the rest of the lab and Eve's glass bio-environment. "You know, something's not right over there."

The tone of his voice made Laura look up. "What?"

"Maybe I'm just seeing things—too much crazy stress or something—but I could've sworn I just saw part of that glass bubble thing that Eve is in sort of . . . *bulge.*"

The statement made Press jerk toward the lab and Eve's bio-environment. "Jesus Christ, Laura—you don't think she could shatter that, do you?"

"No way," Laura said flatly. "That's quartz glass. It's unbreakable and it won't melt until it hits several thousand degrees Celsius. The stuff is used to contain—"

The whole front wall of Eve's habitat *exploded.*

The three of them spun simultaneously, and for a too-long moment, no one moved. A lifetime ago Press had stood with Laura and the members of the first team who had been gathered to apprehend the escaped Sil and had watched a laboratory tape of how as a child, Sil had cannonballed through the window of her smaller glass quarters and escaped. Now many of those people involved in the resulting alien hunt—Stephen Arden and Xavier Fitch, the head of the whole operation, among them—were dead, and the sight of all that glass, so much more this time, brought it all back to the forefront of Press's memory. It was like before—a huge, glistening blast of strangely sharp water, a shower of glitter that razored against the skin and clothes of anyone within range.

Press and Laura both looked to the right and saw the woman in charge of the tether mechanism stagger back, her face covered with bloody cuts. Then the woman's dazed expression cleared and hardened, and she went for the double sequence of buttons that would take care of this alien problem once and for all.

She never made it.

Even with her exceptional speed and strength, Eve was too far away to reach the guard before she would hit the death button. She must have known it would be this way, because before the woman's stride could take her back to the tether mechanism, something flew through the air, a blur that was traveling far too fast to identify until it smashed into the side of the guard's head and knocked her off her feet. The force of the blow tossed her against the wall behind her and it wasn't until she slid down it and didn't get up again that they saw what had done the damage—the lopsided remains of the baseball Eve had ruined the other day.

"The tether!" Laura shouted, and the race was on.

Eve and Press went for the gold mechanism on the wall at the same time. The only reason Press got there an instant before she did was that he was closer—Eve was far, far faster. Still, that wasn't enough. As his hand jabbed toward the button, Eve's fingers closed around his arm; before he could go on the defensive, he went sailing through the air as though he was no more than a bothersome gnat.

He heard more than saw the tether mechanism shatter under the impact of Eve's fist, had a glimpse of flying sparks followed by the stench of heated insulation. The device fell off the wall and crashed to the floor, nothing but a useless, crumpled hunk of metal leaving a few stray wires still attached to the wall. Press tried desperately to shake the fog from his brain and managed only enough sense to pull himself up on one knee and watch Eve as she sprinted across the laboratory; the main locked door might as well have been made of cardboard for all it kept her inside. She kicked it open without any effort at all and vaulted through the opening, disappearing into the corridor beyond.

"Oh, *shit*!" Press heard Dennis cry out. Then the astronaut and Laura were at his side and helping him to his feet.

"Why didn't anyone fire?" Press demanded. Eyes blazing, he glared around the laboratory but none of the guards would meet his eyes. A few feet away, the woman who had been in charge of guarding the tether mechanism was still splayed against the wall; starting at the left temple, the entire side of her face had turned into a black bruise. Her eyes were open and staring at nothing that anyone in the lab would ever know.

"I think the quarters were too close—they were afraid they'd hit each other," Laura said. She peered hard at Press and tried to lift one of his eyelids. "Are you okay?"

"I'm wonderful," he retorted and pushed her hand away. "Grab the DNA compound and let's go."

"We didn't test it—"

"What the hell were you going to test it on, anyway?" Press gripped her by one wrist and tugged her back toward the main lab area, knowing that Dennis would follow. "If she gets to Patrick before we do, we're going to have problems bigger than anything we ever dreamed of. Let's grab our gear and *go.*"

Laura and Dennis didn't have to be told again. A few seconds that felt like eternities, then they were sprinting through the wreck of the main lab door and after Eve, following corridor after corridor while alarms began to scream through the speakers. It wasn't hard to track the life-form—it was BioHazard policy to post a sentry at every half-landing to check identification cards and authorizations; all they had to do was to track the trail of bodies Eve left in her wake. One of them was missing the chain of keys at his belt that no doubt had held a security cardkey . . . and that meant that Eve was going to be able to get all the way outside.

"She won't make out of the building, will she?" Dennis demanded as the three of them jumped over the unconscious man and kept going. "I mean, someone will stop her before she takes off, right?"

"How does she even know where she's going?" Press asked on the heels of that. "This damned place is the biggest tangle of halls I've ever seen."

Laura pulled up, then motioned at a stairway marked EMERGENCY ACCESS ONLY—AUTHORIZED PERSONNEL ONLY. "Let's go this way—the stairwell alarm hasn't been triggered, which means Eve must've taken the elevator." She pulled a security cardkey from her pocket and jammed it into the card reader; an instant later the red light on the device changed to green and the locking mechanism clicked open. "Even if we don't beat her upstairs, we should at least be able to get there at the same time. Come on!"

"Oh, I can't wait," Press said.

Nevertheless, he was the first one through the door.

* * *

Eve lost count of the number of people who got in her way.

There was no doubt that she'd killed some of them, including the woman back in the lab, the one who had been charged with the task of triggering the tether mechanism. But she had no regrets; she had passed the point of no return and she neither needed nor wanted to go back. Tonight she would find what she was, *be* what she was, or die trying. And if that was the way it was meant to be, then a lot of the humans would die with her.

There was no question about finding her way out of the BioHazard complex. The urge to go upward was as strong as the longing deep inside her that was pulling her unerringly toward freedom—every time she turned in the correct direction the sense of impending physical fulfillment grew stronger, and every time she chose wrongly, it faded. It was a built-in homing beacon, destined to lead her out of this place and, ultimately, to her mate.

After such a long time in the bio-environment—literally her entire life—Eve had no idea what to expect when she hammered her way through the final metal door that led to the outside world. Up until now, her entire knowledge of anything beyond the BioHazard 4 hallways had been limited to the programs she'd seen on television. She'd watched everything from sitcoms to soap operas to nature programs, slice-of-life serials to science-fiction movies. But none of it had prepared Eve for her first sight of the night sky.

It was beautiful, stretching endlessly above the complex as she stepped through the wreckage she'd made of the last doorway. *Big sky*—she'd heard that term applied often enough to a state somewhere called Montana, but had never understood it until now. She still wasn't sure she did, but she could at least finally comprehend why someone would say that: so far above, and for her, unreachable . . . yet she felt an undeniable connection to it that the people on this planet would never feel. Her ancestors had come from somewhere out there—*she* had, too. The sky and the concepts behind it and everything it stood for in her existence overwhelmed her for a single, eternal moment, wiping out everything else—the BioHazard 4 complex, the escape from her habitat, Dr. Baker and her associates in pursuit. The silence around her was absolute, and she felt fused with the universe, as though every part of her was finally back where it belonged.

Eve never even saw the soldiers ringing the parking lot around the building's exit, nor did she hear the MP squadron leader's shouted, single-word command—

"Fire!"

"There is unusual activity on the western edge of the compound perimeter, sir."

Colonel Burgess resisted the urge to tell the pilot of the AH-1G Huey helicopter that he had eyes, thank you, and could see that for himself. "Keep your distance," he said instead. "Let's see what's going on but stay high enough not to become a part of it." The man nodded and banked the black-painted chopper, his smooth handling of the stick a good indication of his years of experience; in a few moments he'd brought them to a point where Burgess could focus his binoculars and get a closer bead on the action below.

Watching, Burgess saw their flight here in his mind again in much the same way that a drowning man sees his life flash before him. With Monroe A.F.B. as his destination, they'd taken off from the Pentagon and flown above Washington, D.C. proper. Burgess had had little on his mind but the assignment ahead—let Lennox neutralize the alien threat, then he would neutralize Lennox. But the flight had been an unintentional delight, giving the colonel a panoramic night view of all the monuments that he loved and that stood for American freedom—the Capitol building, the White House, the Lincoln and Washington memorials. These were all representations of his life, and now everything Burgess saw happening on the ground below the helicopter threatened that. Soldiers and military vehicles crawled around the outside of the BioHazard end of the complex like ants attacking a sugar hill while searchlights swept the area and another two dozen men poured out an exit and positioned themselves on the edge of the roof. In another instant, the main door to the building came crashing down—so much for steel-reinforced construction—and out stepped a blond-haired woman who could only be—

Eve!

Burgess leaned forward in the passenger seat, his breath caught in his throat. Bad enough that Patrick Ross was still out there somewhere, but if this alien female escaped and went to him, then all those spectacular symbols back in the city, everything they stood for, would probably be destroyed. She *had* to be stopped here and now—

Machine-gun fire rippled through the night, its bright orange flashes and sound detectable even above the drone of the helicopter. Far below, the woman jerked and fell, then lay facedown and motionless on the concrete.

For a few precious seconds, both he and the pilot thought it was over—

—then everything changed.

Burgess only had to jerk his head and the pilot nodded and knew to pursue.

Eve opened her eyes to a ring of soldiers' faces peering down at her.

For a second she thought she was back in the lab—damn it, she must have been unconscious long enough for them to hustle her back to the lower level and imprison her again. But no . . . beneath the skin of her arms and legs she could feel concrete, warm and rough, unlike anything in the lab. And sparkling from between the gawking faces above her—

Starlight.

There was pain everywhere, but it wasn't debilitating. She felt her insides shift around the pieces of metal and somehow *test* them before pushing them aside, then out. By the time all her wounds had closed and knitted together, the pain was gone and something about her cellular structure had changed permanently, as though her body had learned about the danger of bullets and now could—and would—protect itself. Experience was always the best teacher.

The fools who surrounded her never expected her to come back to life.

Eve took four of them down with one brutal sweep of her arm, then left a moaning, bleeding pile of men when the rest tried to stop her. There was gunfire again—out here these stupid humans would shoot even their own kind—but she hardly felt the bullets; now they were more like bee stings that never penetrated her skin although they did horrible damage to the terribly fragile men still witlessly trying to stop her. The gunfire was escalating but it didn't matter; she crossed the sidewalk and street at a dead run and made for one of the HMMWVs, the military version of a Hummer, parked at an angle on the other side. Yanking the door open, she pulled out the driver before he realized what was happening; another hapless human casualty, the man's body was decimated by his comrades' gunfire before he ever hit the ground.

Then Eve was inside the vehicle and turning the

key, listening to the engine of the well-maintained vehicle as it churned to life. It took a precious three seconds for her to decipher the markings on the gearshift knob and decide which was which of the two foot pedals. She killed the motor once and started it again, this time succeeding in her search for reverse on the transmission. She hit the accelerator too hard and the vehicle lurched backward and hit something—a quick look and Eve saw the front of the Jeep she'd just trashed. She found first, twisted the wheel, and jumped on the gas pedal. The gates were too far away and roadblocked; lights and people and the red-orange flashes of gunfire flew by as she made for the fence at the perimeter, aiming the vehicle for a stretch of it between two metal posts. It came down with a clang and the HMMWV bounced and rocked as it climbed over the twisted pieces.

Then Eve was roaring down the access road and headed for freedom . . .

. . . and Patrick.

"You want to tell me how the hell she learned to drive?" Press demanded as he hauled Laura out of the BioHazard 4 building and toward the remaining HMMWV. He shouted something at the driver and waved his identification; in return the man practically leaped out of the vehicle. The taillights of Eve's HMMWV were just disappearing through the fence when Press, Laura and Dennis clambered into the vehicle, clawing for their seat belts at the same time that Press rammed the gearshift into drive and floored it.

"It's not such a stretch," Laura yelled over the screaming of the engine. They followed the path of the first vehicle through the fence, jerking over the downed section and missing having the tires slashed by a vibrating length of razor wire only because it had come loose and snapped out of their path.

"Think of all the television she's watched—that stupid *Dukes of Hazard* for starters. If you recall, Sil didn't have any problem with a car either."

"Fan-fucking-tastic," Press ground out.

"Television, huh? Well, what else can she do that we don't know about?" Dennis asked anxiously from the back seat. Belted in, he was now fighting to keep the canisters and spray nozzles from rolling all over the place.

"It doesn't *matter* what else she can do," Press interrupted. His jaw was set and his hands were locked on the steering wheel as he concentrated on following the HMMWV. "She's not going to get the chance to try."

"How are you going to catch her?" Laura squinted through the windshield at the taillights far ahead. "What if she doesn't stop—"

"Oh, she'll stop all right," Press said. The glow from the instruments on the dashboard gave his eyes and face a slightly greenish tint. "And when she does, Eve'll be doing exactly what I want—

"Leading us right to Patrick Ross."

"Colonel Burgess, sir," squawked a sexless voice over the helicopter's radio. "We have confirmed the presence of the alien escapee in the first vehicle. Preliminary identification of the individuals in the second gives us Preston Lennox, Dr. Laura Baker, and NASA Flight Officer Dennis Gamble."

"Roger," Burgess said into the radio. He leaned forward and finally saw them far below—the first HMMWV, presumably with Eve inside it, hell-bent to some unknown destination that hopefully would bring them to Patrick Ross. Maybe a hundred and fifty yards behind it was an identical vehicle, this one carrying a team of good old American would-be soldiers determined to destroy both Eve and Patrick. Well, good for them; then he would step in and clean up the mess. Lennox would be no loss to humanity, although it was a damned shame about Baker and Gamble.

"Do not send backup except on my order. This is a preplanned operation." He got an affirmative from the radio operator, then turned his gaze toward the pilot. "Keep your distance," he said. "Let's find out where she's going first, or what she's looking for, before we make any moves. We want to crash this little party at just the right time." The pilot nodded and obeyed like a well-programmed robot, nosing the chopper slightly faster but higher, where they could easily track the action but not be seen or heard.

"We're coming up on Virginia airspace, sir," the pilot announced.

"Wonderful," muttered Burgess. Where the hell was this alien bitch going? "Keep it steady," he ordered. "Don't get any closer than you have to. We're not going down until I give the signal."

Virginia, Burgess mused. What was it about this state that had drawn Eve?

Virginia is for Lovers.

And suddenly, he knew.

Damn it all, the information was right there in the files on Senator Judson Ross—Burgess and his crew had missed it because they'd concentrated on going over *Patrick's* records, not his father's. Patricia Downey—Patrick's mother and namesake—had a summer estate that had been in her family for generations. She had inherited it at age twenty-two when her mother, Patrick's grandmother, had died. But Patricia Ross had elected not to bother with transferring the deed to the property over to her married name, so in the computer search nothing about the place had come up under the name "Ross." A hundred and sixty acres, a house . . . and who knew how many unused buildings?

"I know where we'll end up," Burgess told the pilot abruptly. "It's an estate not far from here. They'll probably go into the house or an outbuilding, a barn or something like it. When we get there, hang back until everyone goes inside, then take the chopper down somewhere out of sight."

Was she being followed? Oh, most definitely. Had Eve not been able to see the other vehicle's headlights in the rearview mirror, she would have *sensed* it. It didn't matter though; she had already been through the worst the puny humans had to offer, and look at how well she'd survived. Not only that, but she was *better* now, adapted to the paltry metal nuggets thrown by their firearms. Toward the end of her time back at the compound, the bullets hadn't even been piercing her skin.

Not the quietest of vehicles, the HMMWV raced down something called the Rock Creek Parkway as Eve pushed harder on the accelerator, seeing the needle on the speedometer climb past eighty-five, then beyond. By the time the Virginia road sign flashed by, the HMMWV was quivering at over a hundred miles an hour and every nerve in her body was screaming as Eve finally neared her destination. Her eyesight picked out the shadow of the oncoming driveway much more quickly than would her pursuers and she slowed the vehicle and skidded onto the tiny side drive, the HMMWV groaning at the hard, overly fast turn. Tires spitting gravel and dust in the darkness, Eve guided the vehicle up the driveway and slewed to a stop.

This wasn't so far away from the base, and yet it . . . might as well have been on the other side of the world. The air was clear and crisp, untarnished by the exhaust from a hundred passing military vehicles every hour. The sky was studded much more heavily with stars, testimony to the layer of haze that must've hung over Monroe Air Force Base. Out here the bright dots of light overhead did not seem nearly so unreachable as they had earlier, and it was too bad that her acute sense of hearing picked up the sounds of a helicopter engine running far out of sight.

It was time to get to what she'd come here for, what she'd been *born* for:

Patrick Ross.

Eve cocked her head, then let instinct take over. There, off in the farthest field behind the house, Patrick was diligently watching over the offspring he'd created thus far. She could feel them just as well as she could feel him, pulsing with life inside their sheaths of tough alien flesh, each coming toward the end of that precious and helpless chrysalis stage. They were so, so good, so *strong*... but the children that she and Patrick would make together would be exquisite.

It seemed like it took only seconds to reach the barn, and Eve paid no mind to the slack-jawed corpse of an old man lying out front. How... quaint, she thought as she fingered the wooden door with its brass hasp and saw light leaking from between a thousand cracks in the old boards. Not nearly as efficient as concrete or metal and twice as useless at keeping her and her kind out—how could it when it didn't even prevent unwanted humans from getting inside?

Eve went through the two-foot space between the door and the barn wall and stopped for just a moment to let her eyes adjust to the brightness of the single lamp sitting off to one side. Gleaming chrysalises hung everywhere, their forms shifting and trembling while the nearly grown brood inside went through the final throes of change prior to rebirth. As miraculous as it was, however, Eve had other things on her mind.

Just a couple of floors above was Patrick—Eve could sense him, could feel him sensing *her.* Finally, she was about to meet her destiny—

—*and mate.*

CHAPTER 20

"What is this place?" Laura asked. "It looks like a farm."

"Haven't a clue," Press answered. He spun the steering wheel to the right and the HMMWV skidded to a stop.

"I know where we are."

Press and Laura turned to look at Dennis. He sat in the back seat looking ashamed, like a small boy remembering something he should've known all along. "It's the old Downey summer plantation—Patrick's mother's place. He mentioned it once or twice a long time ago, but he said they hardly ever came out here since his mother died, always used the cabin in the mountains instead. There's a skeleton staff of servants in the house, but not much more than that since she passed away. I've never been out here before."

Press's mouth was a hard slash in the darkness. "Ah, the perfect place. So this is where we'll also find

Patrick—I knew if we stayed with her, Eve would lead us right to him." He threw open the driver's door. "Let's grab the gear and go."

"Oh boy," Dennis said unhappily. Nevertheless, he handed the spray canisters out to Press and Laura, then clambered from the HMMWV.

"What do you think?" Laura asked. She eyed the house dubiously. Except for the faint glow of lamplight toward the back, it was dark.

"No," Press said. "It's too public, too close to the road. There must be something else—look here." He pointed at the ground, where a path had been beaten in the gravel. It led off into the darkness. "I'll bet if we follow this we'll find a shed or a barn, someplace a lot more private. Come on." The others started to follow him, then Press stopped and looked up at the star-spilled sky. "Do you hear that?"

"What?" Laura looked at him, then at the sky, but it was clear that she was missing whatever Press had picked up on.

When Press looked to Dennis, the man shook his head. "Don't hear a thing, buddy. You're just jumpy, and I can't say I blame you."

"I guess it's nothing." Press shrugged but the expression on his face said he didn't believe that for an instant.

"Ready when you are," Dennis said. He hefted the canister of toxin that Laura had assembled.

"Let's go get this over with, Press." The moon, a full one, had finally risen high enough in the sky to illuminate Laura's white face. "I've got bad memories of the first time and I don't expect this to be much better."

Press nodded and motioned for them to follow. The gravel path ended where the pasture began, its crop long gone fallow. Waist-high weeds and wildflowers gleamed in the white shine of the moonlight, and the broken edges of the greenery clearly showed where the path had been recently used. They didn't bother trying to stay quiet; they all knew the aliens would hear them coming—unless they were otherwise distracted, and Press didn't want to think about that before he had to.

In the daylight, the ancient barn was probably visible for a hundred feet, but at night Press thought it seemed to pop up out of the ground without warning, despite the light spilling from the cracks in the old wood. Three stories high with a hayloft at the top—the damned thing was *huge.* Dark and weathered by God only knew how many winters without care, it looked like the last place in the world he and his two companions wanted to enter, and the beams of light coming from within only made things worse—it was like some sort of strange, golden explosion was taking place inside.

Then they stumbled across the ravaged corpse of Senator Judson Ross by the barn doors.

Laura sucked in her breath and froze; she and Press and Dennis stared down at the old politician, unwillingly taking in the gaping hole in the center of his chest and the blood that was streaked across his wide-eyed face.

"So much for family loyalty," Dennis rasped. He ran nervous fingers along the handle of the machete hanging from his belt. At the same time, Press pulled the tranquilizer gun from his waistband and inserted a loaded dart in its chamber, then boldly stepped over Judson Ross's dead body and pushed through the door of the barn.

Inside it wasn't nearly as bright as they had expected, but it was lit well enough for them to see everything that awaited.

Chrysalises, suspended from knotted ropes of flesh twined about the rafters—at least a dozen of the things, maybe more, hanging there like butterfly cocoons subjected to some sort of radiation to increase their size to monstrous. And all of them glowing a deep, corrupt golden-orange and covered in thick slime, literally *dripping* with it as life pulsed fast and furious within each one.

For a shocked second no one said anything. Then Press exhaled and spoke. "Welcome to the maternity ward from hell. Our astronaut's been a busy boy indeed."

"Patrick's offspring," Laura said. Press glanced at her and saw a mixture of awe and sorrow on her face. "My God, Press—do you realize how many women must have *died*?"

"Obviously more than the newscasters are reporting," Press said grimly. "I mean, *look* at this—I can't even count them all!"

"Well, pardon me if I don't pass out cigars." Dennis swiped a hand across his forehead. "Damn, these things are ugly." He looked to Press and got a confirmation nod; both men swung their canisters around to the front and unlatched the spray nozzles.

"What about Eve?" Laura asked uneasily. "If she finds Patrick—"

"Then we'll deal with it," Press told her. "But I'd rather fight the happy couple and maybe a junior or two than a whole army—these bastards are about to hatch. Come on, Dennis. Let's do it."

The two men took battle stances, feet apart and firmly planted as they aimed the spray nozzles and began pumping the canisters to release the gel-based human DNA Laura had manufactured from Dennis's genes. A fine blue mist erupted from the nozzle tips and floated over the first two cocoons, then Press and Dennis stopped the flow and stepped back.

Nothing happened.

"Oh, shit," Press muttered. "Now we're fucked."

"What?" Dennis stared at Press and then at the two chrysalises. His face twisted in panic. "*What?* What's wrong, you alien motherfuckers? My DNA not good enough for you?" He balled up his fist and would have taken a step forward if Press's hand hadn't come down on his arm to stop him. "You let me live on the *Excursion* just so I could come in here and die in this damned *barn*?" Dennis shrieked. "Well, *fuck* you and your entire butt-ugly species—"

"Dennis, wait." Laura's voice cut through his anger and stopped his tirade in mid-sentence. "Look—something *is* happening. I think we just have to wait for the chrysalis to absorb the gel."

And indeed, the chrysalises were doing that. The two slime-coated cocoons were still moving, but the quality of the shifting had changed—now the unborn hatchlings were shuddering instead of doing the slow, almost sensuous rolling the trio had seen before the spray had hit them. The trembling escalated to a violent pitch, then a rich, burnt-umber glow suddenly spread over the slippery-looking surface of the chrysalises in a pattern that resembled veins in a gigantic yellow eyeball. Something wailed once, then again, high and loud enough to make Laura clap her hands over her ears while Dennis stood there with his mouth hanging open.

"I've heard that sound before," he said in a low, wondering voice. He actually took a step *toward* the two cocoons. "I'm not sure . . . Wait, now I remember! It was on the ship right before I blacked out! It—*yaaaah!*"

Dennis threw himself backward again as half a dozen mottled brown tentacles burst through the outer wall in each of the two chrysalises, flailing wildly at anything and anyone within reach. But the thrashing was growing weaker with each passing second, and at each place where an appendage had torn through the glowing flesh, a white spot of infection appeared. The spots themselves began to spread faster and faster, blossoming outward like drops of colorless liquid atop the reddish-brown shine. The tentacles slowed as quickly as the points of disease spread across the surface of the alien pods and a noxious-looking ooze gushed from the tentacle openings. In less than a minute the two chrysalises were a throbbing, sickly eggshell-white, and as the three of them watched with revulsion, the walls of both cocoons abruptly imploded—

—leaving only sagging, empty sacks of unidentifiable alien flesh.

"Score one for human DNA and the good guys!" Dennis said brightly. Despite the cheerful words, his skin tone was decidedly green around the edges.

Press unslung his canister apparatus and motioned at Laura. "Here," he said. "Take this, and you two nuke the rest of these bastards. I'm going after Patrick."

Dennis didn't need to be told again. While Press hoisted the carry-all straps over Laura's shoulders, Dennis began to sweep the walls of the first level with the toxic gel, aiming high and low and making sure he covered as many chrysalises as he could get to.

Laura tugged at Press's shirt before he could head for the stairs. "Wait, Press. This isn't Eve's fault—remember, she's part human, too. She's just doing what her instincts tell her to, and wouldn't anyone kept a prisoner their entire life escape if they could?"

"Human?" Press's dark gaze flicked to the wilted alien carcasses hanging from the rafters and the other chrysalises around the barn area that were starting to twist beneath the onslaught of Dennis's spray. There was no understanding in his reply, only sarcasm.

"Sure, Laura. I'll keep that in mind."

"*Please,* Press." She was still holding onto his arm, her fingernails digging in as she struggled to keep him from pulling away before she finished having her say. "You don't know her like I do. I made her,

I watched her grow. I know how she thinks, and I *swear* to you there's a human being inside that life-form!"

Press opened his mouth with the intention of suggesting she stuff it, but the nasty words never came out. Who was he to judge? And based on what, besides—money? A million cold, but even at that price, was it worth killing Eve? He just wasn't so sure anymore.

In the end, Press gave Laura a quick squeeze on the shoulders to show his agreement, then raced up the stairs.

Patrick had checked the second level of the barn—filled to capacity like the main floor—then moved to the third floor. Not as full, but there were more than a few pulsating birth pods well on their way to hatching. He had stopped now and then along the way to inspect and caress the cocoons, murmuring encouragement much like a mother talks to the child within her womb. It wouldn't be long now—

Eve was here!

He felt her, sensed her, *smelled* her, as suddenly and completely as if she'd stepped in front of him and run a hand across his face. He knew everything about her all at once . . . even before she stepped into the fourth-floor loft, he could feel the racing of her heart and the desire that was making her breath come in short, hot gasps as she searched for him. The only thing Patrick didn't know before she climbed gracefully over the edge of the loft was what she looked like.

He wasn't disappointed.

Tall, lithe, with blond hair that brushed the line of her jaw like strands of soft corn silk, big blue eyes and a soft-looking, full mouth. She didn't smile, and Patrick didn't expect her to. Instead, they gazed at each other for a long moment, then Eve took a tentative step toward him. Patrick's fingers found the top of his shirt and he pulled it open, ripping the fabric and tossing it aside. Eve did the same, and by the time they met in the center of the room, they were both naked.

Their first kiss was soft and sweet and absolutely romantic. Somewhere in the recesses of his brain there had been moments like this with a woman who was now dead, but Patrick couldn't really remember them. There was only now, and Eve, and this moment that it seemed they had both been expecting for eternity.

Heat surged through him and he felt its match in her. When their arms wrapped around each other and locked, the bizarre and beautiful transformation began; by the time the full lengths of their bodies met, neither Patrick nor Eve were human any longer.

He felt new tips of flesh erupt from his sides, his shoulders and back, everywhere, wildly sensitive and matched one for one by Eve as thick coils pushed from her body and twined with his. Soon the strands of flesh were combining and encircling them both, protecting and quivering while the barn and the rest of the world faded away and became unimportant.

There was only Patrick and Eve, and their driving need to mate . . .

. . . and *create.*

The second floor, Laura and Dennis soon discovered, was nearly as filled with chrysalises as the first.

"Say good night, you ugly little shits," Dennis said with a grimace as they came, finally, to the last two of the alien cocoons, off to the left of the stairway leading to the third level.

"Hurry, Dennis—look at them. We don't have much time!"

He nodded and sent a mist of blue gel skimming through the air to cover the first one. A ropy-looking tendril shifted behind the glowing, murky shell; an instant later, the chrysalis's color went the death shade of bright burnt umber and the appendage within it convulsed. Another few seconds and the alien pod imploded, sending a torrent of brownish muck at their feet.

Dennis sniffed the air, then gave the drooping, dead sack a vicious grin. "I love the smell of burning aliens in the morning," he said mockingly.

"Dennis," Laura said sharply from her stance a few feet away. "We don't have time to waste. The other one—"

Before she could finish, one side of the second chrysalis contorted and tore. An arm, not quite human, not quite alien, broke through and with terrifying speed seized Dennis around the neck.

"Laura!"

That word only, then his air was cut off. He clawed at the scummy thing encircling his throat, but it only tightened its hold and began dragging him backward and toward the split in the side of the chrysalis.

Laura swiveled and brought the spray nozzle of her canister up in a motion so smooth that even Press would have been proud to witness. She made a sound that might've been a snarl and squeezed the handle . . .

. . . but only a pathetic blue dribble came out.

The damned thing was empty.

"Hang on, Dennis!" she cried as she tried desperately to think. Just that small instant of paralysis and the tentacle clutching at him was joined by another, then by three more, and more still, until there were too many to count. Dennis had a moment of elusive freedom while the thing readjusted its hold and he managed to choke out—

"Laura, the knife!"

He saw Laura jump forward but didn't feel her fingers grabbing at his waist. A moment that was surely a year later, and the comforting gleam of the machete blade whipped through the air in front of him as it swung up and cleanly severed the grasping limb around his neck, cutting easily through skin and bone or God knew what else was beneath it. Dennis gratefully sucked in air as Laura began hacking haphazardly at the ropes of flesh, but his relief soon returned to fear—he still couldn't get away because every time Laura sliced off a tentacle, another sprouted from within the chrysalis to take its place. No matter how hard she tried, Dennis was being pulled relentlessly upward and toward the waiting slash in the side of the alien cocoon.

As hardened and experienced as Press thought he was, even he was unprepared for the sight that greeted him on the fourth-floor loft of the barn.

If he and the other members of the tracking team had thought the shining, golden-brown chrysalises that permeated this place were repulsive, the huge, quivering knot of grotesquely interlocked flesh in the center of the loft floor was nothing short of unspeakable. Easily five or six times the size of the smaller cocoons in the lower parts of the building, this monstrosity had the same unearthly amber glow coming from within it, the perfect illumination for Press to make out the two entwined forms inside. Eve was surely the smaller form squirming beneath something bigger and shadowy, with far too many limbs for Press to account for. The thought that his world might someday be filled with these disgusting things was enough to urge him forward, the tranquilizer gun aimed and ready as he circled the strange, alien "love nest" and tried to get a bead on the larger male form. He would have fired just anywhere, but something Laura had said—

"I swear to you that there's a human being inside that life-form."

—stuck in his mind and made him pause and shout instead, "Eve, this is your last chance—get the fuck out of there!"

There was no response, and truly, no matter what Laura claimed, Press hadn't expected one. Dark and light shifted and reshifted inside the nest and Press's eyes widened as he found himself with the best aim he was likely to get to plant a toxic dart in the middle of the male alien.

"Time for *coitus interruptus,*" he growled and squeezed the trigger.

The dart never hit its mark.

A tentacle, long and twice as fast as a bullwhip, lashed out from somewhere beneath the nest and knocked the tranquilizer gun from his hand. With a sense of unreality, Press grabbed for it with a hand gone numb—and missed; he saw it skitter away and out of the dim ring of light thrown by the glow of the alien nest. He heard it bump against the wall somewhere and stop as he stumbled and went to one knee while his gaze shot back to the nest. Fear dropped into his gut as he saw that the tentacle had receded and someone—some*thing*—was staring at him through the break in the nest's side wall. Press started to rise—*need to get to that tranq gun!*—then fell back again as the nest suddenly heaved and bubbled; the tear widened as long, dark fingers grabbed the sides of it and pushed it open in another obscene version of alien birth.

"Oh, *shit!*" Press exclaimed, but he was far too slow to gain his footing and flee from the creature that pulled itself from the slit. Press gaped up at it, speechless, scared beyond anything he'd ever known or expected. He'd thought he knew so much, but the male alien was *different*—a quadrupedal nightmare that chittered and screeched and literally *towered* over him when it rose on its hind legs, so much more deadly and so much *larger* than Sil or Eve or anything Press had ever envisioned. He remembered that shiny brown-gold skin of Sil's, the huge, vaguely reptilian eyes and sinewy, long-limbed movements, but the rest of Patrick—the rest of *it*—was new, and completely terrifying: multijointed legs—it walked on all fours—below a long, flexible neck and winding body out of which sprang a dozen Medusa-like tentacles.

And the whole hideous thing was looming over him and closing in for the kill.

Press yanked the Glock 26 from its holster and emptied the clip straight into the monster.

Ten shots using hollow-point bullets that should have sent the bastard halfway to hell, and they didn't make a damned bit of difference.

The Patrick-alien gave a low growl of rage and started to reach for Press. He cringed away, expecting agony, but a full-throated hiss to its right made the alien pause and swing its head toward the sound. When Press looked, he saw that Eve had emerged from the nest and was striding toward him and her dreadful-looking lover. She was just like Press remembered Sil as being—a fantastic breed somewhere between human, reptile, insect and octopus, all constant, flowing movement. Deformed but oddly beautiful, weirdly sensuous in the way everything about her came together and just . . . *fit*, like something out of some dark, erotic nightmare. And so very, very dangerous as she stepped between her alien mate and Press and hissed again, volunteering to deliver the lethal blow.

There was nowhere to run, no way to escape. All Press could do was stare into the cold color of Eve's enormous glistening eyes and wait for her to strike. He might be defeated and have nothing left with which to fight her, and he might be frightened nearly witless . . . but he would *not* go down silent.

"Oh, yeah, Laura," he said scornfully as Eve

leaned toward him. "Tell me again how Eve's *human*, too."

Incredibly, Eve hesitated. The Patrick-alien made a rough chattering noise and gestured impatiently—*Do it!*—and if nothing else, Press thought that when Eve raised a gnarled hand to strike, she might've seemed just a little reluctant. Her mate, however, came forward in anticipation, crowding in as she was about to strike—

—and was impaled on five spikes of dark, bony columns that burst from Eve's back.

The Patrick-alien bellowed in pain and wrenched itself free. It tripped backward and nearly fell, then crouched as Eve spun to face it, planting herself bodily between her former consort and Press. She hissed wildly, then launched herself at it and the two aliens came together in midair . . .

And the true battle began.

Instantly it was impossible to distinguish one from the other. The noise was indescribable—a sort of ongoing echoing bellows, and the force of their blows was enough to shake the floor beneath Press as, forgotten for the moment, he scrambled sideways to get out of their range. The two creatures rolled and thrashed, then split apart and circled each other, but Eve's next offensive was cut pitifully short when one of Patrick's limbs whipped forward and backslapped her with incredible strength. The impact sent her flying and she hit the far wall of the loft nearly twenty feet away; dazed, she slid down and slumped against the floor.

The Patrick-alien swung its head toward Press for a moment, then dismissed him, apparently convinced that the lowly human no longer posed a threat. Instead, it stalked across the loft and pawed at the nearly senseless Eve until it had turned her body face-up; without preamble, it mounted her, intent on finishing the mating, howling like a victorious hyena the entire time.

Stunned but not conquered, Eve's eyes opened and she stared at Patrick with nothing less than undiluted loathing. Held in place and unable to move, Press blinked, unable to believe it when he thought he saw her smile.

Then he realized why.

A thick, muscular-looking tentacle unfurled from each of Eve's breasts with blurring speed, rising up and encircling Patrick's neck in a viciously tight grip before the huge male alien could do anything to stop them or pull away. With both of them oozing alien blood from a dozen scrapes, the gnarled appendages that served as Patrick's hands released their hold on Eve as he threw himself backward and instinctively clawed at his neck, trying to break the choke hold.

But Eve only pulled Patrick back, nearly shaking him as she put everything she had into this last assault and her would-be lover's strange face finally began to darken.

"They've been in there long enough," Burgess said. "Set her down as close as you can get."

The Huey pilot nodded and brought the chopper to an expert touchdown in the field adjacent to the old barn into which Press Lennox, Dr. Baker and Dennis Gamble had followed the alien Eve. Colonel Burgess unclasped his seat belt, then unhurriedly pulled his bottle of Visine from one breast pocket and gave his good eye a generous drop of the stuff.

That done, he pocketed the Visine and retrieved a small brown case from beneath his seat and opened it. Inside was his personal choice of a weapon: a Mauser-Werke HSC 7.65 pistol and a finely crafted laser scope. This baby dated back to 1941 and with a serial number in the early 700,000 range, it was a collector's item. It took Burgess only a few seconds to snap the custom-made scope on and hold up the gun. The expression on his face was one of savage anticipation.

"Let's hope Lennox is as good as I think he is."

He left the pilot there to wait in the darkness.

Laura didn't know who was screaming louder—she or Dennis—as his head disappeared into the long, moist crack in the chrysalis.

The machete was clearly useless—if she tried to stab at the cocoon she risked cutting Dennis, or worse. She flung it aside then spied Dennis's canister of toxin where it had dropped at his feet when he'd been grabbed by the first tentacle. Laura's fingers were slick with fear-sweat as she scurried over and grabbed at it, finally aiming the nozzle at the point where Dennis's head had vanished into the disgusting pod and squeezing off a cloud of the fine, blue mist. There was no sense standing and waiting for it to work—it either did or didn't—so she dropped the canister and threw her arms around Dennis's waist, putting all her weight into a downward pull, determined to haul him out of the dripping cavity.

The alien cocoon convulsed, expelling Dennis like an unwanted olive pit. The two of them tumbled to the floor, then Laura was up and dragging him bodily out of reach of any more questing appendages.

But there was no need. A second later, the now-familiar burnt-umber glow swept over the chrysalis, followed immediately by the escalating shuddering of disease. No display of flailing tentacles this time—with the side of the pod fractured, the DNA-based toxin was clearly absorbed at twice the rate. Before Dennis could finish wiping the birth slime from his face, the cocoon caved in on itself with a *pop!*, then sagged.

"Thanks," Dennis managed. He staggered to his

feet and held on to the wall for a second. "Thought I was baby food there for a minute."

Laura couldn't resist an impish smile. "Actually, I didn't really do anything, and you'd never have given it a good first meal. The hatchling needed food, but you'd've still been indigestible to it. It would've spit you out anyway."

"Gee, thanks," Dennis said sarcastically, but there was no denying the measure of relief in his voice.

"We need to check on Press," Laura said. "He's been up there by himself for an awfully long time."

"Yeah, and there've been some God-awful noises coming from up there," Dennis said. His gaze flicked to the sagging pods around the walls. "We've just escaped death—hey, let's go do it again!"

Laura grabbed up the canister pack. "Let's hope the third floor isn't as full," she said. "There isn't much left." Dennis nodded then took a quick two steps and retrieved the machete. He and Laura headed up the stairs, taking the risers two at a time and convinced they'd be met by a swarm of alien offspring. But this time luck was with them—only half a dozen or so chrysalises were positioned around the spacious third level and Laura waited impatiently as Dennis sprayed them as quickly as he could. When he came to the last one, the deadly dosage was there but it sputtered alarmingly at the end. Their toxin supply was almost out.

"We'd better hope this is it," he said as the last of the cocoons went into its unearthly pre-death glow, "or we could be into some really deep shit."

"We'll have enough." Laura motioned at him, her gesture nearly frantic. *"Come on."*

"We'll have enough," Dennis echoed as he shouldered the canister and hurried after her. "Provided the next floor isn't full of them, too. We should check down here one more time—"

Something howled horribly upstairs and obliterated his train of thought. He and Laura bolted up the final flight of stairs—

—and never noticed the mild pulse of a golden-brown chrysalis deep in the rafter shadows above their head.

With Eve and Patrick's attention focused on each other, Press grabbed at the opportunity to hustle in the opposite direction and find the tranquilizer gun. A search in his pockets gave him another loaded dart—it would've been just his luck to drop the entire supply in the fight—and he slammed it home, praying that the undersized specialty weapon wouldn't jam when he needed it most.

Spinning back to view the battle, Press gasped as he saw the result of Eve's choke hold on Patrick. The male alien's face had gone almost completely black and had swollen until it looked ready to burst. For a moment it looked like Eve would take care of Patrick herself, then the inflated skin around Patrick's skull abruptly *split.* A line of flesh that was long and repugnantly phallic shot from the center and rammed itself into Eve's mouth, twisting and burrowing and *chewing* on the inside of her face. The tentacles around the Patrick-alien's neck loosened and fell away and Eve's hands beat ineffectively at her attacker as the shape of her face contorted and fell it on itself.

In far too short a time, Eve was still.

"Oh, *fuck,*" Press muttered. Patrick rose from Eve's body and hovered there for a second, as though waiting to see if she would move. Before Press could bring up the dart gun, a noise from the stairwell—Dennis and Laura clambering into the loft—caught both his attention and the alien's. They came over the last step and then Dennis and Laura stood frozen, their gazes tracking around the room to the Patrick-alien and Press, the deflated but still heaving nest in the corner, and finally, Eve's crumpled figure.

"Shit!" Dennis exclaimed. He put a hand out to stop Laura when she would have run forward.

The two halves of his head flapping, Patrick rose to his full height and snarled at them, the sound somewhere between a lion's roar and a wolf's threatening growl.

A *challenge.*

Patrick brought up the tranq gun and fired, aiming intuitively. There was a *crack!* and the dart embedded itself in one of Patrick's forearms. The alien jerked and stared down at it as though wondering why Press would shoot such a thing at him, then the skin around the small wound began to pucker and blanch, the alien's normal amber-colored arm going the pallid, sickly white of infection. As the flesh shriveled and started to fester, Patrick let out a deep-throated groan.

Determined to get the best of the creature while it was weakened, Dennis took four steps and aimed the nozzle of the canister, then squeezed hard on the spray handle. A haze of blue mist erupted, but it was far too small and feeble—Patrick easily jerked backward and out of harm's way. As the mist settled harmlessly to the floor, the alien vaulted forward and shoved Dennis as hard as he could. As Press struggled to load another dart into the gun, Dennis and his now empty canister setup sailed through the air and crashed to the floor fifteen feet away.

Patrick groaned again as the dart in his arm sent its contamination farther up his arm, then the creature cocked its head and held up its other hand. Too late Press saw the machete—Patrick had snatched it from Dennis's belt before he'd struck. Press and Laura watched, thunderstruck, as Patrick swiveled the blade around and—

—severed his own arm at the elbow.

The alien screamed in agony and threw the machete to the side, but whatever pain it had was short-lived. Press, however, was caught off guard by the unspeakable deed for half a second too long—enough time for the Patrick-alien to take three enormous steps toward him, rip the tranquilizer gun from his hand and grab him. Press had a moment of vertigo that reminded him crazily of roller-coasters, then the alien slammed him to the floor using all of its inhuman strength. For Press, the lights damned near went out.

He didn't know how he managed to hang on to consciousness; maybe it was hearing Laura's scream that did it—

"Press!"

—or just knowing that things were headed downhill at locomotive speed and that if they didn't find a way to stop Patrick, there wouldn't be much left to wake up *to.* Press pulled himself upright and made it to his knees, and when he lifted his head he saw Patrick again, this time facing off with Laura. She'd snatched up the machete and was brandishing it like a pitchfork, but the multilimbed creature advancing on her had no problem avoiding her jabs. She tried again but lost her hold on the blade when Patrick's remaining hand zipped forward and twisted it out of her fingers. He flung it away and caught hold of her, intent on dragging the fighting and squirming Laura to that atrocious-looking dome of breathing alien flesh at the other end of the room.

Press scrambled around on the floor for a precious two seconds trying to find the dart gun, then knew it was futile—the fucking thing had probably fallen through a crack somewhere in this pitted old floor. The only thing left was the machete and Press seized it, but how effective would it be against this thing that had withstood everything they could throw at it?

Fuck it, Press thought, and headed for Patrick. He

wasn't about to let Laura become this disgusting alien's next piece of tail.

"Press—wait!"

He almost ignored Dennis, but something in the other man's voice made him turn. One side of his ebony face was bruised and hugely swollen, but the astronaut had hauled himself into a sitting position where he'd landed. He gestured at Press to come back. "Use me," he rasped. "Use my blood—it's our only chance!"

Behind him, Laura screamed again. Press looked back and saw her bite viciously into the distorted arm around her neck, then gag and try to spit out the viscous green liquid that spilled from the injury. He knew he had to do it; by itself, the blade would be useless, but with Dennis's help . . .

Press sprinted over to Dennis and raised the machete. Holding it aloft, he locked gazes with the astronaut and was unable to move.

Dennis punched him in the ankle to break the paralysis. *"Do it!"*

He buried the edge of the machete in Dennis's thigh.

Dennis's scream mixed with another from Laura and below both was Press's own cry of anguish. He pulled the blade free and whirled, saw that Patrick had dragged Laura within only a few feet of the pulsing, fleshy nest. The damned thing would cover them both in a protective sheath that for all Press knew would be impenetrable even to human disease, and he was never going to get over there in time to stop Patrick from pulling her inside.

Press brought the machete up, took one quick rehearsal swipe, then sent the machete hurling end over end through the air.

"Die, you son of a bitch!"

The point of the blade found its target and bit

deep into the muscles running down the center of the Patrick-thing's back.

The alien's screech was like nothing they'd heard before. Infection spilled instantly across the surface of its back, bleeding white into the veins and rippling along the lines of bone and sinew. Still gripping Laura, Patrick collapsed and pinned her beneath his oversized frame, knocking the wind out of her. She quivered once, then was still.

Press dashed toward her, then saw with a jolt that he would never make it in time. Patrick's body convulsed and tore down the middle as his head had done; from the resulting gore-filled cavity rose the same penile appendage that had retreated after destroying Eve—the core alien, the abominable thing that had manipulated both human and alien flesh in order to hide and safeguard itself. Now it was headed for Laura, *his* Laura, who lay unconscious, defenseless, and too fucking far away from Press for him to do anything to stop it.

He started to cry out, then choked it back. Eve, Press and Dennis saw in amazement, had *not* been annihilated. Injured and perhaps even dying, she had nevertheless crawled unnoticed across the floor, and now she flung herself the last few feet toward Patrick's dead shell. As the two men stared helplessly, one of her knotted alien hands buried itself into the fish-white, diseased skin along Patrick's spine. She shrieked as contamination exploded along her arm, finding an instant pathway inside her body amid a half dozen scrapes along her skin. It surged through her system with phenomenal speed, turning her shining, deep-gold complexion into that deathly virulent shade of ivory.

Then, with the last of her strength, Eve pulled herself over Patrick's husk and sank the talon-tipped fingers of her other hand into the alien's core tentacle as it was only inches away from Laura's mouth.

The last of the terrible species turned white and writhed in her grip—

—then the ghastly duo imploded and was no more.

For a moment, Press was too shocked to move, then sensibility returned and he raced over to Laura. But when he got to her he couldn't, *wouldn't*, believe that she wasn't moving.

Or breathing.

"*Please*, Laura," he begged. "Damn it, you come back to me." Press slipped a hand beneath her neck and lifted her head, some long-ago CPR training kicking in when all he really wanted to do was scream. Bending over her, he closed her nostrils and covered her mouth with his, tasting the nauseating alien slime from her bite on Patrick's arm, but feeling, underneath that, the soft lips that he'd kissed many times too long ago. He inhaled through his nose, then exhaled into her mouth, then did it again, watching her chest rise with the pressure of the air he was forcing into her lungs while his mind tried to remember the right ratio of breaths to chest compressions. Should he start chest compressions now, or breathe for her again? Everything was all muddled up and he couldn't find the figures past a year and more worth of memories he'd forced to the background when they'd parted—

Laura and him laughing over dinner and wine in a hundred restaurants—

Laura smearing sunblock on her delicate, peach-colored skin during a trip to the Galapagos as Press admired her figure in a sleek, metallic-green bathing suit—

Laura at his townhouse with him, her body entwined with his and moving like silk beneath the comforter on his bed—

—then he felt the pressure of his lips being returned and realized she was kissing him as she swung her arms up and around his neck. She murmured something against his mouth, but Press wasn't sure he heard it right. Surely she couldn't have said . . .

"Magically delicious."

"Okay, Dennis," Laura said. "That'll hold you until we can get you to a hospital." She pulled back and inspected the makeshift tourniquet she'd fastened around the astronaut's thigh. "Does it feel okay?"

"Oh, sure," Dennis answered through gritted teeth. "Just like a big slab of sliced steak."

"Come on, buddy." Press bent and hooked an arm under Dennis's shoulder. "Up you go—get your weight on that other leg. That's good, just like that." He lifted the other man with a grunt and they both wobbled for a moment, then caught their balance; he was bone-weary and he ached in a dozen places he hadn't known he had. He knew Laura did, too, and Dennis . . . well, he didn't want to think about how Dennis's leg must feel right now. "We've got all our stuff and we're finally done here."

"Let's go," Laura said, leading the way to the stairs and holding on to Dennis's other side as they made their way down to the third floor. "Jesus, I'm so *tired.* I can't wait to get out of here—"

"Hold it right there."

Laura gasped and jerked too hard, making Dennis hiss with pain as the trio halted. Across the room and coming closer was Colonel Carter Burgess. Clutched in one of his hands was a pistol, complete with a deadly efficient laser scope. The laser's red dot had already found and settled on Press.

Press let go of Dennis and steered the injured man's arm to the railing so he could hold on, then stepped in front of his two companions. "Well, well," he said sardonically. "Carter Burgess. They sent you for cleanup, huh?"

"Sorry, Press."

Of course the older man didn't look sorry at all as

he moved closer. "Why, you rat-faced son of a bitch," Dennis said in awe. "You—"

"Take it easy, Dennis. Our friend here is just following orders. After all, we've got a dead hero on our hands. They can cook up some kind of story to blame it on us and get everything tied up in a neat little bundle to hand to the upper muckity-mucks." Press raised an eyebrow. "I'm assuming it's not just me, unless you grew a sudden streak of compassion."

Burgess shrugged. "I've made an executive decision. I'm afraid it would be unwise to let any of you leave this place."

Laura's mouth turned down. "What was it you said—'*There are other staff members in the facility who have skills more or less equivalent to yours.*' I didn't know how serious you were . . . *sir.*"

"Nice little Nazi machine-pistol," Press said cuttingly. "An antique, I presume? What an interesting choice for the all-American military man."

Burgess shrugged again, impervious to both Laura and Press's insults. His gaze on Press was sharp, missing nothing. "I know you've got your gun out, Lennox. Any good agent would have. You can just put it down—I'm wearing an armored jacket."

"I suggest you eat shit," Press said pleasantly. His hand was a blur of speed as he brought the Glock up and squeezed the trigger, aiming for Burgess's head—

The Glock just clicked emptily.

Burgess smiled and took a step closer, the Mauser aimed at Press's chest. "I suppose it's safe to say you didn't count your bullets up there, isn't it? Tough luck—and yours just ran out." His finger drew back on the trigger, but the burst went wild as Burgess was suddenly jerked off his feet. The colonel's escalating scream was cut short by a long, powerful tentacle that had snaked out of the darkness above the stairwell and wrapped around his neck.

No matter what kind of man or monster Burgess was, instinct made both Laura and Press try to grab for him, but Burgess was pulled up and out of reach too quickly; all the three of them could do was stand below and watch in horror as he was lifted up and yanked inside a glowing alien chrysalis. The military man managed one muffled shriek, then the chrysalis heaved and a splash of red hit the inside of the membranous wall, turning the light it gave off a deep, uneven crimson.

"Damn," Dennis said in a bland voice. "I guess we must've missed one."

Overhead, the cocoon pulsed unexpectedly and they all flinched, waiting for tentacles to burst from its sides, or perhaps something much, much worse. Press's hand slid to his waistband, but the only thing that happened was a final shiver as something small and hard dropped out of the pod and landed in front of Press's feet.

"Oh, God," Laura said as she gaped at it. "That's *disgusting*."

Press stretched out one foot and pushed Burgess's glass eyeball with his toe. "Here's looking at you, kid," he said in his best Bogart imitation.

Silence, then Dennis half coughed, half laughed while Laura covered her mouth with one hand to stifle a smirk. "Press, that is *so* bad!" he exclaimed.

But Press just grinned, stepped forward, and crushed the round piece of glass under his heel. Then he yanked the tranquilizer gun from his waistband and brought it up in one liquid motion. "Excuse the ingratitude," he said flatly, and fired.

The final chrysalis gave a piercing wail of death, and this time the trio stayed to watch and make sure it was all over.

Then they descended the stairs and, finally, made their way outside.

CHAPTER 21

Even when the quiet was disrupted by a stream of military vehicles and the churning of a Med Evac helicopter's blades, dawn over the Virginia countryside was a beautiful thing to behold. The sun bled golden over the distant peaks of the mountains and lit up the hillsides slowly, as though it was a gigantic yellow floodlight brought up to full power by the world's most powerful dimmer switch.

Press and Laura had had their bruises and bumps attended to while Dennis, with the six-inch gash in his thigh newly bandaged, sat in the passenger seat of the Med Evac. Laura and Press stood by the door to the chopper, and all three watched without speaking as the members of the clean-up team, a couple of dozen men encased in white protective suits, scurried around like albino ants and carried out the tagged and bagged remains of the chrysalises. On the other side of the field six military trucks idled, their back doors open and waiting to receive the cargo.

"What do they need those suits for?" Dennis asked. His handsome, dark face was creased with worry. "I mean, we were in there without anything—"

"Don't get your bandage wrinkled," Laura said. "They don't need those suits at all—it's just standard operating procedure."

"That translates to a way to spend taxpayers' money," Press put in mildly. He watched a few more men go by carrying cargo, then said, "Gee, I wonder which one of those has Burgess in it?"

Dennis snickered as Laura shot Press a severe look. Press met her gaze without backing down and she had to turn away before he made her laugh—damn it, then she'd end up feeling guilty.

"You know," Press said softly, "I think you were right about Eve."

Laura turned back. "What?"

Press looked at the ground and poked at the flattened grass with his shoe. "About her being human, too—or least partially human. She had the chance to kill me in there, but she didn't. And she didn't let Patrick do it either."

"And she gave her life to save yours," Dennis said. "Whatever else was inside her, we . . . *you* were also a part of her. At the end, she remembered that."

Laura opened her mouth to reply, then closed it as a couple of paramedics came around the corner of the barn and headed for the back of one of the transport vehicles. The gurney they were pushing held Eve, and Laura was thankful that the human part of Eve's metabolism had triumphed in death and retaken her body. Underneath the grime from the barn, she was beautiful again, her skin pure and unbruised, that lovely young face now still and serene. A single tear slipped down Laura's cheek as the medics lifted the gurney into the waiting vehicle, then shut the door with a clang.

"Mr. Gamble, I distinctly remember telling you to lie down in the back."

Laura and Press turned in time to see a pretty woman in a paramedic's uniform hurry up to Dennis and tug on his arm. He came out of the seat willingly, but with a decidedly exaggerated limp that made Press roll his eyes. "Oh, yes, ma'am. Right away." Behind the woman's back Dennis winked at his two friends, then slipped his arm around her and found a snug hold on her waist as she led him to the rear of the Med Evac.

"Once a letch, always a letch," Press said wryly.

"Oh, he's not that bad." Laura hesitated, then glanced at Press. "Is he?"

"I sure wouldn't put my money on it," Press retorted. The chopper's engine hummed to life and Press and Laura ducked and hurried out from under the blades. A few seconds later it lifted off and they saw Dennis waving happily from the rear window as the chopper flew away into the sky.

Something snapped faintly behind them. Press and Laura turned and saw the flag over by the main house, the red, white and blue rolling proudly in the air currents stirred up by the helicopter's departure.

EPILOGUE

"It's certainly a funeral befitting a hero," Laura said.

Press, Laura and Dennis were standing on a hill overlooking Arlington National Cemetery. Their view of the ceremony below was perfect and they could see everything—the full-dress detail for the twenty-one-gun salute, the high-security private box containing the President and First Lady, the rows of dignitaries and military men who'd come to pay their last respects. No doubt the Pentagon Three generals were down there somewhere as well, sitting with hands clasped and bland expressions while their devious little brains cooked up some other nasty trick to play on John Q. Public.

"You sound a little bitter," Dennis said. He shifted on his crutches, trying to get comfortable. He still wasn't used to the pressure under his armpits.

Laura stared at the service below. "He murdered a lot of women. He even killed his father."

"No," Press said. His voice was sharp, perhaps a bit more than he intended. He put a hand on her arm to take away the sting of his tone. "The alien part of him did those things, not the human part. You taught me that, remember? What's remembered today is the human part, the man who went up and walked on Mars—"

"—because his country told him to," Dennis finished for him.

Laura watched the ceremony for a few more seconds, then finally nodded. "You're right, of course. All this," she waved a hand around her, "all these people and the graves here—so *many,* it's all a big . . . *monument* to the things that might have been. When you think about it, it's just heartbreaking."

"You're wrong," Dennis said quietly. Press and Laura looked at him questioningly. "It's *necessary.* Just like *we're* necessary. There are people like Patrick, who get noticed and commended for their bravery, and there are people like all the rest of the men and women in these graves who don't. People like *us.* This monument, as you called it, is for all of us, whether we're seen or not—because we're the ones who give our all to keep our country, and sometimes the world, safe."

Press's hand found Laura's and he squeezed it as Dennis's dark gaze paused on them before he lifted his face to the sun, and the sky, and all the unseen things beyond.

"No matter where the attackers come from."

YVONNE NAVARRO

YVONNE NAVARRO lives in a western suburb of Chicago and is the author of the original *Species* novelization. Since her first published story in 1984, her short fiction has appeared in over fifty publications. *Species II* is her sixth novel, with the most recent two being *Final Impact* and *Aliens: Music of the Spears.* Other past projects include the novels *deadrush* and *AfterAge* and the reference work *The First Name Reverse Dictionary. Red Shadows,* a follow-up to *Final Impact,* will be published in November 1998. She yearns for heat and sun, and plans to fix this problem by relocating to Arizona.